# AMBUSH!

The colonel leading the advancing regiment sent recon in first. The recon moved carefully and cautiously. But they seldom investigated more than twenty yards on either side of the old highway. It was a mistake.

As soon as the recon teams passed, the Rebels slipped out of their holes and reset the Claymores and placed C-4 at selected sites . . .

The first tanks of the long column appeared and the Rebels let them rumble past, allowing them to roll deeper and deeper into the trap . . .

"Now!" Ben Raines said, and Cooper fired the Armbrust. The rocket slammed into the side of a tank and turned the inside into a fiery death for the crew. Up and down the mile-long stretch of highway, explosions shattered the quiet. A rattled regimental commander screamed orders to retreat.

But it was too late. In their haste to retreat, the tanks and trucks were twisted up in a death lock. Now it was a turkey shoot for the Rebel troops . . .

# TREASON
## IN THE
# ASHES

## WILLIAM W. JOHNSTONE

PINNACLE BOOKS
Kensington Publishing Corp.
http://www.kensingtonbooks.com

PINNACLE BOOKS are published by

Kensington Publishing Corp.
119 West 40th Street
New York, NY 10018

All Kensington Titles, Imprints, and Distributed Lines are available at special quantity discounts for bulk purchases for sales promotions, premiums, fund-raising, and educational or institutional use. Special book excerpts or customized printings can also be created to fit specific needs. For details, write or phone the office of the Kensington special sales manager: Kensington Publishing Corp., 119 West 40th Street, New York, NY 10018, attn: Special Sales Department, Phone: 1-800-221-2647.

Pinnacle and the P logo Reg. U.S. Pat. & TM Off.

ISBN-13: 978-0-7860-2024-9
ISBN-10: 0-7860-2024-5

First Printing: April 1994

10 9 8 7 6 5 4

Printed in the United States of America

"The first requisite of a good citizen in this Republic of ours is that he shall be able and willing to pull his weight."

—Theodore Roosevelt


"Behold, I show you a mystery; We shall not all sleep, but we shall all be changed."

—The Bible

# Prologue

*Mexico*

So this is how it ends, Ben thought, as the sun began gradually casting its light over the land. He stared at the Nazi firing squad, staring back at him. Then that old familiar recklessness filled him and he grinned at the line of men.

"I believe I will have that last cigarette you offered me, Volmer," Ben called. "If the offer still holds."

Peter Volmer, leader of the Nazi Party in what used to be known as America, looked at Jesus Hoffman, self-proclaimed Fuhrer, and the man nodded his head. "Give him a cigarette."

"His hands?"

"Untie them," Hoffman said. "What can he do now? He is a mere shell of what he used to be. The interrogations have weakened him and his knees tremble with fear. Go on. This could be amusing."

"Stand the men at ease," Volmer ordered the thirteen men who made up the firing squad. He walked across the courtyard and up to Ben. Volmer untied Ben's hands and handed him a cigarette.

Ben flexed his hands several times before taking the cigarette. "They're really bad for your health, you know?" he said with a smile.

"You won't have to worry about that for very much longer, General Raines."

"I guess not." Ben bent his head to take the offered flame from a cigarette lighter. He got the tip glowing red hot and then suddenly jammed the lighted end into Volmer's right eye, grabbed the Nazi's pistol from his holster, and scrambled over the low part of the crumbling adobe wall.

Volmer was rolling on the ground, screaming in terrible pain, both hands to his blinded eye. From the balcony of the hacienda, Fuhrer Jesus Diguez Mendoza Hoffman screamed, "Shoot the son of a bitch!"

But Ben had vanished from sight.

The next thing he knew, he was face to face with a very startled Nazi SS man. He wasn't startled long. Ben shot him twice in the chest. He ripped the submachine gun from the dead hands and tore off the full ammo pouch, then he took off at a dead run for the main house. Ben didn't think he had a snowball's chance in hell of getting out of this pickle alive, so he had made up his mind to take some Nazis with him.

Ben was not nearly so mentally and physically worn out as Hoffman and Volmer thought. He had resisted the drugs and the brainwashing, and for some reason, the few physical beatings had been half-hearted.

Ben heard running feet behind him, and he scrambled out of sight. The footsteps stopped, the door to the room flung open and a tall, rangy SS officer stepped inside. Ben drove the butt of his submachine gun into the man's belly, bringing him to his knees. One more blow broke the SS man's neck. Ben opened a canvas pouch and smiled. Grenades. He took those and the dead man's clips, all fully loaded.

Dragging the body to the other side of the room, Ben stood for a moment, staring at the corpse. "Well . . . why not?" he muttered. He and the dead man were about the same size. He stripped the body and put on the hated black of the SS, wondering why there was so little pursuit of him and virtually no gunfire since he'd jumped over the low wall of the execution site.

After dressing the dead man in his own uniform, he squatted down beside the body for a moment. "Might work," he muttered, and slung both submachine guns and the ammo pouches over his shoulder, and took out two grenades, pulling the pins and holding down the spoons. "Achtung! Achtung!" Ben yelled, then added in German: "Here he is."

Ben quickly put one grenade under the man's belly and the other one beside his head and got the hell away from that area.

Ben entered a storeroom and closed the door just as the grenades blew. He sat down wearily behind some crates and boxes and thought: How in the hell did I ever get into this mess?

Ben remembered the ambush by the Nazi kids, some of them as young as eight or ten, somewhere in New Mexico, he thought. The damn drugs he'd been force-fed during his captivity had really screwed up his thinking and memory. That and his time on what he'd heard called a "sensory-deprivation" machine—whatever the hell that was. The important thing was, Ben had fought it and won. He knew he was in Mexico, but how deep into Mexico he had no idea.

Now everything began coming back to him. The year-long war with Jesus Hoffman and his Nazis. They'd come out of South America with grand plans to take control of what remained of the United States. Ben Raines and his Rebels had kicked that nightmare right in the head.

Ben wondered how long he'd been in captivity? Weeks, surely. Maybe months. He wondered how the war was going? Who was winning? Was it over? He shook his head. No, not as long as just one Rebel lived, the fight for freedom would never be over. And he knew for a fact that one Rebel was damn sure alive.

Ben Raines.


A voice shouted out in German: "Here he is. The man is dead. Ben Raines is dead!"

So far, so good, Ben thought.

"Get the Fuhrer out of here!" a voice filled with panic screamed, just as hard gunfire slammed the early hours of the day. "Paratroopers. Look!"

Interesting, Ben thought, sitting amid the mops and buckets and crates and boxes.

Ben heard cars and trucks crank up, the sounds of what seemed to be hundreds of running feet. Just to be on the safe side, Ben removed the SS officer's shirt. If those were his people parachuting in, he sure didn't want to be mistaken for a Nazi and catch a Rebel bullet.

Ben smiled as he heard his son, Buddy Raines, yell, "Where is my father, you goose-stepping son of a bitch?"

The reply was given in German. Ben winced at the sound of a blow. His son was built like a tank and possessed enormous strength. If he'd struck the man, the man was now seriously hurt.

"Where's the General?" he heard Jersey yell.

"I'm in here!" Ben yelled, standing up.

Silence in the hallway. But outside, the battle was raging. Angry Rebels were apparently taking few, if any, prisoners. The sounds of screaming and moaning was loud even through the thick walls of the old hacienda.

"Did you hear that?" Beth's voice drifted to him.

"Where's here?" Corrie demanded.

Ben tapped on the door. "Right here, gang. I'm coming out, so ease up on those triggers." Ben opened the door and stepped out into the hall. He looked at his team, at his son, and smiled. "Took you long enough to get here. Where the hell have you been?"

# Book One

# One

It had long been said that when the United States stumbles, the world staggers. Whoever said that knew what they were talking about. The beginning of the end came not suddenly, but in a quiet, insidious manner. As silently, slowly, and carefully as a leech crawling across the edge of a straight razor to get to a drop of blood. The seeds of collapse, which would eventually lead to the end of what was once the greatest nation on the face of the earth, came with a lessening of morals, a country misplacing its values. A few people did see what was happening but their voices were ignored, and in some cases, stilled permanently by Big Brother Government. Our political leaders had moved us too far to the left, trying to be all things to all people, all the time. Our Great Nannies in Washington bankrupted the citizens trying to do that which they should have known was impossible.

There was no one *thing* or *happening* that led to the collapse of America. No historian will ever be able to point the finger of guilt at any single person or government program or world event.

But the signs were there. Evidence was all around that many citizens were worried. Americans were buying guns in record numbers, in the face of liberals frantically launching programs to disarm Americans. Many Americans were stockpiling emergency food and water and ammunition. But instead of our elected and appointed officials trying to determine *why* these thousands and thousands of people seemed to be preparing for some sort of Armageddon, the government sent armed federal agents in to seize the weapons and prosecute and jail (and sometimes kill) those who felt they had a constitutional right to own weapons. The national press belittled the men and women called "survivalists," mocking them and downplaying their warnings and actions. Liberals were prancing about, waving their hankies and shrieking that more money must be gouged from already overburdened taxpayers to pay for more social programs.

The warning signs were in place, and there were people who read them with alarming clarity. Writers wrote books about the end of civilization. Those men and women were immediately branded as nuts and kooks (some were), racists (some were), right-wing lunatics (some were), and enemies of America (most were not). Federal agents followed them, bugged their phones, and read their mail.

Most members of the press, liberal to the core and completely out of touch with the true feelings of millions of Americans, could predictably be counted on to lean to the left, weeping and blubbering and sobbing about those terrible guns and how the government should forcibly disarm the law-abiding, tax-paying citizens. Finding a true conservative among the national press, print and broadcast, would have been a real test of sleuthing.

So now, at the beginning of the last decade of the millennium, those men and women who felt the nation was teetering on the edge of collapse went about their business of preparing for the end quietly, staying away from groups who sought the limelight. These people had sensed, accurately, that it was too late. Nothing could be done to save America. The nation had sunk into an undrainable cesspool, and the politicians, both liberal and so-called conservative, and the press (always liberal) were skipping merrily along, hopping from turd to turd, blissfully unaware that beneath their feet lay collapse, chaos, and anarchy.

To many Americans who did not walk around with their heads up their asses, it was inconceivable that those in power could not see the end fast approaching.

In his last published book before the world exploded, Ben Raines wrote, "As a nation, we lost our way. We lost sight of one very important item: America must come first. We must first solve our many problems here at home, then, and only then, turn our attention and resources to other countries. That sounds hard and cruel, but if we are to survive as a nation, we must keep jobs at home and see to the needs of Americans first. We cannot be the world's problem solver and we must not become the world's policeman. We can't afford to be either."

But of course, the politicians ignored that and critics branded Ben and others like him as racist, right-wing lunatics.

Religious fanatics in the Middle East (and other

places) declared America the "Great Satan" and openly called for terrorist attacks against the U.S. And what did our great leaders do about these madmen? Why, nothing, of course. Finally terrorism struck the U.S. (as Ben Raines and others predicted it would) and the press was outraged. Never once did the know-it-all network commentators suggest we go over and bomb the shit out of the host country. That might involve some collateral damage (that means civilian dead). Of course between 1939 and '45, we had civilian dead in Berlin, Dresden, Cologne, in Holland and France and Belgium, England, the Philippines, Japan (to name only a few of the countries involved), but the press seems to have forgotten all about that. We still won the damn war. And it just never dawned on our Great Nannies in Washington, D.C. that to fight terrorism, you must think like a terrorist and act like a terrorist. And we had military units trained to do just that. But the sobbing sisters and hanky-twisters set up such a squall at just the thought of it that it was never really considered seriously.

Race relations in America began to deteriorate, finally reaching their lowest point in several decades. Riots became commonplace. The police, never enough of them, and now unable to enforce the law because of recent court decisions, could not hold back the violent tide. Los Angeles blew up. New York turned into a battleground, as did St. Louis, Detroit, Miami, and Atlanta. Much to the disgrace of this nation, our capital, Washington, D.C., became the most dangerous city in America.

A few people in prominent positions, like Ben

Raines, said, "Why don't you just shoot the god-damn punks and put an end to this crap?"

"You racist, right-wing, NRA, gun-loving, un-compassionate person!" came the collective shout from thousands of liberal throats.

"Naw," the law-abiding, tax-paying, so-called "silent majority" said wearily. "He's just voicing aloud the thoughts of millions."

There were many injustices inflicted upon minorities by whites in positions of power. There were also injustices inflicted upon whites by people of color. Minorities were justifiably angry about the lack of jobs. Whites were angry about quotas and promotions based on race and gender and not seniority and/or ability. Minorities demanded respect—loudly. Whites responded by saying that respect is not handed out on demand—it must be earned. Blacks (by now the name had been changed to African American) appeared on TV talk shows dressed like something out of the Congo and wondered why many whites smiled.

One white author appeared on a national talk show dressed in a Viking helmet and kilt, and carrying bagpipes. He said he was of Scandinavian/Scotch/Irish heritage and was just dressing like his ancestors. The black host was not amused.

But she should have been. She should have known that it has to work both ways. If it won't work both ways, it won't ever work.

We all should have had a sense of humor. And we all should have believed that we were Americans first, last, and always. And we should have known if we didn't pull together, it just wasn't going to work.

And in the end, it didn't.

# *Two*

The Rebel assault force that came in by land and air routed Hoffman's troops and quickly moved Ben out of there and into a secured area. Two hours later Ben was back in Texas. Doctor Lamar Chase, a man who had been with Ben since the formation of the old Tri-States, ordered his doctors to check Ben out, head to toe. He got a clean bill of health.

Ben was not a man who wasted time. By late that afternoon he had flown in all his batt coms . . . at least those that had responded to the call.

"We're all over the country, Ben," General Georgi Striganov told him. The Russian and Ben had once been mortal enemies—until Ben kicked the Russian's ass and forced him to lay down his arms. Now the Russian Bear was one of Ben's closest friends and allies in the drive for freedom and the quest for democracy.

"Anybody heard from Tina?" Ben asked.

"Last word we got was that she and her 9 Battalion were up near the Canadian border," Buddy told his father.

Tina Raines was Ben's adopted daughter.

"Colonel West?"

"At last report, West and his 4 Battalion were pushing hard to her last reported site," his son told him.

Ben had learned, much to his shock, that he had been in the hands of Hoffman's Nazis much longer than he originally thought. He was completely out of touch with what was going on.

But it wouldn't take Ben Raines long to get back into the saddle of command.

"The foreign troops?"

"All the European troops were called back home to help put down rebellion in their respective countries," Ike told him.

Ike McGowan, the stocky ex-Navy SEAL, was another who had been with Ben since the outset.

Ike continued, "The troops from Iceland got chewed up pretty bad. They requested to be assigned to various of our battalions and Cecil granted them permission."

General Cecil Jefferys, a black man, was second in command of all Rebels, and another of Ben's closest friends. Since suffering a heart attack during the Alaskan campaign, and undergoing bypass surgery, Cecil was in charge of Base Camp One, a huge section of what had once been known as Louisiana, now spilling over into much of what had been called Mississippi. Base Camp One was the only area in the battered nation that was totally, one hundred percent crime-free. Rebels did not tolerate crime . . . of any sort. And since they did not tolerate it, they had none. The Rebel philosophy toward crime was very simple, and very deadly.

Ben sat down on the edge of a battered old desk.

Everything in the nation was old and battered and scarred; the only area in the entire country that had been producing anything for years was Base Camp One. "Let me see if I have all this straight," Ben said. "While we were chasing Hoffman's goose-steppers all over the damn country, the thugs, punks, outlaws, war lords, and trash in the nation got together?"

His batt coms nodded their heads in agreement.

"Everything we accomplished over the years is right down the toilet?"

"That's it, Ben," Ike said. "We're back to square one. And we've taken a hell of a beating in running off Hoffman. Some battalions are down to quarter-strength. We're tired, Ben. Just flat worn out."

"I know," Ben said. "Believe me, I do. Equipment?"

"More than we can use in a lifetime," Colonel Rebet told him. "We've captured hundreds of thousands of tons of supplies and equipment from Hoffman and his allies. Everything from boots to tanks."

Ben nodded his understanding and turned to Corrie, his long-time radio operator and member of Ben's personal team. "Get this out to all batt coms: Hold your positions and get some rest. Find out if they need air drops and what they need in the way of supplies."

"They need everything from SAMs to sanitary napkins," Corrie quickly informed the General.

Ike rolled his eyes and looked toward the ceiling. Georgi looked embarrassed. Buddy quickly began studying his big hands. Pat O'Shea, the carrot-topped, freckle-faced, wild Irishman who commanded 10 Battalion ducked his head and took a sip of whiskey from a small flask.

"See that they're supplied," Ben ordered. "Promptly."

Ben had blown the theory right out the window that women could not perform well in combat. Two of his batt coms were women, and many of his most feared Scouts, Night-fighters, Pathfinders, and Rat Pack members were women. The female motorcycle Rebels, called the Sisters, were under the command of Wanda. And they were savage fighters.

"Yes, sir," Corrie said with a smile.

"You find something amusing about all this?" Ben demanded.

She laughed at his expression. "Good to have you back with us, General."

Ben smiled. "It's good to be back." To the room of batt coms: "Are we going to have to regroup and redefine battalions, people?"

Ike shook his graying head. "I don't think so, Ben. Beth has prepared a list of all battalions and their strength. But General Payon has taken his Mexican troops back across the border to deal with what is left of Hoffman's people. So you can see that we're really cut down in size."

"Casualties?" Ben asked softly.

"Thirty to thirty-five percent of Rebels dead or unaccounted for," Ike said without hesitation.

"Damn!" Ben let the word explode from his mouth.

For a man pushing middle age hard, Ben was in excellent physical shape, still possessing enormous upper body strength and maintaining a trim waistline. His thick hair was cut short, and now salt-and-pepper. He was not handsome in the pretty-boy way, but more a man's man with rugged good looks. He was also very much a woman's man. He had known for a long time that his personal bodyguard, the beautiful, dark-eyed, part-Apache, Little Jersey, was in love with him. But Ben had let that remain strictly platonic, and always would. Jersey knew that too, and contented herself with just being close to the man.

Ben had suffered through several May/September romances, and knew they seldom worked. He had buried the only woman he had ever truly loved, Jerre, on a lonely windswept hill in the Northwest, after a particularly brutal campaign. The entire Rebel camp knew of their years-long stormy and rocky relationship. They also knew it was a closed book.

"Get some rest," Ben abruptly ended the meeting. "In the morning, all you batt coms list your needed supplies and start them moving toward your location. I don't want anybody to do anything except rest and relax for a week. It's going to take me that long to assess the situation and make plans." He paused and grinned. "And for me to get myself squared away. I'll see you all at breakfast. Dismissed."

As was his custom, Ben was up long before dawn, walking the silent camp. Jersey had alerted the sentries that Ben would be taking his walk shortly—so easy with the trigger fingers. He had slept soundly for seven hours— about two hours more than what he usually got—and awakened refreshed. He showered and shaved and dressed in clean BDUs. Ben wandered to the mess area and got a mug of coffee. He knew Jersey, Beth, Corrie, and Cooper were all around him, but leaving him alone until he signaled he wanted company.

Ben sat down on the tailgate of a pickup truck, rolled a cigarette, and smoked, drank his coffee, and let his thoughts wander.

After his meeting with the batt coms, he had gone over field reports. The Rebels were in bad shape. The worst they'd been in a long time. They were not demoralized, not since his return, anyway. They were just tired. Battle weary.

Ben wandered back to the mess and got a coffee refill and returned to the truck tailgate. He was lost in memory, thinking back over the years. Remembering the final year before the collapse.

The end came during the last few years of the millennium. History clearly points out that the last decade of any millennium is always the most violent, the most volatile, the most unpredictable, the most subject to tumultuous change.

History sure was right.

America had become embroiled in other countries' civil wars around the globe. And Americans were very weary of being the world's policeman. America had troops in Haiti, several countries in Africa, Central America, and we had thousands of troops in Eastern Europe. And, Ben thought, we shouldn't have been in any of those countries.

Americans were being taxed to the point of open rebellion. Crime had soared to an unprecedented level. Gangs roamed the cities and had spread out into the smaller rural communities. And still the petunia-plucking liberals in congress refused to allow the law-abiding, tax-paying citizens to protect themselves adequately. God forbid a person should take a life just to protect his own, or the lives of his or her family, and under no circumstances should lethal force ever, ever, *ever,* be used just to protect property. How *awful!* Dreadful.

Like so many others, Ben had sealed up his guns in weatherproof containers and buried them. He recalled looking toward Washington and the Democratic president who had signed the bill and said, "Fuck you all!"

Jails and prisons were filled beyond capacity. Unemployment was high. Discontent among the hard-working, over-taxed Americans was running at a fever pitch. And there appeared to be no end in sight to how far the liberals would go to disarm law-abiding Americans and kiss the ass of the criminals.

"We must give the oppressed and the poor and those whose propensity it is to break the law more money," cooed the liberals.

Taxes went up again.

The president grinned and ate another Big Mac.

"Sit down," said his wife, the unelected czarina of the nation. "You look stupid."

For once she was right.

The American people (those who never did believe in Camelot) soon learned that the President of the United States, nearing the end of his first term, and elected because of his promises to reduce government, lower taxes, provide all things to everybody whenever they wanted it (all without raising taxes) had lied every time he'd opened his mouth on the campaign trail.

So what else is new?

It had long been said that if five million taxpayers stopped paying taxes, the government would soon cease to function. A grass-roots movement was started to do just that. Thousands signed up and thousands soon became about ten million with the majority of them refusing to pay taxes according to the current tax structure, which by now was not just the highest in the nation's history, it was obscene.

The government threatened to put them all in jail. But that was a hollow threat and those in the tax revolt knew it. There was no place to put hundreds of thousands of men and women.

"We'll pay fifteen percent of our gross income," the leaders of the Fair Taxation movement said. "No deductions. But we won't pay over fifteen percent."

The Federal government sent in agents to crush the movement. But this time the American people were determined to stand their ground and fight for what they believed was right and just and fair. Several thousand heretofore tax-paying and law-abiding citizens were shot to death and many, many more were wounded during the nationwide raids. Men, women, and children.

The men and women who had joined the fair taxation movement had not done so without expert study of what it would take to run the government and fund what they believed were needed programs. Some programs were going to be cut down in size, only a few would be cut out altogether. Pork barrel programs and general government waste would have been hard hit. Government programs would not be run by government employees, but by retired members of the business community and volunteers. Economists had proven time and time again that more revenue would be collected for the government's coffers by a flat income tax for everyone, with no exceptions and no deductions. That's all the members of the Fair Taxation movement wanted: for everyone to pay their fair share.

And they were, by God, not going to pay any more income tax until that happened.

Then the president ordered federal agents to move in and seize the members' property and possessions for back taxes, and to try to physically arrest the members.

It was by far the worst decision any sitting president had ever made.

The Fair Taxation members chose to defend their property and themselves. And why not? It was their property. They worked for it. The federal government had no right to attempt to take it from them by force.

After hundreds of bloody shoot-outs all across the nation, dozens of them in every state, many of the FBI, ATF, Secret Service, IRS, Justice Department agents, and Federal Marshals threw down their badges and said, "No more." They were sickened by the sight of dead children, sprawled in pools of blood, lying by their parents' side. Dead parents, shot to death by federal agents. Dead parents who had broken . . . what laws?

The President of the United States then went on TV and said that he was just, "Terribly, terribly sorry about all this violence. But if the men and women who were killed had obeyed the law, none of this would have happened. And," he added, holding up a finger, "if the American people had turned in their guns as had been ordered by new federal legislation, those poor children would still be alive."

That is liberal logic at work, folks. Go figure.

Then one of the president's aides, who was just barely old enough to shave, took his Walkman earplug out of his ear (where he had been listening to a rap song titled "Kill the Pigs and Rape the Bitches"), handed the president a Twinkie and the press conference was over.

But this time it backfired. The nation's press finally got around to doing some unbiased public opinion polls and found the majority of Americans shocked and sickened by the sight of dead children and the cold, savage callousness of federal agents. The American people were aroused to a point unequalled in American history.

Many Americans began calling for the president to be impeached. Many more began arming themselves, openly defying the new federal anti-gun laws. Others openly signed on with the Fair Taxation movement. Still others called for calm and for a total overhaul of the machinery of government in general and for revamping the tax system in particular—go with a flat tax for a couple of years. See if it will work.

It would have worked. But it was too late. It was just too late. Americans began choosing sides, and this time bullets would replace words.

Revolution was in the air. Not just in America, but all around the world.

Ben Raines sat in his house, in his easy chair, and watched the news on TV. He lifted a martini glass toward the set. "It really isn't your fault, Mister Pres, but you're going to get the blame for it. Not that it's going to make any difference in the long run. It's all over."

Ben went outside and dug up his cached guns.

Some say that the President of the United States broke under the strain. No one will ever know for sure because the whole goddamn world blew up twenty-four hours later. The only thing that history recorded about that last day is that the President of the United States had a meeting with the Chairman of the Joint Chiefs of Staff. The meeting was tape-recorded and for a time was preserved and removed to the new Capital of Richmond, Virginia after Washington, D.C. took a direct hit during the limited nuclear strikes exchanged between various countries around the world. The tape was lost the year after the move.

"I want troops sent in to put down those pockets of resistance around the country," he told the General.

"No," the Chairman of the JCs said. "You won't use my people to kill any more American civilians."

"I gave you an order."

"And I said no."

"You're fired!" the Commander in Chief shouted.

"All right," the general said with a smile. "Throw me out of your office."

The president wasn't about to tangle with the general, even though the general was a good ten years older than the president. The pres did not want to get the shit beat out of him.

The president buzzed for security. None came. He stalked to the door of the Oval Office and looked up and down the hall, expecting to see his

Secret Service guards. Instead, he saw armed Marines, Army Rangers, and Navy SEALs.

The Secret Service was not going to take part in the killing of more American citizens. They had met with the Joint Chiefs and bowed out.

For the first time in the nation's history, a coup d'état was taking place in America.

The president returned to his desk and sat down. He stared at the general for a moment, then sighed. "I only wanted what was best for all."

"I know that, Mister President. But you should have known that the nation cannot afford to be all things to everyone."

"We are our brothers' keepers," the pres went biblical.

"Horseshit!" the military man, totally worldly and one hundred percent realist, replied.

"You can't hope to get away with this."

"I wish to God I didn't have to."

"The American people elected me."

"Not the majority of them," the general reminded him. "And those who voted for you certainly didn't think you would order children butchered."

"I didn't want that to happen. My God, what kind of a man do you think I am?"

"One who is out of a job," General Harold Coyle replied.

# *Three*

Corrie walked over to Ben and broke into his thoughts. "General Payon just radioed in, sir. Jesus Hoffman is dead. Positively identified. Ecuadoran troops shot down the plane he was in. Hoffman and nearly all of his top people dead."

"That's the good news." Ben laughed. "Now tell me the bad news."

She smiled in the murky light of pre-dawn. "Heavily armed gangs all over the nation. Hundreds of thousands of men and women. Not like the ones we kicked ass before. These are para-military types. Most of them, anyway. Disciplined, organized, and well-trained."

"Where the hell did they come from?"

"Doctor Chase has a theory about that."

"Doctor Chase has a theory about everything. He once told me that rice has no nutritional value."

"Doctor Chase hates rice."

"I know. That's why he said it. Go on."

"He thinks that many of these people are thugs and the like who have managed to escape from foreign countries and make their way over here. Once here, they organized, stayed low, and began training their people. Now they're surfacing."

"I don't doubt that's part of it. Have you learned anything about what is happening in Africa?"

"Everything bad you can possibly imagine."

"That bad, huh?"

"That bad."

"I predicted that, too," Ben muttered.

"Yes, sir. I know. In a book of yours called *Out of the Darkness.*"

"You read it?"

"Yes, sir. Enjoyed it immensely."

"I haven't seen a copy of that book in years."

"All your books have been reprinted and have been required high school reading for the past two years," Corrie said, stepping back.

"They *what?*" Ben shouted, spilling coffee down the front of his shirt.

Rebels began running out of tents, scrambling from under six-bys and other heavy vehicles, all armed and racing toward the general.

"Relax," Ben shouted. "Stand easy. Everything is all right. Go get breakfast." He turned to Corrie. "Some of those books are damned sexy, Corrie. Whose bright idea was this?"

"General Jefferys. He had people edit out the rough spots, though." She grinned. "But not in the copy I have."

"Why wasn't I told about this?"

"Because Cecil is in charge of public education and didn't feel it necessary," Doctor Lamar Chase said, walking up. "You should be flattered, Ben. It's not every day that a writer of such dubious pulp that you managed to get published is immortal-ized."

"You're too kind to me, Lamar."

"I feel charitable this morning. I'll revert to my normal self by mid-morning, I assure you."

"With any kind of luck, I'll be fifty miles away by then."

Chase grinned. "Sorry. But the only place you're going is to the hospital."

"I had a check up yesterday!" Ben protested. "I checked out just fine."

"A very perfunctory examination. No, Ben. This time you're going to be in my capable hands."

"God help me," Ben muttered. But he knew better than to argue. In almost any army in the world, a doctor can order the captain of a ship off the bridge and to his quarters or sick-bay, ground a pi-lot, and put a general to bed.

For the next two days, Ben was in the MASH hos-pital tent, and Doctor Chase put him through a gru-eling examination. Grudgingly, the doctor admitted that Ben was in excellent health (for a man his age) and released him back to duty.

In his makeshift office, Ben began once more poring over reports. None of them looked good. True, Jesus Hoffman and his goose-stepping, Nazi army had been anti-climactically smashed and ground under the boot-heels of the Rebels and their allies, but in the year it had taken the Rebels to do that, a dozen or more threats to peace and rebuild-ing and some semblance to order had sprang up.

"It never ends," Ben muttered. "It just never ends."

He picked up a wad of reports, dealing with warlords and cults: Al Rogers, who had settled in the midwest part of the nation and boasted an army of five thousand. Dangerous and well-equipped. Bandar Ali Shazam Baroshi, a self-proclaimed black messiah with a following estimated at four to six thousand, also in the midwest part of the nation. Carl Nations, an extremist far to the right, hates people of color, and has a following of several thousand, located in West Virginia. Jeb Moody, located in Central Illinois—following of about five thousand. Political leanings unknown. Carlos Medina, Arizona/New Mexico, militant hispanic. Hates all anglos. Jake Starr, located in what was once called Florida. Drove off or killed all people of color. Strength: about five thousand.

Ben sighed and laid the reports to one side. There were at least two dozen more files on groups still waiting to be read. They could wait for a little while.

Ben stood up and stretched. He was restless, eager to get on the road. But he had promised his people a full week of rest and would hold to that promise. He walked to the huge wall map and studied it for a time. There were several dangerous groups that had sprung up here in Texas. Ned Hawkins and his New Texas Rangers were roaming the state, dealing with them. For all the trouble that had taken place inside what used to be called Texas, this state would probably be the first to re-establish law and order, thanks to people like Ned and those who served with him.

The rest of the country was in chaos—the best word Ben could think of to describe the condition of what used to be the United States of America.

Almost all of the carefully set up Rebel outposts had been overrun by the gangs of thugs and punks and trash that had surfaced while the Rebels were fighting Hoffman and his Nazis.

"Bastards," Ben muttered.

"Who are you cursing now, Raines?" Doctor Chase asked, stepping into the office. "Oh, don't let me stop you from venting your spleen. It's good for you."

Ben turned and smiled at his long-time friend. Chase was too old for the field—he had to be in his seventies—but he refused to leave the field, and Ben had stopped asking him to do so.

"Fresh pot of coffee over there," Ben said, pointing.

Chase poured a cup of black coffee. He sat down in front of the desk and watched Ben fidget for a moment. "Getting restless, are we?"

"Yes," Ben admitted, cutting his eyes to his personal team as they entered the office and spread out. Jersey was always close, her CAR ready.

"Well, calm yourself. The people need their promised week of rest." He looked at Jersey, looking at him. "Girl, don't you ever relax your guard?"

"No," she told him, and sat down, her back to a wall.

Chase harrumphed and looked back at Ben. "I saw you working while I had you in the hospital. Have you reorganized?"

"I'm almost through. Very few changes. I'm pretty much going to leave things as they are." He looked at Corrie. "You have news, Corrie?"

"I just spoke with Thermopolis. He's all set up

back in Arkansas. Fully operational. They had to do a little ass-kicking but nothing serious."

Ben nodded.

Beth, Ben's organizer, said, "I'll have situation reports ready for you in a few minutes. We're spread pretty thin, General."

"The Hummer is sittin' on ready, General," Coop, Ben's driver said. "It's been completely reworked, inside and out."

"My Thompson?"

"Ready," Jersey said. "Is there an original part left in that thing, General?"

Ben laughed. "I doubt it. It won't qualify as an antique."

"You would," Chase muttered, and left the room.

"Crusty old bastard," Jersey said.

"I heard that, you damn Apache heathen!" Chase roared from the outside.

"Go sit on a candlestick," Jersey retorted.

Ben sat down, laughing so hard he had to wipe his eyes. Conditions were back to normal.


Rebel planes were kept busy that week of rest for the ground troops. They flew in supplies to a dozen different locations around the country, working around the clock. Those men and women who had chosen a life of crime and had staked out parts of the nation as their own little kingdoms heard the roaring of engines overhead and knew something was up . . . and that something was not going to be good for them.

"That honky, racist, pig bastard Raines is coming

after us, " Bandar told his people. "We've got to be ready for them."

"That damn nigger-lovin' Ben Raines is gettin' ready to move against us," Carl Nations told his people. "It's root hog or die time."

No one could really fathom Ben. One just could not fit Ben Raines or his Rebels into any particular political slot. The Rebels were of all colors, all races, all religions. But first, last, and always, they were Americans, even though the nation of America, per se, no longer existed. Many Rebels did not agree with Ben's philosophy one hundred percent, but they all agreed with it in general.

It was a hard time, and it took hard people to wage the long fight to bring the nation back into some sort of structured order. All Rebels shared many philosophical points; but all shared one thing in common: they were not so much interested in the fine points of law as they were in order and justice. Nearly all could clearly remember when criminals had more rights than the law abiding. That was never going to happen again.

On the fifth day of the Rebels' stand-down, in every encampment around the country, Rebels were getting restless, itching to get back into the fight. Those that had family and friends back in Base Camp One had written their letters. They had cleaned their weapons and washed their clothing and taken care of equipment. The tanks and trucks and APCs and Bradley Fighting Vehicles and Hum-Vees were ready to roll.

On the sixth day, a Saturday, Ben told Corrie, "Radio all the batt coms to have religious services early tomorrow and make sure all the Rebels know when and where. We roll at 0900."

"Yes, sir. What's our objective, General?"

"That nut up in Oklahoma. Jesse what's-his-name."

"Jesse Boston."

"Yeah, Boston." Ben picked up the file on Jesse Boston and studied it. Most of the information the Rebels had gathered on the various warlords and self-proclaimed rulers had come from victims of their brutality or from members who had been captured . . . usually the latter. Jesse Boston. Alias. Real name unknown. Age, approximately thirty-five. Boasts of having spent more time in prison than out. Convicted murderer and thief. Was in prison when Great War broke out. Escaped in the confusion and since that time has bragged of all the evil deeds he's done. He and his bunch overran and took over a small town southwest of Oklahoma City."

Ben closed the folder. "Well, now, Mister Boston," he said softly. "We'll just see about bringing your little empire down around your ears." He raised his voice and said, "Corrie? I want Buddy's 8 Battalion and Jim Peters's 14 Battalion with my 1 Battalion on this run."

"They're both short, sir."

"I know it. Our usual complement of artillery will roll with us."

"Right, sir."

"Beth, plot us a course."

"I already have, sir."

Ben looked over at her. "Now, just how did you

know where we were going? I didn't know myself until this morning."

"I guessed." She smiled. "I know the type of person you dislike the most. I have compiled a listing over the years, ranking the types from one to ten, one being the highest. Jesse Boston tops the list."

"Why doesn't that surprise me?"

Beth smiled coyly and returned to writing in her ledger.

Ben stood up and walked to the door. Jersey stepped in front of him, blocking his way. "Aren't you forgetting something, General?"

"What?"

Cooper tossed Jersey Ben's Thompson, then web belt with ammo pouch. She handed the articles to him and he dutifully hooked the belt and took his Thompson. "I'm surrounded by a thousand Rebels, Jersey," Ben said with a smile. "And then, I do have you shadowing me."

"I don't have eyes in the back of my head, General," she replied without cracking a smile.

"Right," Ben said drily. "Shall we proceed with our walk?"

"Certainly." She stepped aside.

Father Riley, the Catholic priest assigned to Ben's 1 Battalion, fell in step with him.

"Padre," Ben said. "Have you written your sermon for Sunday's mass yet?"

"Oh, yes. We're moving out to smite the Philistines hip and thigh?"

"No. But we're going to kick their asses from here to eternity."

The priest laughed. "It's amazing how many more confessions I hear just before a campaign."

"A person is dead a long time, Padre. I guess," Ben added. "Maybe the soul goes to Heaven or Hell or someplace in between at the moment of death. I don't know and neither does anyone else. Including you." Ben said the last with a smile.

Father Riley smiled. He wasn't about to get into an argument with Ben, and he knew that's what Ben wanted. Ben would argue with a stump . . . and usually win.

Riley looked at Jersey. "I want to hear your confession this evening, young lady."

"If I have the time," Jersey hedged.

"She'll be there," Ben said. "Cooper will escort her."

"I'm not Catholic, General!"

"That doesn't make any difference, does it, Padre?"

"Not a bit." He looked at Cooper. "I'll be glad to hear your confession, son."

"Can I listen?" Jersey asked.

"She can't listen in, can she, Father?" Cooper asked.

"No," the priest said, laughing. "I won't even know it's you, Cooper."

"What do I say?" Cooper asked.

"You tell him all your sins, dummy!" Jersey said. "If you've been mean to someone, thought bad thoughts about someone, lusted in your heart, you confess it."

"Then what does the priest do with that information?" Cooper asked.

Jersey, a wicked glint in her dark eyes, whispered in Cooper's ear: "The priest tells God!"

"I'm in real trouble," Cooper muttered.

# *Four*

The religious services were over, the Rebels mounted up and ready to roll out of the staging area. As was his custom, Ben walked up beside the long lines of trucks and Jeeps and Hummers and tanks. At one time he knew the name of every Rebel in his command. Not so anymore. There were many new faces. Many of those who had survived the assault on the old Tri-States years back were gone. Dead, permanently disabled, retired back to Base Camp One. There were few in the ranks now who had survived the long years of war.

By all rights, Ben should not have been one of those who survived. He was known for taking incredible chances. He'd been shot several times, stabbed more than once, survived assassination attempts, kidnapped, tortured. But he always came through and returned to lead his people. He was back now, leaner and meaner than ever before.

Ben realized he was a living legend, and not just among his troops. The name of Ben Raines was known all over the world. He was equally loved and feared and hated. At the end of the brief but deadly

Great War that exploded worldwide, hundreds of thousands of thugs and punks and human slime had roamed the ruins of the nation, preying on the very old, the very young, the sick, the helpless. Ben Raines and his Rebels had tracked them down and killed them.

Now it appeared they had it to do all over again.

Ben walked the line, his Thompson slung, Jersey one step behind him to the left, her M-16 at the ready. Corrie walked beside Jersey, to her right, wearing the backpack radio, headset in place. Beth and Cooper behind them.

As Ben neared the head of the long column, Buddy and Jim Peters joined him. "Scouts out, son?" Ben asked, knowing full well they had been gone for several hours.

"Left two hours ago," his son acknowledged.

Ben's 1 Battalion would spearhead, as always, with tanks ranging out ahead of him, between Ben and the scouts, Jim's battalion in the center of the long column, Buddy's battalion in the drag. Tanker trucks, carrying fuel, were spaced among the three battalions.

Ben glanced at Cooper and he and Beth ran on ahead, to ready the Hummer. "We should make about a hundred miles today, considering the condition of the roads," Ben said. "And providing we don't get our asses ambushed," he added drily. He looked at Buddy and Jim. "Let's roll."

It was slow going. During the year-long battle with Hoffman's Nazis, many of the bridges and overpasses had been blown by the Rebels to slow the enemy advance. The Rebels made seventy-five miles the first day, fifty miles the second day, and slightly over eighty miles the third day. They encountered no hostile forces.

"We're going to pass through a small town in the morning that is filled with people who are not going to be thrilled to see us," Corrie informed Ben that evening.

"Oh?"

"Scouts report that these people don't even want us to enter their town."

"Is there a bypass?"

"No, sir."

"Then we'll go through the town. Tell the leaders of this group we are not looking for any trouble."

"They've been told that, sir."

"And?"

"They said to keep out or fight them."

"Oh, shit! What's their problem?"

Corrie could not hide her grin.

Ben sighed. "Come on, Corrie. Give."

"They're hippies, sir."

"You're kidding? Like Thermopolis and his bunch?"

"Sort of. But totally non-violent. They don't believe in guns or eating meat or wearing leather and things like that."

"That's admirable of them. I applaud them for it. But you said they were going to fight us—how?"

"With a protest march."

"Oh, shit!"

"Yes, sir. At least that."

* * *

BEN RAINES SUCKS read the white banner with large black words that stretched from one side of the road to the other.

Buddy walked back to his father. "Father, what is that horrible sound coming from the town?"

"Acid rock, son."

"I beg your pardon?"

"Music of the 1960s. Or maybe the '70s. I wasn't in the country so I'm not sure."

"That's music?"

"They think so. Listen to that chanting."

"ONE, TWO, THREE, FOUR. WE DON'T WANT YOUR FUCKING WAR!"

Buddy could not understand why his father was smiling. "That takes me back," Ben said.

"Father, this is ridiculous. We're not asking them to fight with us. We just want to drive through the town."

"Brace yourself, son. I assure you, you have never seen anything like this. Let's roll on through."

BEN RAINES IS A BABY-KILLER, proclaimed another banner, stretched across the old highway.

NIXON EATS SHIT, said another banner.

"Nixon?" Cooper muttered. "Oh, President Nixon. But that was more than thirty years ago!"

"That's where they're living, Coop," Ben told him. "In the past."

"My God!" Corrie blurted. "Look at that crowd."

"Thermopolis would love this," Beth said.

"In a way, he would," Ben said. "But Therm knows that having freedom sometimes means fighting for it. How did these people escape the Nazis?"

"They ran," Corrie told him.

"Well, that's one way to do it."

MAKE LOVE, NOT WAR, another banner read.

The column inched forward. "Don't run over anybody," Ben urged.

Many of the Rebels had their cameras out, taking pictures of the crowd. Most of the hippies were middle-aged and beyond.

"This is pathetic," Beth said.

"Oh, in a way, I suppose it is," Ben said, taking a flower offered him by a gray-haired man. "Thank you," Ben told him. "But they're happy with their way of life and I'll bet you they have no crime, they're all healthy and they all work together. I wish the whole world could adopt their ways."

"That would be neat," Cooper said. "I wonder if they believe in free love."

"Boy, it's back to confession for you," Jersey told him.

"I'm sorry I brought it up," Cooper muttered.

"Don't kill our babies, Ben Raines!" a gray-haired woman shouted, standing close to the Hummer.

"How old is your baby, lady?" Ben asked.

"Forty-one."

"Incredible," Ben muttered. "Get us the hell out of here, Cooper."

"I'm tryin', General!"

The town must have held about five hundred aging hippies. Ben had yet to spot one who wasn't at least sixty years old. And they had blocked the road, standing ten deep.

After a few moments of listening to protest songs that Ben hadn't heard (thank God) in more than twenty years, he lost his patience. "I've had all I can tolerate," he said. Ben stepped out of the Hummer and let a full clip of .45 caliber slugs cut the air over the heads of the protesters. The line of colorfully dressed men and women broke ranks in one hell of a hurry and cleared the street. Ben got back into the Hummer. "Now drive on through," he said.

The roads were so bad that the Rebels only made about fifty miles that day before having to pull over for the night. They always stopped early, to give them time to scout the country and set up perimeters, for the land called America was once more enemy territory for the Rebels.

"You think those old hippies will come out here and make trouble?" Cooper asked Ben.

"Oh, no. They made their point, albeit a couple of decades late, and they'll leave us alone. I'm ninety-nine percent sure of that. I don't want to hurt any of those people."

"We going through Dallas or cut around it?" Corrie asked.

"I'm going to let the Scouts answer that," Ben said. "There shouldn't be a whole lot left of the city."


"Negative on Dallas," the scouts radioed back the next morning. "I get the distinct smell of Creepies."

"10-9," Corrie asked for a repeat.

"Creepies. Night People. The smell is strong."

"I heard it," Ben said. "Damn!" he whispered the word. "I thought we were through with those cannibalistic bastards. Pull the convoy over, Corrie. Set up for long-range traffic."

When she was set up, Ben said, "Burst transmission, Corrie. To all batt coms. Inspect the larger towns and cities for Creepies. I think they have returned."

"Creepies?" General Georgi Striganov said, up in Tennessee.

"Creepies?" Colonel West said, from his location in Iowa.

"Creepies?" Ike said. "Again?"

"I thought we wiped them out?" Thermopolis said, from his HQ Company location in Arkansas.

"Let's go to Dallas," Ben told his people. He looked at his son. "Spearhead, Buddy."

Dallas was a ruined city, having been bombed and burned twice by the Rebels, but still, life survived there. In a manner of speaking.

Some Rebel doctors had opined that the constant and prolonged eating of human flesh caused the unusual smell associated with the Night People, or Creepies and Creeps as the Rebels called them. Whatever caused the stench, it was unmistakable, and it hung over the ruins of Dallas.

"I hate these bastards," Jersey said, standing beside Ben.

"No more than I do," Ben replied, his eyes watching as a human form flitted from ruin to ruin a few hundred yards away. "But that isn't a Creep."

"So they've managed to coexist with, ah, more normal people?" Jim Peters asked.

"Probably as procurement agents," Ben replied.

Cooper spat on the ground at that.

"Back off and make camp," Ben ordered his battalions. "Double the guards and stay alert. The Creeps hate us as much as we hate them."

Ben and his Rebels first encountered the Night People years back, about the same time the Libyan terrorist, Khamsin, and his army invaded North America. Khamsin and his terrorist hordes were eventually destroyed, but the Creeps clung to life and the Rebels fought them for years, only recently having decided they had finally rid the land of the cannibals. The Rebels were wrong. The Night People were back . . . or more precisely, had never gone away, just buried themselves and waited and recruited.

And what other old enemy has returned? Ben silently questioned that evening, sitting in the darkened den of a once fine home just outside of Dallas. The Creeps can't be the only ones. My God, are we going to have to repeat everything we've done?

Ben sighed and shook his head. Probably, he concluded. At least a part of it.

"Creeps outside the camp," Jersey broke into his thoughts, speaking from the archway leading into the den. "Looks like they're massing for an attack."

Ben stood up smoothly, Thompson in hand. "Here we go again, Jersey."

"Let's do it right this time," Beth, the quiet one, said. "Let's take first things first and hunt them down like the dangerous rabid animals they are, and destroy them once and for all. Make damn sure the job is finished. Then we tackle the warlords and punks."

Beth had lost a very close personal friend to the Night People, and she hated them with an intensity that bordered fanaticism.

"All right, Beth," Ben said. "That's a good idea."

The old and very familiar chanting from the throats of the Creeps began drifting to the Rebels. "Die, die, die!" they chanted.

Even though the Rebels had faced the Night People many times, it was still a chilling sound coming out of the darkness of dead of night.

"Ready flares," Ben spoke softly and Corrie spoke quietly into her head set mic.

Ben did not have to ask if the Rebels were in place. He knew they were.

"In sight now," Corrie relayed the message.

"Hold fire," Ben said. The rancid smell of the Creeps assaulted his nostrils and he grimaced. "No doubt about who it is."

"Bastards," Beth whispered the word.

Cooper sat behind an M-60 machine-gun. For all his clowning, he was as fine a combat soldier as Ben had ever seen. Jersey was fearless in combat, a savage, merciless fighter who gave absolutely no quarter. Beth and Corrie were solid soldiers with no backup in them.

"Flares up," Ben ordered, and the night was suddenly bright under the artificial light.

"Jesus!" Cooper broke the momentary silence as Ben and the others were stunned into silence.

The ground on all sides was filled with hundreds of robed and hooded Night People, all well-armed.

The Rebels were going to be outnumbered about five to one.

So what else was new?

"Fire!" Ben shouted.

# *Five*

The Rebels laid down a withering rain of lead, the slugs ripping into flesh and slamming those Creeps leading the assault back against their friends, dead and dying. The Creeps climbed over the bodies of their dead and continued running toward the encampment, screaming out their fury at the hated Rebels.

The second wave met the same fate as the first wave. Within seconds, the area around the Rebel camp was littered with bodies, three and four and five deep. The Night People fell back to regroup and plan a new strategy.

"They do the same damn thing every time," Ben said, changing clips. "Eating human flesh not only causes them to stink like rotting meat, it must also affect their minds. When this little altercation is over, I want these twin cities burned to the ground. We'll use the captured napalm from Hoffman to bring this place down."

"Do all the cities this way?" Corrie asked.

"Every one of them. We'll take them one at a time, throw up a loose line of Rebels around them, and then destroy the ruins. And we start first thing in the morning. Corrie, bump Base Camp One and have planes readied. I want them here early."

"We're going to surround Dallas/Fort Worth with three short battalions?" Beth asked.

"As best we can. Have gun ships come in right after the planes drop their payloads, Corrie. Eyes in the sky."

Corrie went to work and Ben waited for Cecil's objections. They were quick in coming.

"General Jefferys at Base Camp One," Corrie said, handing Ben the headset.

"Go ahead, Cec."

"Are you out of your mind, Ben?" Cecil's voice boomed in Ben's ears. "You can't surround Dallas/Fort Worth with three short battalions."

"We will be spread rather thin," Ben admitted.

*"Rather thin!"* Cecil yelled. "That's, by God, the understatement of the decade. Three short battalions covering an area fourteen miles west to east, on both sides, and six miles deep on both ends. It can't be done, Ben."

Ben smiled at Corrie. "Cec has been busy with his little ruler, hasn't he?"

Ben keyed the mic. "Your transmission is garbled, Cec. I'll talk to you later. Just get those birds up."

"The birds are up, Ben. And you're lying about garbled transmissions. I won't even ask you to be careful, because I'd be wasting my breath. Base Camp One out."

"General Jefferys is slightly pissed, General," Jersey ventured an opinion.

"I would say so," Ben said with a smile.

* * *

The prop-job planes arrived just after dawn and began circling while Ben and his Rebels were getting into place as quickly as humanly possible, and that took a good hour working at break-neck speed. No more attacks had come out of the night, as the Creeps melted back into the ruins of the twin cities. It had always been a mystery to Ben and the others why the Night People insisted on living in the burned-out, bombed-out ruins of cities. Over the years, those places had consistently proven to be death-traps for the Creeps.

The planes would strike the outer limits first, along I-20, I-635, I-820, along the Northwest Parkway and I-35, creating a wall of flames, then work inward toward the ruined hearts of the twin cities.

"Spread thin *is* sort of an understatement," Ben said with a mocking smile.

"No kidding," Cooper said.

Ben and his personal team were all that stood between life and death for the Creeps who might try to bust through their location at a junction along Highway 77, just south of Dallas.

The next team was half a klick away on Hampton Road.

"Bump the planes," Ben said. "Tell them to go to work."

A runway had been hurriedly cleared southeast of the twin cities and trucks containing aviation fuel had been rolling all night to reach the siege site.

The crumping sounds of bombs exploding on contact with the ground reached the Rebels; those closest in felt the ground tremble under their boots.

Flames seared every living thing and then leaped hundreds of feet into the air.

"Don't you just love the smell of napalm in the morning?" Cooper said with a smile, knowing Jersey would have something smart-ass to say about it. "It's so invigorating."

"I worry about you, Cooper," Jersey called from the other side of the highway. "I think you're losing it."

"Nothing is going to come through that," Beth said, her voice soft in the gasoline-scented air.

"There will be holes between the flames," Ben said. "Just like that one right ahead of us. See it."

"Here they come," Cooper yelled, over the crackle of flames eating everything in their path. He pulled back the bolt on his .50 caliber machine gun.

Corrie, Beth, and Jersey lay behind M-60 machine guns. Ben squatted behind a Big Thumper. "Fire!" he shouted, and let the Big Thumper start banging out 40mm anti-personnel grenades.

Within seconds it was carnage in front and slightly below their position on the overpass. The machine gun slugs ripped bodies and the 40mm grenades shredded flesh from the bone.

The Creeps had no place to run that wasn't lethal for them. The raging flames lay hot behind them, and the guns of Ben and his team stood in front of them. They chose the guns, and died.

The rattle and slam of machine guns and the roar of the grenades lasted only a moment, then fell silent. The ground before Ben and his team was littered with the bodies of the dead. Ben sat down and pulled the plugs from his ears.

"This is one hole that won't be used again," he said, rolling a cigarette. "One person eyes front, the others relax for a moment."

As the team began to settle down from the brief fire-fight, the sounds of heavy firing and the booming of mortars and rockets striking their targets faintly reached them over the crackle of the flames, all mingled with an occasional, very faint scream of burning pain.

No Rebel could work up even the slightest amount of sympathy for the Night People—not even the religious leaders of the Rebels—Protestant, Catholic, or Jew. They all supported Ben's plan to purge the earth of the Night People.

The twin cities were pounded with napalm from the planes and with Willie Peter from Rebel artillery all that morning and into the afternoon. At four o'clock that day, Ben called a halt to the shelling and the bombardment. Even from where the Rebels had backed up to, they were still covered with grime and soot from the monstrous blaze that stretched for miles.

Back-fires had been set to help contain the blaze and as wide an area cleared as best they could—behind the controlled burn—by careful burning and blasting.

The collapsing of burned-out hulks of buildings would continue far into the night and the next day, and it would be several days before the twin cities cooled down enough for any Rebel to enter, if Ben wanted them to go in—which he did not.

"No," he told Buddy, lowering his binoculars and casing them. "Maybe we didn't get them all—I'm sure they had quite an elaborate underground system—but we cut them down to a manageable level. We'll let the combat engineers enter in a few weeks and locate and seal off any entrances and exits the bastards might still have working. We're through. Let's go shower and get this stench off of us."

The fires continued to burn out of control all that night, and they were still burning when the Rebels pulled out the next morning, giving the cities a wide skirt.

The Rebels crossed over into what had once been the state of Oklahoma early that afternoon and pulled over to bivouac just across the line, the Red River behind them.

They made camp in the ruins of a small town about nine miles inside the line. Their objective was about a day and a half straight north, and Ben felt sure that Jesse Boston knew they were coming.

Buddy sat down on a stool beside his father, who was eating his dinner while sitting on the floor of the old home. "Scouts are within a few miles of Boston's location," he said. "They report a heavy concentration of well-armed and seemingly well-disciplined men and women."

"So our information was correct."

"It appears that way."

"Estimates on size of force?"

"Hard to say. They guessed at four to five thousand, not counting kids and slaves."

Ben fixed his son with a hard look. "Slaves?"

"Yes. Several hundred of them at least. And they are not treated well."

Ben nodded his head. Light was fading and the

camp was secure. Few people, with the exception of the Creeps, would dare attack a Rebel encampment. Before making camp, the Rebels secured everything within a mile of the camp site, oftentimes ranging out two or three miles, or more. Sentries were dug in hard before dark and anything that moved was suspect. Approaching a Rebel camp at night was not only foolish, it was oftentimes lethal if one did not know the right words.

Ben was not in a real peachy mood that early evening along the Oklahoma line. Everything the Rebels had managed to accomplish over the bloody years was unraveling. During the year-long war with Hoffman's Nazis, the thugs and punks and slime had emerged, knowing the Rebels were tied-up fighting the goose-steppers and could do nothing to stop them.

Buddy Raines had walked past his father and saw the storm-clouds on his father's face and had passed the word: Leave the general alone.

Ben drank his coffee and brooded, his thoughts mixed and often dark. One part of him said to pull back and enlarge the area of Base Camp One; take in three or four states and just let the rest of the country go to hell.

But he knew he couldn't do that. He couldn't have a single oasis of freedom surrounded by anarchy. It might work for a time, but not for long. He had discussed this very matter with military leaders from those foreign countries who had sent personnel in to help fight the Nazi hordes. They were all doing what Ben and his Rebels had originally set out to do: purge the land of criminal types. Forever.

But was that nothing more than a wonderful, impossible dream? Sometimes Ben thought so. Like right now.

Ben was no dreamy-eyed idealist. He had seen that peace and stability and reason and order could prevail. The living, working proof was Base Camp One. Thousands and thousands of people living and working side by side and getting along like clockwork.

So why in the hell wouldn't it, couldn't it, work nationwide? What was he doing wrong? Everything or nothing?

What was he supposed to do? Kill everyone who didn't subscribe to the Rebel philosophy?

People had seen, witnessed firsthand, how harsh the Rebels could be; still certain types persisted in flaunting lawlessness in the face of terrible penalties . . . and those penalties more often than not meant death.

What in the hell did he have to do to prove to people that obeying the few laws the Rebels had on the books was better than breaking them? That if one obeyed the law, their overall lives would be far better. What did he have to do to get that through their heads?

Ben smiled for the first time that evening as he realized he was asking himself questions that humankind had been asking for thousands of years. And no one had ever come up with a workable answer or solution.

Ben rolled a cigarette and freshened his coffee. "All right," he muttered, only the few members of his personal team close enough to hear the words. "Maybe what we're doing is not the best way, but it's the most effective way I can think of. I don't have time to hold hands with the lawless and spout fancy words about their poverty-stricken childhood and how it was society's fault that they turned bad. To hell with that crap. It was bullshit when the country was more or less whole, and it's still bull-shit."

Jersey smiled and cut her eyes to Beth. Beth was smiling. The women looked at Cooper. He was smiling as he looked at Corrie. She had a grin on her face, too. Ben Raines had made up his mind and his team knew they were only a few hours away from kicking ass.

Ben Raines could be as compassionate as any human being could be toward those he felt deserved it. To those standing under the umbrella of lawless-ness, he was a dark avenging angel, cold, ruthless, and savage.

Ben lifted his eyes to touch the gaze of Corrie. "I want gunships up in this area by noon day after tomorrow, Corrie. I want artillery in place to shell Mister Boston's little kingdom. Get Pat O'Shea on the horn and tell him to move his 10 Battalion out now. He's right on the Kansas line and that should give him time to get in place north of Boston's ter-ritory. Buddy's battalion will flank to the west and Jim Peters's battalion will flank east. We'll be in position to the south. I want a show of force that will scare the shit out of Boston and his people. I will not have this nation divided. I will bring this country back together. I will, by God, do that if I have to kill every lawless son of a bitch in the land. Before I die I will see this nation put back together and working."

"Yes, sir!" Corrie said, and turned to her radio.

"All right!" Cooper said.

Beth smiled and reached for her journal.

Ben picked up his Thompson and looked at Jersey.

She smiled. "Kick ass time!"

# Six

"Holy shit!" one of Jesse Boston's lieutenants said, looking at the activity in the sky.

Jesse's eyes were scanning the skies, far in the distance—too far away for his limited range ground-to-air rockets—helicopter gunships hovered. Higher up, but still out of range, the old slow PUFFs lazily circled.

A member of Jesse's inner circle panted up. "We just received a bump from our patrols. We got artillery all around us, Jesse. Big stuff. Everything from 105s to 155s. We got tanks on all borders. Main battle tanks with 105s. And fuckin' Rebels everywhere."

Jesse sighed. He had managed to convince himself and his followers that once they grew as strong as they had, Ben Raines would leave them alone. Now he knew he'd been lying to himself all along.

"Jesse!" the shout turned him around. "Over to the radio shack. Ben Raines wants to talk to you."

Jesse sighed and started the walk toward the communications building.

The town where Jesse had settled had once held

about twenty thousand decent, law-abiding people, and was some thirty-five miles southwest of the ruins of Oklahoma City. It once had a fine university, but Jesse and his followers had little use for anything like that.

"This is Jesse Boston. Go ahead."

"Pack it up, Jesse. You're finished," Ben's voice was calm out of the speaker.

Jesse stood for a moment, staring at the speaker in disbelief. He lifted the mic. "What did you say, Raines?"

"I said, you simple-minded shit, to pack it up. You're finished."

"Just who in the hell do you think you are, Raines?"

"The biggest kid on the block, Jesse. You want to fight?"

"I might just do that, Raines."

"Then that makes you a fool. I have four battalions of Rebels with me. I have gunships and PUFFs. I have artillery that can lay back twenty-five miles and drop rounds down any chimney you care to point out to my forward observers, and I assure you, they are watching your little kingdom as we speak. You still want to fight, Jesse?"

"Shit!" Jesse muttered. He keyed the mic. "Damnit, Raines. You don't have the right to do this. This ain't . . . well, it ain't constitutional."

"Yeah, that's a word you punks got to use quite a bit back in the good ol' liberal days, isn't it, Jesse?"

Jesse wisely said nothing.

"The Constitution no longer applies, Jesse. The only law in the land is what the Rebels enforce."

"Your goddamn law, you mean."

"You could say that, Jesse."

Again, Jesse was silent.

"Turn your slaves loose, Jesse. Right now."

"And if I don't, Raines?"

"My people start coming in at night and cutting throats. And my people are the best in the world at doing that."

Those in the room looked at Jesse, some with open fear in their eyes, others with cold defiance.

"He's bluffin', Jesse," one said. "I say we stand our ground and fight."

But Jesse shook his head. "No, Nick. He's not bluffing. Ben Raines doesn't bluff." He keyed the mic. "And if I turn the slaves loose, what then?"

"We sit down and I explain to you and your lieutenants the very simple rules of living under Rebel law."

"There ain't no goddamn way I live under your rules, Raines."

"Is that your final say, Boston?" Ben's voice was very hard out of the speaker.

"You got it." Jesse waited for a reply that did not come. Ben had broken off.


Jesse and his several thousand followers braced themselves and waited for the attack that did not come. By the end of the third day of the standoff, they were nervous and extremely tense, even though not a single shot had been fired from the Rebel side. Jesse and his people had labored long repairing the town's utility plant and had enjoyed electric lights—until Rebels slipped in and sabotaged the power plant, then melted back into the darkness like ghosts after plunging the town into darkness. To make matters worse, Rebels had then doctored the town's water supply. Now everybody had the shits. Then the Rebels sabotaged the sewer system which Jesse and followers had worked so long to get back in order. All the commodes were backed up and everybody was forced to dig latrines and throw up some sort of covering to serve as an outhouse.

Jesse Boston sat on the hurriedly carved-out wooden plank in his tent bathroom and cursed Ben Raines as the splinters dug into his ass. "I hate you, Ben Raines. Goddamn you, I hate you so bad I can't even think of enough cuss words to describe how I feel."

He reached for the rack where the squares of old newspapers were kept. It was empty. Jesse put his elbows on his bare knees, his face in his hands and said, "I hate you, Ben Raines."


"Men and women coming out under a flag of truce," Corrie said to Ben.

"All right. Let's see what we have."

Jesse had released the prisoners. "Is this all of those being held captive?" Ben asked a man.

"Yes. Those of us that are left," he added bitterly.

"Say it all," Ben said.

"We were a striving little community until Jesse came along. We couldn't fight him."

"Why not?"

"We don't believe in guns, General Raines."

Ben shook his head. He started to say some pretty hard things to the man, then thought better of it. "Get them over to the medics," he ordered. "Patch

64

them up until somebody else comes along and enslaves them. Just get them out of my sight." Ben turned to leave.

But the man wouldn't let it go. "We aren't all like the Rebels, General. We're not all brave and know how to fight."

Ben whirled around, his eyes blazing. "And you think all of us were born that way? Well, do you?"

The man, who obviously had not been treated all that badly—he bore no marking of abuse and looked to be in reasonably good health—backed up under the hawk-like gaze of Ben. "We have our beliefs, General."

"So did they," Ben responded, pointing all around him at the Rebels. "They were just average people when the Great War came. Nurses, bankers, clerks, secretaries, farmers, mechanics, salespeople, teachers. They worked in insurance, stocks, you name it. Just average people. But when they looked around them and discovered brute force and violence staring them in the face, they realized that all the liberal bullshit they'd been force-fed by the news media and the talk show hosts and the network commentators and the government and the hanky-stompers . . . fed them since birth was just that: bullshit. So they met violence with violence. Nobody enslaved them. You can't be enslaved standing there with a gun in your hands and the willingness to use it." Ben stuck a blunt finger in the man's now pale face. "My people are fighting and dying to reclaim this nation. So don't you get all up in my face and talk peace and love and non-violence. It isn't even a noble thought anymore. Someday, maybe. But not now. So mister, you and your people go get checked out by the medics. And then you scatter. Don't you ever let me see any of you again. Move!''

"We are all followers of the great guru Bagwumg Marsheeree," a woman said. "We believe that . . ."

Jersey poked her in the butt with the muzzle of her M-16. "Carry your ass, lady," she told her.

"Do you have any rice cakes?" a man asked Cooper.

"Any what?"

"Move!" Jersey told the man.

"What the hell is a rice cake?" Cooper asked.

Ben got on the horn to Jesse. "You ready to talk now, Boston?"

"Yeah," Jesse said wearily. "I'm ready to talk. How do we set this up?"

"You walk out of there heading south on Highway 81. Unarmed. I'll be waiting."

"Can I bring anyone with me?"

"Your co-leaders."

"You got any diarrhea medicine?"

Ben chuckled, then keyed the mic. "Yeah, Boston. We'll fix you up. Come on."

Within moments, Jesse Boston and a dozen other men were walking down the cracked old highway toward Ben's location. They were a sorry looking bunch. And they were awed by the mighty machines of war in Rebel hands. They looked at the clean-shaven and disciplined troops and were very happy they had chosen not to tangle with these very competent looking people. Rebel medics dosed them with anti-diarrhea medicine and escorted them to an old home that had been cleaned out and was serving as Ben's CP.

Ben pointed to chairs and the outlaws sat. Ben said, "I'm probably making a terrible mistake, but I've decided not to have you shot."

Relief was immediately evident on all faces.

"But," Ben continued, "now I have another problem: what to do with you."

"How about just letting us go?" a man asked hopefully.

Ben smiled.

"We got kids in yonder who need doctors real bad," another man said.

"We're not at war with children. Have them brought out," Ben told him, pointing to a radio. "That is set on the CB frequency you've been using to communicate with your roaming patrols. Which, by the way, are now all dead. They chose to mix it up with my people. Bad mistake. Get the kids out of there."

Jesse Boston slowly shook his head. "We didn't know what had happened to those patrols. We thought you people might have taken them prisoner."

"We don't take many prisoners, Boston," Ben informed the man. "Rebel policy."

One of Boston's co-leaders shuddered. "I can't speak for no one but myself, General Raines. But as for me, whatever you want me to do, I'll do," he stated quietly. He had looked Rebel might square in the face and it had scared the crap out of him . . . with the help of the doctored water supply.

"You going to try us in your court of law?" another asked.

Ben shook his head. "No. I'm just going to disarm you except for bolt action rifles and shotguns to use for hunting. Not that you really have to hunt. There are thousands of cattle roaming around here. Free for the taking. You can ranch, farm, raise gardens, and become decent citizens for once in your life. We'll help you open up schools and a hospital. We'll bring you up to date on vaccinations and medical checkups. All we ask in return is that you become useful, law-abiding citizens."

"Our past?" a man asked.

"Forgotten."

Jesse Boston leaned forward. "Raines, I killed a man just before the Great War. I was serving time for it."

"Where?"

Jesse blinked. "Where?"

"Yes. Where did you kill the man?"

"In a honky tonk just outside of Oklahoma City."

"So it was trash killing trash?"

Jesse smiled and shook his head. "Boy, you bring it all down to the basics, don't you, Raines?"

Ben returned the smile. Sort of like a mongoose looking at a cobra. "I do try."

"In your eyes, we're all white trash here, aren't we?"

"Until you prove otherwise, yes."

"Long as we kill each other, that's all right, isn't it?"

"That's one way of putting it, yes."

Boston leaned back in the chair. "You're the hardest son of a bitch I ever saw in my life, Raines, and I have known some bad ol' boys. They don't hold a candle to you."

"Thank you."

"Goddamn, Raines! It wasn't meant as a compliment."

"I know it. But that's the way I choose to take it."

"What's the chances of joinin' up with you people," a man asked.

"Not very good until I test your loyalty and you prove to me you can keep your word."

"That's fair," another man spoke.

"Raines," Jesse said. "Are you telling me that if we're good little fellows for a time, say a year, and play by your rules, you'll rearm us and make this a Rebel outpost?"

"Probably."

"And what is to prevent us from returning to our, ah, outlaw ways?"

"The sure and certain fact that should you do that, I will hunt you down and either shoot you or hang you. Probably the latter. And I think you all know I will do exactly what I say I'll do."

"Well," one of Jesse's men stood up. "I was raised on a farm. I kinda miss it. I'll turn in my M-16 and ammo and keep my .22 and shotgun. You boys can find me and my woman over on Highway 19, along the Washita. Thank you, General Raines."

"You're welcome.

One by one the men left Ben's makeshift office, until only Jesse Boston remained. Ben waited on him to open the ball.

Boston sighed deeply. "You'd really hunt me down and shoot me, wouldn't you, Ben Raines?"

"No," Ben said softly, as his eyes burned with a predatory glow. "I'd hang you."

## Seven

The children had been inoculated, the men and women given physicals, and the Rebels pulled out. Just before they left, Jesse walked up to Ben.

"You know, Ben, this isn't going to be half bad. For the first time in my life, I'm on the side of law and order, and I won't have to be looking over my shoulder twenty-five hours a day."

Ben smiled. "That's what you think, Jesse."

"Huh?"

"Within seventy-two hours, every punk and thug and worthless piece of human crap in a two hundred mile radius will know that you and your bunch have thrown in with the Rebels. They'll know that you now have medicines and proper food and up-to-date radio equipment and everything else that goes with joining up with us. And they'll be coming in to take it from you. Just like you people took it from that pathetic bunch that was here before."

Jesse paled as the truth in that hit him hard. "But we don't have anything to fight with, Ben. We can't fight off renegades with .22 caliber rifles and shotguns!"

Ben laughed and patted the man on the shoulder. "Relax, Jesse. Your weapons are stored in that warehouse out on 39, just at the edge of town. I was only testing you."

Jesse stared at Ben for a moment, then burst out laughing. He wiped his eyes and stuck out his hand. Ben shook it.

"We'll do our best to keep our end of the bargain, Ben."

"I know you will."

"How?"

"When I discovered that Boston really was your name, I sent people to the old Oklahoma State Prison to see if they could find your real records. They got lucky and found them. You only killed that one man, Jesse. And you claimed it to be self-defense."

"It was! I'll swear on the Bible it was."

"I believe you. I talked with some of those dip-shits you turned loose. They admitted you were the one who stopped the beatings and the rapes and punished the men who were responsible. That told me volumes about you, Jesse."

Jesse rolled a cigarette and said nothing.

"Then some of your own people told me about you setting up a zoo for the children in your camp. Taking care of the animals yourself. How many dogs and cats do you have, Jesse?"

He mumbled something.

"Beg pardon?"

"About a dozen!" he admitted.

Ben laughed. "Jesse, I won't deny that you're probably a mean bastard to tangle with in a fight, but you're not a *bad* bastard."

"Just don't let that get out, Ben. It would ruin my reputation."

Ben grinned. "Hell, Jesse. Those with you who are worth saving already know it!"


Ben and his Rebels moved northeast, toward the ruins of Oklahoma City. Scouts had reported back that the smell of Night People was very strong amid the tangle of twisted girders, burned-out buildings, and piles of brick and stone. They saw no signs of human life during the short run from Jesse Boston's location to the city. Not one single sign.

"Creepies ate them," Jersey said, disgust in her voice.

"General," Beth said, "was there any evidence of the Night People before the Great War?"

"Not to my knowledge, Beth. Cannibalism was a very rare thing. But I have a suspicion the Creeps were around, although not in the numbers we've had to fight. I think they probably preyed on hitchhikers and runaways. Back when civilization was more or less functioning, about two hundred thousand people a year just dropped out of sight. Vanished. And that was in the United States alone."

"Why?" Corrie asked.

"Oh, marital problems, loss of jobs, unable to pay their bills. All sorts of reasons. Kids ran away because they couldn't, or wouldn't, get along with their parents, or peer pressure became too great. Again, there were a number of reasons. When I was just a kid, back in the '60s, that's when things really began to unravel. We got involved in a war that no one wanted and the politicians wouldn't let the fighting men win. After Vietnam, everything seemed to go downhill. About twenty-five years after Vietnam, the whole goddamn world fell apart."

"Ben Raines?" the man asked, standing on Ben's front porch.

"That's right."

The man held up a badge. "I'm Bond, FBI. This is Reno, Secret Service." Reno showed Ben his badge.

Ben took out his wallet and found his social security card. He held that up. The government agents were not amused.

"May we come in?" Reno asked.

"No," Ben told him. "But it's a nice day. We can sit out here on the porch."

Ben sat down and pointed to chairs on the enclosed porch. "I'm not going to offer you coffee or iced tea or soft drinks. State your business and then get the hell off my property."

"You're not very friendly, Mister Raines," Agent Bond said.

"Should I be? This is not the first time federal agents have been around, questioning me and making a nuisance of themselves. I used to have a dog. She was a very nice dog. The last time people like you came around, they blatantly and arrogantly ignored my "no trespassing" signs and let her out of the fenced-in yard and she was run over. I had to have her put to sleep. I don't like you people and I don't give a damn who knows it. By the way, have you shot any tax resisters today?"

Both Bond and Reno flushed.

Ben wouldn't let up. "You people have a quota? What is it, a point system? Five points for an adult and two points for a kid?"

"Your writing has become very inflammatory, Mister Raines," Reno said. "You're calling for open and armed rebellion against the United States government."

"You're damn right I am. We've got to stop this insanity before it's too late. And if the only way to do it is by overthrowing the government, let's get it on."

"Your publishing company has agreed to cooperate with us, Mister Raines," Bond said. "They will no longer be publishing your works."

Ben laughed in the man's face. "I wondered when the government would get around to pressuring them. So now freedom of speech is restricted. I knew it would happen. Hell, boys, that won't stop me. I'll just self-publish and peddle my books out of the trunk of my car."

"No major chain will be carrying your *Doomsday* series, Mister Raines," Reno informed him. "They have voluntarily agreed to cooperate with us."

"I just bet they have," Ben said sarcastically.

Bond hastened to add, "Of course, your western books are not affected by this order. Your government does not in any way wish to restrict your making a living." He said all that without cracking a smile.

Ben laughed in his face. "Close the gate on your way out," he told the agents.


Oklahoma City loomed before the Rebels. Ben came out of his bitter remembrances and pointed to a huge shopping mall coming up off to the right. "Over there. I want to prowl around some."

Ben stepped out of the Hummer and stretched. Teams of Rebels were quickly converging on what was left of the shopping center. Ben walked toward the mall entrance, not missing a step at his son's shout.

"Come on, Dad! Wait up. The damn place is not secure."

"So let's secure it," Ben called over his shoulder and kept walking.

Buddy ran up to him and did what very few Rebels would dare do to Ben Raines: he grabbed Ben by the arm and spun him around. "Goddammit, Dad. What's the matter with you? What turned you so angry all of a sudden?"

"Well, boy," Ben said, his eyes blazing, "on the way up here, among other things, I was recalling how, a few years before the Great War, good, decent, tax-paying citizens became afraid to leave their homes at night to go shopping, because the malls were not *secure*. The streets were not *secure*. And just before it all blew up in our faces, even the *homes* of good, decent, tax-paying men and women were not *secure*. Now, son of mine, I am going to go into that old mall and do some window shopping amid the ruins. And if there is anybody in there who might like to attempt to mug me, or molest me, or fuck with me, I am going to *secure* that mall in the manner we should have done years back. If the goddamn government hadn't taken our guns away from us, that is. Thanks to the goddamn liberal Democratic Party. Now let go of my arm."

Ben stalked away.

"He was telling us about how federal agents used to come to his house," Cooper said, hurrying along after Ben. "It really, really pissed him off."

"The recalling of it?"

"Yeah," Jersey said. "I've been with your dad a good many years. I know all the signs. Nobody better jack around with him."

"Buddy!" Jim Peters, commander of 14 Battalion yelled. "Recon says the Creeps control the ruins of the city and gangs of punks control all the suburbs, including this old mall."

"Oh, hell!" Buddy muttered, just as Ben kicked in what remained of the mall's electric doors and stalked inside.

"Hey you!" a shouted voice stopped Ben just inside the huge old mall.

Ben turned to face half a dozen young men, all wearing the most outlandish of clothing. "We're the 89th Street Bombers," one told him. "I'm called Prince. This is our turf. You get the hell out of here, dude." He was wearing tennis shoes that had battery operated flashing lights on them.

Ben laughed at the sight.

"You laughin' at me, pops?" the punk said.

"Yeah," Ben told him. "What the hell are you supposed to represent, an early Christmas?"

"Say what?"

"Forget it. Get out of my way."

"I think you need to be taught a lesson, pops," the same punk said. "And we's just the ones to do that. I think I'll cut your ears off and make a necklace out of them."

"Then I would have to say you have extremely lousy tastes when it comes to jewelry."

"You 'bout a smart-assed mother-fucker, ain't you?"

Ben smiled. "Don't press your luck, punk."

"Don't you be callin' me no punk, mother-fucker."

"Look at all them soldiers over yonder," another punk said. "And they's cunts with 'em, too."

"You the Rebels, ain't you?" the first punk asked Ben.

"That's right."

"Well, you just carry your asses on outta here. 'Fore we show you what bad really is."

Ben chuckled. "Punks never change."

"I warned you 'bout that!" Prince said.

"You punks work with the Night People, don't you?" Ben asked. "You raid out in the country for humans and in exchange the Night People leave you alone. Isn't that right?"

"What's it to you?"

"I find that practice quite odious."

"Huh?"

"I think you should stop doing that immediately."

"Or you'll do what, pops?"

"Kill you," Ben said calmly.

Before the Prince of Punks could respond, Buddy called, "Punks coming up behind you, Dad. And more coming in to back up this punk pack."

"You take care of them, son. I'll handle Prince and those with him."

"Say what?" Prince asked.

"Are you hard of hearing, stupid, or a combination of both?" Ben questioned.

"The General's pushing hard," Cooper whispered.

"No kidding?" Jersey returned the whisper.

"You know how he hates punks," Beth said.

"Hey, Prince!" one of his followers said, slowly looking all around him. "We is surrounded, man."

"Prince!" the shout came from behind Ben. "They's tanks outside. All over the place. Must be three or four thousand soldiers."

Prince glared at Ben, and Ben smiled. "You still want to cut off my ears, you punk bastard?"

"Man, why for you pushin' at me so hard?"

"Because I despise worthless punks like you, that's why."

"You honky, racist son of a bitch!"

Ben laughed. "Look around you, punk. Look at the Rebels. All races, all religions. I don't see anything but blacks in your punk pack. So who is the racist?"

One of the gang members very slowly squatted down, conscious of a hundred guns on him, and laid his AK-47 on the floor. "I'm out of this, Ben Raines. And you is Ben Raines, ain't you?"

"That's right."

"You let me get my shit together, and I'm gone like a cool breeze, General."

"Get gone, then."

"You won't shoot or hang me?"

"Why should I do that?"

"I got family down in Mississippi. My mama's down there. I want to see her."

"That's Rebel-controlled territory now. Stick around. There'll be planes coming here tomorrow.

We'll fly you back and you can start a new life . . . if you want to."

"For real?"

"For real."

Another young man said, "I'm from Natchez. Can I go back with Ernie?"

"If you want to start over and change your ways, yes. But you both better understand Rebel law and be willing to play by the rules."

"I was going to go to college and be a teacher, then the Great War tore everything apart. But I'd still like to teach. You got colleges down there?"

"Several of them. You and Ernie get outside."

Prince cussed the two men. They did not look back as they hustled out of the mall.

"Prince, this is crazy!" a shout came from behind the Prince of Punks. "They'll kill us all. I don't want to die."

"Then join them other traitors," Prince said, his eyes never leaving Ben Raines. "I don't need cowards with me."

"Coward ain't got nothin' to do with nothin'," a gang member standing close to Prince said. "We talkin' good sense here, man."

"Then get away from me!" Prince shouted.

"Naw," another punk standing close said. "I ain't livin' under Rebel rule."

"Good man," Prince said. "Some of us are gonna get hurt, but I think we can beat these do-gooders."

"Then start the dance," Ben said softly.

"I believe I will," Prince said, and lifted his Uzi.

# *Eight*

More than half of the gang dropped their weapons and hit the littered mall floor. The rest died where they stood as the entrance to the huge old mall hammered with gunfire.

Ben lifted his Thompson and stitched Prince from left to right, fighting the rise of the powerful old SMG as he held the trigger back.

It was over in two heartbeats. Prince and those who chose to stay with him unto death got their wish. Some of those who chose to live were sobbing in fear as they lay amid the litter. Others were so badly frightened they peed their dirty underwear.

They all realized just how hard Ben Raines was when he said, "Drag the bodies outside and burn them. Interrogate the others and find out what they know about the Creeps and their location." He took a few steps to stand over a gang member who was praying, huddled in a ball on the floor. "You're calling on God?" Ben said, his voice as sharp as tempered steel. "You've helped in forcing hundreds of people to a horrible death by cannibals and you're actually calling on God? Get up, you son of a bitch!" he shouted.

But the man was shaking so badly his knees would not support his weight. He lay on the floor and stared in horror at his dead friends sprawled all around him. He continued to mouth heavenly cast supplications.

Ben looked at those Rebels gathered in the mall. "We became lax over the past few years. Lax enough to cut too much slack to the criminal element. All that ended today. From this moment forward, we give outlaw gangs one chance to surrender. If they refuse, we strike, and we strike hard. Any questions?"

There were none.

"Fine. Now I'm going window shopping." Ben turned and began walking slowly up the long corridor of the mall, his personal team with him.

Buddy waved toward a group of Rebels, pointing a finger. They took off at a run, racing ahead of Ben.

It was bright outside, and the mall was illuminated by a wide skylight, much of it still intact after all the bloody years. The floor was, of course, littered with everything imaginable, empty beer cans and wine and liquor bottles most prevalent.

"Prince and his punks were very fastidious folks," Ben remarked.

"Yes," Beth said, kicking away a pair of extremely filthy underwear. "And hygienic, too."

"Those two who wanted to try our ways," Cooper said. "You think they'll work out, General?"

"No. But we'll give them a chance. They'll last about a month back at Base Camp One. The first time they step over the line down there they'll get a bullet and that will be the end of it."

Ben stopped in front of a bookstore and looked in through the glass, remarkably still intact. The place had been trashed, torn and ripped books ankle deep on the floor.

"If they won't want to read the books," Corrie said. "Why don't they just leave them alone?"

"Because they contain knowledge," Ben told her. "And certain types of people are very much afraid of that. They think if they destroy the words, everybody else will become as them. Dictators have practiced that misguided theory for centuries."

Ninety-nine point nine percent of all Rebels were voracious readers. Reading was stressed in Rebel schools, beginning in most Rebel homes as soon as the child was able to hear words being read to them. The older Rebels had watched a nation slide away from reading and they were determined that would not happen in their new order. Everywhere they went, Rebels gathered up old newspapers and shipped them back to Base Camp One, where they were carefully cataloged and put on microfilm, to save for posterity. Someone had to preserve the history—not just of what used to be America, but the world—and that job fell to the Rebels.

Rebels were not just very capable warriors. They were historians, teachers, medics, and just about anything else one could think of.

As they walked the huge mall, the Rebels found others of Prince's gang in hiding. Very few offered any resistance. Those that did, died. Those who wisely surrendered were disarmed and rousted outside. At first, a few of the gang members resisted

Rebel attempts to extract information from them. They soon learned that the Rebels had highly sophisticated ways of interrogation and were not at all hesitant to use them. Before noon of that day, the Rebels had learned every location of the Creepies in the ruins of Oklahoma City. With the aid of a city map, Rebel artillery was quickly brought up and ranged in.

Ben carefully spread his four battalions out and the thunderous bombardment began. It would continue throughout the night. Long before dusk settled around the land, the city was blazing from the hundreds of rounds of Willie Peter dropping in.

The Creeps tried to escape the towering flames. The Rebels shot them down.

Other gangs had been found on the outskirts of the city and the survivors brought in. They sat under guard in the parking lot of the old mall and were awed by the massive firepower in the hands of the disciplined Rebels.

Under the glare of powerful lights, electricity provided by huge generators, the gang members were hosed down and deloused before being given physical examinations by Rebel doctors and medics. With the slam and boom of artillery in the background, Ben read the preliminary reports.

"Some of these gang members have more diseases than could be found in a garbage dump," Ben said.

"Many of them too far gone to be effectively treated," the doctors told him. "You have two choices, General."

"I know what they are," Ben said shortly. "Turn them loose and let them die. I won't waste our medical supplies on these people. They chose their way of life, so to hell with them."

To say that Ben Raines was a hard man would be the understatement of the millennium.

A gang leader who went by the name of Pookie said, "That Ben Raines is the meanest son of a bitch I ever seen in all my life!"

His brother, Mookie, said, "That man tole me if he ever seen me again he was gonna shoot me right between the eyes. I axed him what I was 'pposed to do? He said find me a nice piece of ground, grow a garden, and live decently and respect the rights of others. Shhittt! I ain't no fuckin' farmer."

"You is now," his brother told him. "If you ain't, you stay the hell away from me."

"Hey, brother!" Mookie shouted at a passing Rebel.

The Rebel stopped and stared in disgust at the former gang member. "I am not your brother."

"You black, man!"

"The similarity ends there, I assure you. What do you want?"

"How long you been with that mean honky bastard?"

"I assume you mean General Raines. And if you call him a mean honky bastard again, I'm going to shoot you."

"Now wait a minute. Shit, man! I got a right to an opinion, don't I?"

"Only if you would allow a white person to refer to you as a nigger."

"Say what?"

"You heard me."

"Well, that don't make no sense."

"No. It probably doesn't to the likes of you," the Rebel said. "That is the reason I am what I am, and you are what you are."

"You 'bout a goofy talkin' an' a goofy actin' nigger! You know that?"

The Rebel smiled . . . thinly. "If you have nothing else to say, I'll be on my way."

"That's cool. Go on. You carry your zebra ass, man. Lick the boots of whitey. When the New Africa rises up, you ain't gonna be part of it."

"How wonderful for me. I can't tell you how relieved I am to hear that."

Buddy was standing in the shadows and heard the conversation. The Rebel stopped by Buddy's side. "Did you hear that idiocy, Colonel?"

"Yes. It's sad."

"Five or ten years ago it would be sad. Now it's stupid. New Africa! Jesus Christ. When are people like that going to understand that if we don't all pull together, we're all going to fail?"

Ben was leaning against a truck fender, standing in the darkness and listening. It flung him back in memory. Back to a time when he'd confronted some local black militants just outside his home town— back when he'd had a home town. Just a few days after the world had exploded and there wasn't a stable government left in any country around the globe.

"You been riding high and mighty, Ben Raines," one man had told him. "Big shot writer always criticizing people on welfare."

"I don't always criticize people on welfare, Henry. And color has nothing to do with it. There are more whites on welfare than blacks. I criticize those people who have one baby right after another and expect the taxpayers to foot the bill. But that's all over now, isn't it?"

"But you meant black people, didn't you?"

"No, Henry, I didn't."

"I say you're a liar, Mister Ben Raines."

Ben had paid a visit to the local sheriff's office the day he'd come out of his sickness and had taken an old Thompson SMG from the gun rack, trying his best to ignore the bloated and stinking bodies. He'd also taken two .45 caliber semiautomatic pistols and all the ammo and clips for the pistols and SMG that he could find.

Now he'd run up on one of the most militant and white-hating black men in the parish.

Ben sighed. "Henry, back off and leave me alone. It's a brand new world now, Henry. So stop hating whites and blaming them for all your troubles."

"I'm out of this, Ben," one of the men with Henry said.

"Fine, Lucas. You and I have always been friends."

"Me, too," the others said. "Come on, Henry," one urged. "You know Ben Raines hates the Klan as much as we do. Why start trouble now?"

"Ain't nobody around to read your goddamn trashy books now, Raines," Henry said.

"That's a fact, Henry."

"And no law, either."

"That, too, is the truth."

Henry pointed a finger at Ben. "So I'll tell you something. I killed that goddamn deputy Harrison . . . the one who beat me that time. Shot him dead yesterday."

"He caught you selling dope and you resisted arrest, pulled a knife on him. He hit you twice with a flashlight. He should have caved your head in and left you for the ants to eat." Ben was very blunt, as was his custom.

"You goddamn racist honky son of a bitch!" Henry grabbed for the pistol in his belt and Ben stitched him with the Thompson. Henry was dead before he hit the asphalt.

"My God, Ben!" Lucas said. "You've killed Henry."

Ben looked at the man. "You think I wanted to, Lucas?"

"I think you were mighty quick to shoot," another man said.

"You maybe wanted him to shoot me before I opened fire?"

The men walked away without answering. They left Henry's body where it lay on the street.

Ben shook away the memories of years past and forced himself to return to the smoky air outside of the ruins of Oklahoma City. Buddy spotted him and walked over. "What are we going to do with these gang members, Dad?"

"I don't know, son. I don't see that we have much choice except turn them loose and hope for the best. Have any of them professed any desire to join us?"

"No. For the most part, they are a sullen and uncooperative bunch."

"We'll have to fight them someday. Or someone will."

"What were you thinking about, Father? You appeared to be deep in thought."

"Oh, of events long past. Racial hatred. Social injustice—real and imagined. Problems the Great War should have solved, but didn't."

His son smiled. "Heavy mental ponderings, Father. Did you arrive at any solutions?"

"Unfortunately, no."

"Father . . ." Buddy hesitated. "Have you ever considered clearing out perhaps half a dozen states in our southern area and just letting the rest of the country go to hell?"

Ben laughed. "Oh, yes. Many times. I was thinking about that just the other day."

"And?"

"It wouldn't work. We would be fighting a never-ending series of hit and run raids all along our borders. It would be another case of the so-called have-nots against the so-called haves. And that's one of the reasons this country went down the toilet in the first place. We elected a socialist for a president and a bunch of wishy-washy assholes in Congress. They mandated that big government be all things for all people all the time."

"A classless society, Father?"

"Something like that."

"That won't work."

"Of course, it won't work. Looks good on paper, but try to put it in practice and it tears the country apart. In any society there will always be those who have more than others. Either by luck, inheritance, or just plain hard work. And there will always be those who will attempt to take what is not theirs."

"Not down in Base Camp One," Buddy said.

Ben chuckled softly as he rolled a cigarette under the disapproving eyes of his son. "And do you know why we have so little of that in any Rebel controlled area?"

"Because we won't admit just anybody who comes along."

"That's right. So consequently, we are not a democracy. You know as well as I of the hundreds of thousands of people scattered throughout this country who refuse to join with us; who would rather live without protection, without medical care, without hope, because they refuse to follow the few laws we have on the books."

"And it never ceases to baffle me," Buddy said.

"You know something, son? It never ceases to baffle me, either."

# Nine

The Rebels pulled out, leaving behind them a confused and very disarmed bunch of gang members. Some of them would heed Ben's warning and try to live a life free of crime, but Ben knew that most would not.

The last thing Ben did before leaving the still-blazing ruins of Oklahoma City was to blow up the old shopping mall.

"Shit, General!" Mookie said. "I ain't got no home."

Ben looked at him in disgust and walked away.

The long Rebel column headed west for a few miles, then turned north on 87. The highways had deteriorated badly and if the Rebels could average twenty miles per hour they considered themselves lucky. They saw no signs of human life. The Creeps had been ranging out farther and farther in their hunt for food, and those people who had not been taken for brunch had cleared out.

All along the route, towns had been destroyed, much of that having been done by the Rebels, several years back. Vance A.F.B. had been looted so many times the Rebels did not even stop. Enid was in ruins. The Rebels were only a few miles south of the Kansas line before they spotted the first signs of human life.

"Scouts report smoke coming from the houses up ahead," Corrie said. "The townspeople have a pretty good defensive line thrown up around the town and the scouts say they are prepared to defend."

"Tell the scouts to back off and make no hostile moves. Wait for me."

Ben reached for a map case and Beth said, "Just about fifteen hundred population before the war, General. Approximately ten miles south of the Kansas line."

"Thank you, Beth," he said with a smile.

"You're welcome, sir."

"Scouts report about three hundred men, women, and children in the town," Corrie said. "Men and women heavily armed."

"Any flags flying?"

"No, sir."

Ben halted the long column about a mile from town and drove on up to the scouts' position, about three hundred yards from the first barricade. He took a bull horn.

"This is General Ben Raines of the Rebels. We mean you no harm. We have doctors with us if you need medical attention. I repeat: we mean you no harm. We're Rebels."

There was no response from those behind the barricades. The Rebels could see where a dirt road had been worn in the earth, leaving the main highway and circling the small town.

"They're talking on CB," Corrie said. "Channel sixteen. They don't believe we're the Rebels."

Ben listened to the people talk back and forth.

"I tell you, I heard General Raines was taken prisoner and shot down in Mexico," a man said.

"If that's those damn Nazis," another said, "I'd rather die right here than join them."

Ben cut in. "Listen to me, people. I am Ben Raines. Field Marshal Hoffman and all his top people are dead. The Nazis have been defeated and are no longer any threat. But the Night People and the roaming gangs of thugs are a problem. We just cleared Dallas/Fort Worth and Oklahoma City of those types. My battalions are working all over this nation cleaning it up, again. If we were unfriendly, with all the firepower we have, don't you think I would have already opened fire? Now, I don't know what else I can do to prove to you that I am Ben Raines."

A man's voice came over the CB. "Back before this nation fell into the hands of democrats, what was the first book you wrote?"

Ben laughed. "The first book I wrote, or the first book I had published?"

The voice chuckled. "Spoken like a true writer. Come on in, General Raines."

Ben and his team walked the few hundred yards to the now opened gate. A man stepped out and Ben narrowed his eyes. "Well, I'll just be damned! Bill Block." He jogged up and stuck out his hand.

The man laughed and took the hand. "Good to see you, Ben. My God, man, it's been years."

"Ten years, at least. The last writers' convention, I believe. Down in . . . San Antonio, I guess."

"That's it. Tell your people to come on in." He pointed. "Good place to set up tents right over there on the flats. Come on, you old hoss thief. Let's talk western books for a time."


Bill Block had been a very successful writer of men's adventure and was just hitting his stride when the world blew up. Like Ben and a few other writers who had the courage to stand up to a fast-growing socialistic government in America, Bill Block had been hassled more than once by federal agents.

"I tried to call you after you didn't show up at the last convention down in Beaumont," Ben said. The men were sitting in the den of a small, but very neat home. "But your phone had been disconnected."

"Goddamn government fell on me, Ben. After I wrote *The Fall of Freedom*, I really started getting hassled. Federal agents came in and seized all my records, all my manuscripts, all my equipment. Bastards charged me with sedition and held me in federal custody for weeks. No bail, no communications with anybody. You remember Nickie, over in Missouri? They did the same thing to him. And they were coming after you, too, Ben. But the bastards were afraid of you. They knew you were armed and would shoot if they got too heavy-handed. Then, too, you had a hell of a following. The government was afraid of you, Ben." He grinned. "You stuck it to those bastards, Ben. I'm proud of you."

"What ever happened to Langhorn?"

"The government shut him down, Ben. During

the last days before the Great War, the federal bully boys went after every writer who dared preach rebellion. They always came at night, kicking in doors, slapping people around. They shut down Bob. They jailed Mike. Hell, they killed Clet. Then they were coming after you. But it's the funniest thing, Ben. All the senators and representatives and appointees who kissed the ass of the last president and went along with all his gun-grabbing and socialistic programs . . . what's happened to them?"

"Those that aren't dead are in hiding."

"In hiding?"

"Yeah. From me. I swore I'd nail every son of a bitch that voted for those programs that crippled this nation."

"Have you found any of them?"

"Eight, so far."

"And?"

Ben's eyes were humor-filled. "I dealt with them."


Rebel intelligence was the best in the world, but due to their relatively small numbers, they could not be everywhere at once. What the Rebels did not know was that many of the nation's senators and representatives had survived the bloody years and were living and working in upstate New York, in the Adirondacks. Unfortunately, few conservatives had survived and those men were not included in the gathering. Senators Hanrahan, Benidict, Arnold, Ferry, Ditto, Goahy, and others of their left-wing ilk, along with Representatives Fox, Crapums, Rivers, Hooter, Lightheart, Holey, and a host of others who leaned so far to the left it was unbelievable they could even stand upright, were just about ready to implement their grand plan of putting the nation back together.

A mercenary army had been training in very isolated spots in Canada for several years. Their commanders said they were now ready to take on the hated Rebel army and their most despised leader, Ben Raines.

"I just hate Ben Raines," Lightheart said, stamping his foot.

"I do too," Harriet Hooter said, stamping her foot.

"Racist, sexist, honky son of a bitch!" Rita Rivers said, stamping her foot.

"I just hope to hell MacDonald's gets back in business soon," the only surviving ex-president of the now defunct United States bitched.

"I now officially call the first joint session of the new Congress of the United States to order," I.M. Holey solemnly intoned, banging the gavel. "First order of business is . . ."

"Kill Ben Raines," an avowed liberal shouted.

"Publicly crucify Ben Raines!" another liberal squalled. "Make him suffer!" This one was on record as stating that any kind of violence sickened him.

"Pull out all his fingernails and toenails and then hang him by the neck and let the vultures eat him!" a former representative from Massachusetts screamed. He had been the first one to sign the bill outlawing all violence on American TV.

"Drive a stake through Ben Raines's heart!" one of the former senators from New Jersey shouted.

The speaker let the men and women vent their spleens for a time and then once more banged the session to order. "The question is this: are we prepared to declare war against Ben Raines and the Rebels?"

"Yes!" the gathering of men and women shouted.

The speaker adjourned the session and everybody went outside to grill hamburgers under a replica of the Golden Arches.

Now, just how a group of avowed liberals, who all their lives had espoused non-violence, could justify putting together a mercenary army to wage bloody war is anybody's guess. But since most liberals think of themselves as a reborn combination of Joan of Arc, Jesus Christ, Carrie Nation, and Aristotle, and firmly believe they sit on the left side of God, it's not that difficult to figure.

Ben Raines, on the other hand, was more in step with Diogenes the Cynic.

The next few months were going to be very interesting.

General Paul Revere smiled when he received orders to make ready to march against Ben Raines. He'd been waiting for this moment for several years. He was ready, and his army was ready. There was no doubt in Revere's mind that his army could and would crush Ben Raines and his stupid Rebels. Revere did not share the lofty thoughts of the men and women down in what used to be called America. He was a professional soldier, among other things, and had been all his life.

This war was to be a very personal affair with Revere. He knew Ben Raines; had known him for years, although the two men had not seen one another for nearly twenty-five years. Had soldiered with him in 'Nam—under his real name. Ben Raines had been responsible for him getting court-martialed and pulling stockade time.

It had never occurred to Revere that Ben Raines would object so strenuously to his knocking off some Vietnamese tramp. Truth was, Ben didn't care how many grown Vietnamese women he bedded down, but raping and sodomizing a nine-year-old girl was more than Ben could take. He had pistol-whipped Revere and handed him over to the MPs.

Revere had sworn to someday kill Ben Raines. He had busted out of the stockade before they could ship him back Stateside for hard prison time, and made it over into Thailand. There he ran a black-market operation until the war ended and then drifted to Africa, working as a mercenary. He had fought all over the world: Central America, South America, Africa, the Middle East, Northern Ireland, and was fighting in Eastern Europe when the Great War came.

Revere was a sorry excuse for a human being, but he was a damn good soldier. Those dimwits down in the Adirondacks had promised him he could be general of all armed forces after he defeated Ben Raines and the country was restored to order.

Revere had gotten a big kick out of that. He knew America would never be what it was. Not in two lifetimes. He shared that much with Raines.

Those silly ninnies down in the mountains actually thought that if Ben Raines was defeated, all the people in what used to be called America would come rushing to them, bowing and scraping and kowtowing and asking them to "Please lead us out of this terrible mess."

Revere had plans of his own for America. After Raines was dead and buried, he'd kill those stupid politicians and he would be King of America.

There was only one little hitch to those plans of Paul Revere. One small obstacle standing in the way.

Ben Raines and fifteen battalions of Rebels.

"It may not be the thugs and punks you should be worried about, Ben," Bill Block told him at supper.

"Oh?"

"We had some people come through here last week. Came down from Canada. They told some pretty wild tales about this huge army being formed up in the eastern part of the country. Thousands and thousands of men, under the command of someone called Paul Revere. You heard anything about that?"

"Not a word. Did these people seem stable to you?"

"Oh, yes. Very much so. The only thing that I didn't put any credence to was the story that a bunch of liberal politicians who escaped the bombing of Washington and then the fall of Richmond was running the whole show out of a place in the Adirondacks."

Ben shook his head. "My people scan every

known frequency, Bill. Twenty-four hours a day. We'd have heard something."

"Maybe not, Ben. Everybody knows you people have the most sophisticated equipment in the world. Anyone smart enough to put together a huge army would have enough sense to stay off the air, except for short-range CB talk."

Ben finished the meal in silence. Over coffee, he said, "So that's where they went."

"Who went where?" Bill asked.

"All those goddamned liberal politicians that I couldn't find to hassle like they did me, that's who. Everyone knows that after the military kicked the president out of the White House, he went hard underground with about fifty of those bastards and bitches who helped destroy this nation. He, and they, never surfaced in Richmond, either."

"I can't say that I blame them," Bill said drily. "Knowing that you had a noose for them."

"Oh, hell, Bill. I didn't kill them. Most of them were too old for me to kick their ass, so I just told them what I thought about them and warned them if they ever set foot in any Rebel-controlled area, I would hang them."

"Did they believe you?"

"Oh, yes, indeed."

Ben excused himself and returned to his temporary CP, informing Corrie what Bill had said. "Check it out, Corrie. Drop scouts in at the edges of the Adirondacks, north, south, east, and west, and have them work inward. Burst transmission only and only at pre-set times. Get them moving, Corrie. I have a bad feeling about this."

# Ten

Ben told the batt coms with him to stand their troops down and rest. Corrie got on the horn and brought in all of Ben's commanders.

"Funny thing," Ike said, as he and Dan Gray rode back with Ben to the CP. Ben's Rebels had quickly cleared a strip for the planes just outside of the small town. "All the gangs just seem to have dropped out of sight."

"Uh-huh," Ben replied.

Dan Gray said, "And not a sign of the Creepies. One day we are fighting gangs and Creeps, the next day—nothing."

"Uh-huh," Ben said. Then he smiled. "Just because a group of people is slightly out of step with the norm doesn't make them bad people."

"I beg your pardon?" Dan asked.

"Just thinking out loud, Dan."

"Another cargo plane coming in," Corrie said.

"That'd be Georgi and Rebet," Ben said. "Tina and West should be here within the hour."

"Do you have any idea what is going on, Ben?" Ike asked.

"Just a hunch," Ben said, cutting his eyes to the stocky ex-Navy SEAL. "I swear, Ike, you're looking more like a basketball every time I see you."

"Hell, I've dropped ten pounds, Ben!"

"Drop ten more," Dan, the ex-English SAS man suggested with a smile.

Ike and Dan exchanged insults all the way back to the CP. At the CP, Ben wandered off, waiting until all the batt coms arrived to start the meeting.

Cecil Jefferys, second in command of all Rebel troops, and administrator of the huge Base Camp One, flew in just behind Georgi and Rebet. Ben greeted his old friend warmly.

"What's the skinny on this, Ben?" Cecil asked.

"Big trouble, I'm afraid, Cec. And to make matters worse, it's been happening right under our noses. I want to brief everyone together. Go rest up for a time."

Ben had pulled Cecil out of the field after a series of heart attacks and open-heart surgery. Cecil had objected, but not too strongly. He knew that Ben was right. The ex-Special Forces man realized his days in the field were, for the most part, over.

A runner found Ben and handed him a folded piece of paper. Standing alone, Ben read the message and then crushed the paper in one big hand. It was another report from the scouts who had parachuted into the Adirondacks.

Ben delayed the meeting until the next morning. He wanted confirmation from another patrol in the New York mountains. He was hoping it would not come, but it did, followed by a third, then a fourth confirmation.

"Son of a bitch!" Ben said.

* * *

Ben sat on the teacher's desk in a classroom of the old school building and looked at his batt coms. They were a tired-looking bunch. The week's stand-down had just not been enough. Most of these people had been in sustained combat for years, and it was telling on them all—even Ben, he reluctantly admitted.

But there damn sure was no end in sight.

Ben sighed and said, "The American flag will be hoisted tomorrow morning in a small town in New York State. The town will be proclaimed as the new capital of the United States of America."

The men and women in the room looked at him as if he had lost his mind.

Ben continued. "The first item of business will be the formal declaration of war between the United States and the Rebels."

"What?" Ike blurted.

"The country is once more in the hands of President Blanton."

"Oh, shit!" Ned Hawkins, commander of the New Texas Rangers, said.

"Who is vice president?" Cecil asked.

"Harriet Hooter."

Cecil laid his head down on the desk. He didn't know whether to laugh or cry.

Thermopolis, the hippie turned warrior, stood up and said, "Now wait a minute, Ben. Just hold on. This is a paper government, that's all. How can they declare war on us without an army to back it up?"

"They've got an army," Ben stunned the group

into silence. "With most of it in place, all around us."

"I'm confused," Greenwalt, commander of 11 Battalion said.

"It gets worse," Ben assured them. "For the past two or three years, that pack of hanky-stomping liberals have been recruiting and training an army up in Canada. Three full divisions of combat-ready troops, under the command of General Paul Revere."

"Paul Revere?" Dan Gray blurted. "My word!"

"I don't think the original has returned from the grave," Ben said with a laugh. "But that is not the worst of it."

"Three full combat divisions is not the worst of it?" West, commander of 4 Battalion blurted. "When we're down by thirty-five percent. What the hell is the worst of it, Ben?"

"I believe they have also recruited many of the roaming gangs of thugs and punks, and also the Night People."

No one said a word for a full minute. Cecil raised his head from the desk and said, "Who are the known senators and representatives, Ben?"

Ben named all that he knew.

"Oh, shit!" Cecil said, and once more put his graying head on the arm of the desk.

Even the Englishman, Dan Gray, the Irishman, Pat O'Shea, the Mexican, Raul Gomez, and the Russian, Georgi Striganov, knew of those individuals.

When the cussing faded out, Tina Raines, commander of 9 Battalion, said, "I have a suggestion, Dad."

"What is it?"

"Nuke their asses."

"You're not serious, kiddo?"

"The hell I'm not!"

"Let's take a vote," Buddy suggested.

"Now wait just a minute," Ben protested.

"You set the rules up yourself, Ben," Doctor Chase reminded him. "You can't vote and neither can I. But the rules clearly state that your decisions can be overridden by voice vote."

"I haven't made any decisions, Lamar," Ben said. "But if a vote is what my batt coms want, it's fine with me, and I'll adhere to that decision."

It was seven for and nine against nuking the new government of the United States.

Several of the batt coms exchanged a few heated words, but as always, in the end, the vote stood with no hard feelings.

"That's why, on the way in yesterday, you made that comment about 'a group of people slightly out of step with the norm,' isn't it, Ben?" Dan asked.

"Yes. Blanton and his ilk would eagerly embrace the Night People. They'd shake hands with the devil to get rid of us. I'm going to open a line of communications with Blanton. I am going to tell that bastard in no uncertain terms, that if he sends troops against Base Camp One or Thermopolis's HQ in Arkansas, I will use either nuclear or germ weapons against him. Let's have a vote on that."

It was unanimously in favor.

Thermopolis raised his hand. "I'd like for my HQ Company to be pulled back into Base Camp One, Ben. For safety's sake. And I'd like to give the order for them to start packing up and pulling out today."

"Granted," Ben said. "Good idea. Everything will be consolidated."

Thermopolis left for the radio shack just as Corrie entered the room. "President Blanton on the horn, General. He wants to talk to you."

"Good," Ben said. "We'll get a few things settled right off the mark."

"Raines," President Blanton's voice rolled out of the speaker. "This is your president speaking. Are you there?"

"You're not my president," Ben told him. "I sure as hell didn't vote for you."

"Oh, I simply despise that man!" Harriet Hooter said, looking at the startled expression on Blanton's face.

"He's such a brute," Blush Lightheart said.

"Now you listen to me, Raines," Blanton blustered, as best he could, which wasn't all that well.

"No, you listen to me," Ben said. "You put Mister, Ben, or General in front of that name. You got all that?"

"Order the man killed," Senator Benidict burped, looking around him. He couldn't remember where he'd put that quart jar of moonshine.

"I concur," Senator Tutwilder said, still looking very much like a drunken TV evangelist about to stick his hand up the dress of a fallen angel.

"I'll have you shot?" Blanton screamed into the mic. "You, you . . . ol' pooter!"

"Who pooted?" Senator Benidict asked. "It wasn't me."

Ben cocked his head and looked at the speaker for a moment. He blinked, shook his head, looked back at Ike. "Did he say what I think he said?"

"I think he called you an ol' pooter," Ike said, scarcely able to contain his laughter.

Jersey got so tickled she had to turn her back and walk away. But not before her muffled giggling got to about half the batt coms.

"General Pooter!" Tina blurted, then bent over in laughter, holding her sides.

Ben knew he'd be a long time living this down. He keyed the mic. "Blanton? Are you still there?"

"I'm here, Raines."

"Well? What the hell do you want? You called me, remember? Get to it. I don't have the time to waste listening to you blather."

"I demand your unconditional surrender, Raines."

Ben thought about that for a moment. Then he lifted the mic. "Go fuck yourself, Blanton."

A sort of choking noise came over the speaker. Then a racket that sort of sounded like bodies hitting a floor. It was an accurate guess. Blush Lightheart and Harriet Hooter had fainted.


The news had spread like an unchecked forest fire around the Rebel encampments, all over the nation. General Raines had told the re-emerging President of the United States to go fuck himself.

But the humor was going to be short-lived, for General Paul Revere and his divisions were on the move out of Canada.

"We've got time to get ready," Ben told his batt coms. "Scouts report they're coming in by truck convoy."

"So they have no planes," Dan Gray remarked with a smile.

Everybody knew what he was smiling about. Immediately after the Great War, as soon as the Rebels were organized, they swept the nation, taking everything that wasn't nailed down. What planes they couldn't fly to storage in the desert, they crippled. In all of North America, Raines's Rebels had the only air force . . . such as it was.

After Blanton had gotten over his shock at Ben's remark, he had radioed back and Ben had laid it all out for the man, in very blunt, no nonsense terms.

"He's bluffing!" Senator Hanrahan puffed up. "He wouldn't dare use nuclear or germ weapons."

Despite what the nation came to think of the man, Blanton was far from being stupid. He just didn't have a hell of a lot of common sense. He shook his now entirely gray head. "No. Ben Raines is not bluffing. I despise the man, but I've studied him extensively. He is a brilliant tactician, a warrior unequalled, and he does not bluff." He looked at his liaison between he and General Revere. "Stay out of what is called Base Camp One. Under no circumstances enter Mississippi or Louisiana."

"But he hasn't claimed all of that yet!" Rita Rivers complained.

"He will," Blanton said.

And Ben did. Not only did he claim all of Louisiana and Mississippi as Rebel controlled territory, he also claimed Alabama and Texas and began shifting missiles around. He knew he surely had spies among some of his civilian people, so Ben openly relocated the missiles.

Blanton and his hanky-stompers got the message—loud and clear.

"Ol' pooter" just didn't seem strong enough to describe the president's feelings toward Ben Raines. "That son of a bitch!" he muttered.

The president ordered Paul Revere to halt and hold his position until he worked out a new plan of battle.

"*He's* going to work out a battle plan?" one of Revere's aides questioned.

"It appears that way. Relax. There's no rush. We have all the time in the world."

Revere had considered just killing Blanton and his people and taking over, but had quickly rejected that. About half of his ranks—including some top commanders—were filled with Blanton fanatics. Any move against Blanton would bring on a bloody and self-defeating mutiny within his divisions.

Those people amused Revere and he felt scorn toward them. And yet in a strange way—amid all the hate he felt toward the man—he admired Ben Raines. The Blanton supporters were avowed liberals, totally opposed to violence and professing a terrible aversion to guns. Yet here they were, all hot to kill Ben Raines and wipe the Rebels from the face of the earth.

At least Ben Raines knew what he was and didn't change philosophies every time he changed his underwear.

While Revere's legions were held up several thousand miles away from Ben's Rebels, those in Base Camp One were working around the clock in the producing of instruments of death and destruction. The Rebels had literally billions of rounds of small arms ammunition. Teams flew all over the nation burying hidden caches of ammunition, grenades, mortar rounds, food, water, and clothing. They stockpiled fuel and hid vehicles amid the ruins of small towns.

Blanton would soon learn that he had made a terrible mistake in throwing down the glove to Ben Raines. Blanton's forces outnumbered the Rebels; but the Rebels were long accustomed to fighting overwhelming odds—and winning.

Blanton knew little of war. The Rebels were experts at it. Probably the best fighters in all the world. Blanton was fighting to resurrect a dream, an ideal, that recent past history had proven to be disastrous as well as totally unworkable. The Rebels were fighting to preserve a form of government that worked for them. And they weren't about to roll over and give it up.

Not as long as there was just one Rebel left alive.

That was something that the Blanton's of the world had yet to learn. But they were about to.

The hard way.

# *Eleven*

The Rebels were waiting. They were ready. Spring had turned to summer and the Rebels were now fully rested and wondering what the holdup was.

The holdup was simple: President Blanton didn't know jack-crap about military tactics, and neither did any of his staff or any of the senators and representatives that made up the new government of the United States.

After weeks of laboring over writing tablets—the lined kind—President Blanton finally said to hell with it and radioed General Revere. "Attack!"

General Forrest, commander of Division One, looked at the one word battle plan and said, "That's it? Attack?"

General Holtz, Commander of Division Two, shook his head. He was speechless.

General Thomas, Commander of Division Three, said, "You have to remember, he wasn't much of a president either. Although I wouldn't want many of my people to hear me say that."

"Are those people going to stand and fight, Tom?" Revere asked the career military man.

"Yes. They're fanatics. Dedicated to the ideals of Blanton. Die for the cause. Take a punk to lunch types."

Revere nodded his head in agreement and moved to the map on the wall. "There are only a few bridges left over the Mississippi, and Raines has those wired to blow. Start moving the people out, straight west, staying in Canada until you reach Thunder Bay and then cross over into the States. Division One enter there. Division Two will cut south at Winnipeg, Division Three will cross the border south of Regina. And you can bet Raines will be waiting."

General Revere eyeballed his three top generals for a long moment. "Gentlemen, do not underestimate Ben Raines and the Rebels. Don't try to second guess him, don't try to outmaneuver him, and for God's sake when the Rebels run, *do not* chase them. They're masters at guerrilla warfare. They've perfected ambush to a fine art. We're not going to win this one in a short time. Be prepared for that. This war is going to last years. Ben Raines and his Rebels will *never* surrender. Never! They will fight to the last person and they'll go down snarling and biting. They have to be wiped out to the last person."

"That isn't possible," General Holtz said softly.

"I know," Revere acknowledged. "This country will always be at war with some number of people calling themselves Rebels. But we've got to cut them down to a manageable size. Right now they're eagles. We've got to reduce them to no more than pesky mosquitoes. And we can do that."

"What do you estimate our losses will be at the conclusion of this affair?" General Thomas asked.

"About fifty to sixty percent."

The generals were stunned. Finally, General Forrest managed to say, "You're saying we are going to lose the equivalent of two divisions, Paul? Two full divisions of men and women."

"Yes."

"But how can that be?" General Thomas asked.

"The three of you, and your families, have isolated yourselves from the outside for years. Deep in Canada's north woods. Hell" he grinned, "it took me a damn year to track you down. You don't know about Ben Raines the way I do. Look, living where you have you're all familiar with the wolverine. You know what they can do; how ferocious they are. Just imagine fifteen battalions of them, their natural skills honed by years of warfare. Warfare in which they were *always* outnumbered. Yet, always won. Raines's Rebels are the finest equipped army in the world. They lack for nothing." He smiled. "No, my friends. This war will not be a short one. Months, at least; probably years."

"And they know we are on the move," General Holtz stated.

"Oh, most definitely," Paul said. "We'll be watched every mile of the way. Expect to be hit the instant we cross over the border." He paused, his expression thoughtful. "Or before we cross over the border," he added. "No one has yet been able to predict what the Rebels will do. And that is something that should be kept in mind."

112

\*\*\*

"Speaking as your president, General Raines," Blanton again radioed Ben. "I command you to lay down your arms and surrender."

"I do not recognize you as President of the United States," Ben told the man. "How many times do I have to tell you that?"

"I was elected by the people!"

"You were elected by a minority of the voters and that was years ago. Washington is still hot from a nuke strike. Richmond is a ghost town in ruins. For years now, Base Camp One is and has been the only stable area of government in America. However, I will accept your surrender, Homer."

"My surrender? *My surrender!* To hell with you, Raines. You arrogant son of a bitch!"

"That beats an ol' pooter, I suppose," Ben replied, then signed off.

"Scouts report massive troop movement westbound along Canadian Highway 11," Corrie told him. "First column, commanded by a General Forrest, approaching Thunder Bay. About three hundred miles out. They can't cross at Sault Ste. Marie."

"They committed to Thunder Bay, then. That would be Matt Forrest. He's a good, decent man. One of the few military men who supported Blanton back when. Forrest is strictly by-the-book and did not approve of special operations people such as Rangers, SEALs, LRRPs, and so forth. He doesn't have much imagination. Who is commanding the second division?"

"A General Holtz."

"Walt Holtz. Another good man. I knew him in Vietnam when he was a shavetail lieutenant. He's also by-the-book. Division three?"

"General Tom Thomas."

Ben sighed. "All good decent men. No bad guys among them, unless it's this General Paul Revere. And I never heard of the man. Has intelligence come up with anything on him?"

"Nothing that hasn't been passed along to you, sir."

"Which so far amounts to nothing."

"When are we going to tangle with them, General?" she asked.

"Ike is in that vicinity with West and Striganov. That's up to him. Get him on the horn while I get a cup of coffee."

"Go, Ben," Ike said a moment later.

"How's it look?"

"Grim. We're not going to be able to stand and slug it out with these people. Too many of them. My latest intel says a minimum of three divisions, sixty thousand men, and probably a backup division, or two. The only crossings open for several hundred miles are Thunder Bay, one south of Winnipeg, and another south of Regina."

"All right, Ike. You take the Thunder Bay crossing. I'll shift Dan, Rebet, and Greenwalt south of Winnipeg. I'll take Jim Peters and Jackie and plug up south of Regina. Good luck."

Ben turned to Corrie. "Let's roll. Break camp." He looked over at Jersey.

She smiled. "Kick ass time, General."

"Yeah," Ben said. "But whose ass is going to get kicked?"

* * *

While Ben and the others raced to get in position, the remaining nine battalions were to be spread out along I-94, from St. Paul west to Miles City in Montana. Artillery was rolling northward day and night. Special Operations people were working planting explosives on bridges.

"I want teams sent into Canada to blow every bridge they can," Ben ordered. "We'll cut Revere's supply lines. We know he has only limited aircraft. That will hurt him. I want every bridge blown between Medicine Hat in Canada south down to West Yellowstone and from Duluth down to Madison. And I mean every bridge. We'll hold until that is done. Then we'll start slowly falling back until we reach I-90. Revere will be unable to go east across the Mississippi, and unable to go west. He's not going to go north. There is nothing up there Blanton wants. He'll have but one direction: south. We'll be harassing him all the way. And that's just over two hundred and fifty miles from the border to I-90. He's going to pay in blood for every mile he gains. I-90 is the line, people. We're going to hold there for as long as we can. By the time his divisions reach that line, we'll have cut them down significantly." I hope, Ben silently added.

"Now then," Ben continued taping the orders for burst transmission. "We'll have Creeps and punks all around us. So we're going to be fighting on all sides. We don't know who we can trust, so trust no one. Don't take any food or water from civilians. Watch yourselves at all times. As they used to say in the movies, this is it. Good luck."

Ben walked to a wall map and stared. He shook his head. "Fifteen short battalions stretched out along a nine hundred mile front," he muttered. "I've got to find us an edge. But where?"

"Our spies in the States say that Raines is moving his people up to I-90," Paul Revere was informed. "He's blowing bridges east and west." He used a grease pencil to mark the locations on a map.

"He's putting us in a box," Revere said. "But he can't believe he can contain us there. He's stretched too thin. That's almost a thousand miles. He's pulling something. It's a ruse. But what kind of a ruse?"

But Paul Revere was getting ahead of himself. He was seeing things that weren't there; trying to think like Ben. Which is exactly what Ben wanted him to do. Ben wanted the man off-balance and unsure.

"What the hell is Raines up to?" Revere muttered, staring at the map.

Waiting, in a small town sixteen miles south of the Canadian border. Ben had spread his three battalions out, stretching them thin and digging them in deep, then daring them to move. If he could pull the ambush off, General Tom Thomas was going to learn the hard way about the dirty art of guerrilla warfare . . . and that was something Ben knew the man was not schooled in. Actually, none of the division commanders knew much about ground combat. General Holtz was Army aviation for most of his career, Matt Forrest was in the Pentagon, tied to a desk, and Tom Thomas was basically an artillery officer, but like Matt, had been assigned to the Pentagon for years.

Ben didn't like doing this. He found the idea of fighting true Americans repugnant. But somehow those three fine officers had been persuaded to join Blanton's team.

Ben sighed in frustration. Blanton himself was more than likely a good man, believing strongly that what he advocated was the right way for the battered nation and its equally battered citizens. But Blanton was a true liberal, right down to the core, believing in more government control of people's lives, while Ben believed in a minimum of government interference in the lives of citizens.

Ben had finally realized that the two philosophies could never peacefully coexist. One side had to dominate. And Ben was determined to be on the winning side.

Revere's forces were now openly transmitting, and the Rebels' scanners were monitoring them constantly. Ben now knew exactly where Revere's forces were going to enter the States, and what they planned to do. Revere's divisions had tanks and artillery; the Rebels had better tanks—although not as many—and longer range artillery.

Ben's dug-in and camouflaged troops were equipped with antitank weapons and mortars. The troops of Revere's third division, under the command of General Tom Thomas, were only a few hours away from learning some hard lessons about tangling with Raines's Rebels.

"Crossing the border," Corrie said softly.

Ben nodded his head. He did not have to ask if

everyone was in place and ready. He knew they were. This time, no one bitched about Ben's being in the middle of the action. They all knew Ben would not have paid the slightest bit of attention to their protests.

As the first tanks approached the presumably deserted little town, the tank commanders did not button up. The town had been checked out by Revere's recon the day before when it really was deserted, and reported that back.

The tanks rumbled through without incident.

Just north of the town flowed a creek, running high now because of the spring rains. Once that bridge was gone, there would be no crossing for miles in either direction. Ben smiled as the men and equipment of the third division took the bait and swallowed the hook.

The members of Ben's personal team looked at him; they knew that smile. It was the smile of an eagle about to sink its talons into prey.

The minutes ticked past and the rumble of tanks and trucks continued.

"Fire," Ben said.

Corrie spoke into her headset and the two-lane bridge north of town blew into hundreds of chunks. Two trucks carrying troops were caught on the bridge and the men and equipment disappeared into the running waters of the creeks.

Dozens of rockets were fired and impacted against their targets. Mortars began thudding out rounds. One third of Thomas's division was caught on the south side of the creek, most on the open road, some in the town. They didn't have a chance.

Tanks and trucks erupted in an inferno of fire as

flame and fuel-air rockets struck their targets. These rounds spewed highly flammable liquid all over their target upon impact, then the explosives blew, creating a deadly, hellish nightmare. Snipers, using .50 caliber Haskins rifles, laying back a mile and more, created more havoc. Some of the Rebel snipers were using special rounds, with a hardened tungsten-carbide penetrator inside the projectile, capable of penetrating four inches of armor and then blowing up.

If there was a dirty trick the Rebels didn't know, it was because it hadn't yet been thought of.

All General Thomas could do was stand on the north side of the overflowing creek and watch and listen as his forward units got creamed.

"That dirty, sneaky, ambushing bastard!" Thomas said.

Thomas was learning about Ben Raines. The hard way.

# Twelve

As the other forward units of Revere's forces entered U.S. territory, they got a short, bloody, and very brutal lesson in Rebel ferocity.

Revere quickly shut them all down and told them to dig in and wait for orders.

"What the hell is happening out there?" Blanton shouted into the mic, just moments after receiving the first battlefield reports.

"I tried to warn you about Raines, Mister President," Revere spoke calmly from his CP, a couple thousand miles away. "But you wouldn't listen. You just simply cannot fight the Rebels on any type of conventional basis and expect to win. It isn't possible."

Blanton was silent for a moment, which for him was nothing short of a miracle. He'd been in love with the sound of his own voice for years.

"Go to scramble, Mister President," Revere said. "The Rebels are listening."

"They're going digital," Ben said.

"I've got it," Corrie said.

"Hearts and minds, Mister President," Revere said.

"What do you mean?"

"Bluntly put, sir, it means give me your hearts and minds or I'll burn your house down and kill your firstborn."

"You mean," the president said, "kill all of Ben Raines supporters?"

"That's it exactly."

"Yes, yes!" Harriet Hooter shouted. "Destroy all those right-wing, gun-loving jerks."

"Isn't this exciting?" Blush Lightheart cooed.

"But what about the children?" Blanton asked.

"Who cares?" Senator Ditto said. "Little rednecks grow up into big rednecks."

"That's right," Representative Crapums said. "The only way we'll ever have peace in this nation is to kill everyone who owns a gun. Except those on our side, that is," he quickly added.

"Kill all those racist bastards!" Representative Rivers shouted.

Blanton was again silent. Order and stability had to be restored in the nation. My goodness, me. Just let a little war break out in the country and look what happened: the people actually started to believe that they could run the nation without politicians. That just wouldn't do at all. The American people couldn't govern themselves. That was ridiculous. They were actually shooting people out there for stealing and other silly little things like that. He'd heard that rapists were being castrated. How awful. Made him nauseous for hours. Caused him to spit up his Twinkie. No, no, no, no! The American people could not govern themselves. They had to have a firm hand on the reins of government. His hand, naturally. He was born to lead. Everyone told him so. Even his wife. Occasionally.

And it was all Ben Raines's fault. Every bit of it. Goddamn rabble-rousing, right-wing, redneck peckerwood.

Blanton opened his mouth to speak and then remembered he first had to key the mic. He always forgot that. Too many other pressing matters on his mind. "All right, General Revere. Do it your way."

Revere smiled. "Thank you, Mister President. Thank you very much."

"Hearts and minds," Ben said. "Now it gets rough, folks. If I let it. Corrie, get me Blanton on the horn. No! Forget that. I don't want him to know that we have equipment capable of descrambling every transmission they send."

"Surely he has enough sense to realize that?" Jersey added.

"Don't bet on it," Ben replied with a smile.

All along three fronts, General Revere's forces had been stopped cold by the Rebels. Those few who managed to escape the initial three-pronged ambush and return to their lines told tales of absolute horror and terror.

"It just seemed like the Rebels were part of the earth," one said. "They just rose up out of the ground and turned everything into an inferno."

"I've never seen such accuracy with artillery and mortar," another said.

"I never so much as got a glimpse of the Rebels," a platoon leader wrote in his report. "They were like ghosts. The fire was not centralized, but came from all around us. How they managed to do that without hitting their own forces is a mystery to me."

Paul Revere called for a meeting with his three division commanders. Revere either did not realize it, or did not care, that this move was only giving Ben time to strengthen his own lines.

"The president has given us carte blanche in dealing with the Rebels," Revere told the men. "Hearts and minds, gentlemen. That's the way to defeat Ben Raines."

"General Revere, these are Americans we're fighting," General Holtz pointed out. "Now, while I strongly agree that this nation must be reunited, killing civilian supporters of Ben Raines is repugnant to me and could easily backfire."

"President Blanton okayed the killing of civilians?" General Thomas asked.

"He has put the order in writing and that paper is being couriered to me at this moment." Revere knew the "hearts and minds" program was a dangerous one to put to these generals. While many of the troops were solidly loyal to him, many of them loyal to Blanton and his idealistic concept of government, still others were loyal to Generals Thomas, Holtz, and Forrest. "But before we implement the program," Revere said smoothly, "flyers are being printed and will be distributed throughout the nation, air-dropped by light plane. They will tell the long-suffering American people that we are not the enemy. Ben Raines is. Raines offers aid and comfort only to those who support him. We offer aid and comfort and amnesty to all people.

We are not going in willy-nilly, killing women and children. I want that understood."

The three generals relaxed. Those were the words they wanted to hear.

General Holtz said, "The American people should be advised that we did not start this war. Raines's Rebels ambushed us."

*"Exactly!"* Revere said. "The American people must understand that we did not come here as invaders, but as liberators. Raines and his Rebels are the oppressors, not us. Now, we will have to kill some civilians. And I don't like that one little bit. No, sir. I'm going to shed some tears before this campaign is over. I see that. Some of these poor, misguided fools who support Ben Raines will fight us, and we'll have to fight them. I hate it. And I'll be giving the orders with tears in my eyes. But . . ." He held out his hands and shrugged. "America must be reunited. This great nation cannot be allowed to dissolve into warring factions. It must be restored, and if spilling civilian blood is the only way, then so be it."

Hearts and minds. And the first three he hooked were men who should have known better.


A scout brought Ben a leaflet, a disgusted expression on his face. "You want to read some shit, sir," he said. "This is it." He handed Ben the leaflet.

A MESSAGE TO ALL AMERICANS FROM THE PRESIDENT OF THE UNITED STATES, HOMER BLANTON (A CHRISTIAN MAN AND A TRUE GOOD OL' BOY

IF THERE EVER WAS ONE): MY FRIENDS, I WISH I COULD SIT DOWN AND HAVE A PERSONAL CHAT WITH EACH AND EVERY ONE OF YOU. BUT THAT IS IMPOSSIBLE. THE FORCES OF EVIL THAT PROWL THIS GREAT NATION UNDER THE COMMAND OF BEN RAINES PREVENT ME FROM DOING THAT. BEN RAINES, THE GREAT SATAN (AND A REGISTERED REPUBLICAN, TOO), AND HIS ARMY OF MALCONTENTS CALLED THE REBELS, HAVE PUT ME UNDER A DEATH SENTENCE. THIS HANDFUL OF REDNECKS AND BEER-BELCHERS AND GUNFREAKS HAVE PARALYZED THIS NATION, SPREADING FEAR AND HATE WHEREVER THEY GO. BEN RAINES AND THE REBELS PREACH WAR WHILE I SPEAK SOFTLY OF PEACE, BROTHERHOOD, FREEDOM, AND A CHICKEN IN EVERY POT (ALWAYS REMOVE THE SKIN BEFORE YOU COOK IT; THE SKIN IS NOT GOOD FOR YOU. MY WIFE TOLD ME THAT).

I HAVE SENT THE UNITED STATES ARMY, UNDER THE COMMAND OF GENERAL PAUL REVERE (AND YOU KNOW WHO HIS GREAT-GREAT-GREAT-GREAT-GREAT GRANDDADDY WAS) TO FREE THE GOOD CITIZENS OF AMERICA FROM THE TERRIBLE GRIPS OF ANARCHY. THEY BRING WITH THEM FOOD AND MEDICINES AND HOPE AND CONDOMS AND ALL SORTS OF OTHER REAL NEAT STUFF. AND IT'S FREE. YOURS FOR THE

ASKING. OF COURSE, YOU'LL PAY FOR IT LATER WHEN I RAISE YOUR TAXES, BUT WE DON'T HAVE TO TALK ABOUT THAT RIGHT NOW.

WE NEED YOUR HELP, GOOD CITIZENS OF AMERICA. WE NEED YOUR SOLID MIDDLE-CLASS MINDS AND VALUES TO HELP US DEFEAT BEN RAINES. BEN RAINES IS A REAL SHIT-HEAD, AMERICANS. HE'S A BABY-KILLER. HIS REBELS RAPE AND PILLAGE AND PLUNDER AND DO ALL SORTS OF OTHER REAL BAD THINGS. BEN RAINES DOESN'T EVEN GO TO CHURCH AND HE HATES RAP MUSIC. HE LISTENS TO THAT OL' CLASSICAL STUFF. YUKK! BEN RAINES IS A HEATHEN AND HIS REBELS ARE THE HORDES OF EVIL. THEY MUST BE STOPPED. AND WITH YOUR HELP, BEN RAINES AND THE REBELS WILL BE STOPPED. GOD IS ON OUR SIDE. I REALLY, REALLY, REALLY BELIEVE THAT. CROSS MY HEART AND HOPE TO DIE.

GENERAL PAUL REVERE AND THE UNITED STATES ARMY WILL BE ADVANCING THROUGHOUT THIS NATION, STOPPING ALONG THE WAY TO TALK WITH YOU AMERICANS, TO SEE WHERE YOU STAND IN THIS STRUGGLE FOR FREEDOM AND EQUALITY FOR ALL, AND TO TAKE YOUR COMPLAINTS AND TO OFFER YOU FOOD AND MEDICINE AND HOPE FOR THE FUTURE. PLEASE COOPERATE WITH THESE SOLDIERS OF FREE-

DOM. AND DON'T BE ALARMED IF SOME OF YOUR NEIGHBORS AND FRIENDS ARE TOTED OFF IN HANDCUFFS. I PROMISE YOU THEY WON'T BE HARMED. BUT IT IS OUR STRONG BELIEF THAT ANYONE WHO AGREES WITH THE PHILOSOPHIES OF BEN RAINES AND THE REBELS HAS A REAL MENTAL PROBLEM. WE MUST ATTEMPT TO RE-EDUCATE THESE MIS-GUIDED SOULS AND BRING THEM BACK TO THEIR SENSES. THOSE UNFORTU-NATE PEOPLE WHO FOLLOW BEN RAINES HAVE BEEN BRAINWASHED. THEY ARE TO BE PITIED AND THEY ARE TO BE HELPED.

I PLEAD WITH ALL TRUE AMERICANS TO STAND BESIDE YOUR PRESIDENT AND HELP US DEFEAT THE EVIL GREAT SATAN BEN RAINES AND HIS ARMY OF BUTCHERS AND BABY-RAPERS AND OTHER STUFF TOO AWFUL TO MEN-TION HERE.

HOMER BLANTON, PRESIDENT OF THE UNITED STATES.

Ben shook his head and handed the oversized leaflet back to the scout. "You raped any babies lately, Sergeant?" he asked with a smile.

"Are you kidding, sir!" He held up the paper. "This guy is a nut."

"No, not really. He just has very bad advisors. He always did. He listens to the wrong people and ob-viously is still listening to the wrong people." Ben pointed to the leaflet. "How many of those things were dropped?"

"Millions of them, I guess. All outposts and recon and scout teams outside our battle zone are reporting the ground covered with them."

Ben fingered the paper and arched an eyebrow.

The scout smiled. "Yes, sir. That's what our people are using them for. We're saving them for emergencies."

Ben laughed. "Corrie, be sure that Blanton knows how the "Evil Empire" is using his leaflets. That ought to really make his day."

Those around him thought the president was going to have a stroke when he received word about how the Rebels were using his leaflets. His face turned red, his eyes bugged out, and he jumped up and down, flapping his arms. It was a pretty good imitation of Big Bird.

"The Rebels are doing what with the leaflets?" Harriet Hooter asked. Her eyes bugged out at the answer and she said, "That's disgusting!"

"The man obviously has no class," Rita Rivers sniffed. Lack of class was something she should know about, since before being elected to Congress she'd been arrested for prostitution four times (among other things) and it was said she could suck a dick with more power than a vacuum cleaner.

She and Blush Lightheart really had more in common than they thought.

"I want that damn Ben Raines *killed!*" Blanton shouted. "I want him dead, dead, *dead!*"

Peace, brotherhood, freedom, and a chicken

(skinless) in every pot. Right. Just as long as you agree with me. Blanton wasn't as far apart from Ben Raines as he thought he was.

# *Thirteen*

Ben had used the lull in fighting to strengthen his own positions and also to make certain that the towns and the ruins of small cities within the battle zone were cleaned out of Creeps and punks aligned with Blanton. The Rebels were working against time and they were not gentle with any gangs living amid the ruins of the cities. It was classic search and destroy.

While the Rebels were busy purging the battle zone, Revere was working swiftly to rebuild his divisions with replacements gathered from all over what had once been called the United States of America. It came as no surprise to Ben to learn that thousands and thousands of men and women were racing to join Blanton and his Forces of Independence and Brotherhood. He had to smile at the abbreviation of that—FIB. Ben wondered if Blanton had caught it. He doubted it.

"The forces of FIB," Jersey said. "How come we always get to fight the loonies?"

"They think the same about us, Jersey," Ben told her.

"I don't understand it, General," the young woman said. "I have never understood why others hate us so."

It was a quiet time in Ben's CP, everything that could humanly be done toward the defense of their zone had been done. Now they had to wait.

"You have to try to understand the liberal mind, Jersey," Ben said, as the others in the room turned and listened.

Jersey, who had known nothing but war since childhood, said, "What's to understand? They're a bunch of damn nuts and kooks."

Ben laughed and refilled his coffee cup. He rolled a cigarette and said, "But Jersey, to people like Blanton and his followers, we're the nuts and kooks."

"That's what I don't understand, General," the small, shapely, dark-eyed beauty said. "We're the ones out here trying to establish order, bring stability back to the land, put people to work, do all the things that make a nation whole. Now up jumps this Homer Blanton—who I just have vague memories of—and he starts running his damn stupid mouth about us being baby-killers and possessed by the devil and all kinds of the most ridiculous crap I have ever heard."

Ben smiled and took his Desert Eagle .50 automag from leather and laid it on the table. "Let me see if I can show you how the liberal mind works, Jersey." He looked around the room at the young faces. Every member of his personal team was in their mid-twenties; middle teens when the Great War erupted. He pointed to the pistol. "What is that, Jersey?"

She stared at him for a moment. "Well, hell, General! It's a pistol."

"Nothing else?" Ben asked.

"No."

"It isn't evil?"

"General," the usually quiet Beth said, "how can a piece of metal be evil? It can't think or reason."

Ben chuckled. "But to a liberal, a gun is an evil thing."

Corrie shook her head and said, "A gun by itself cannot be evil. The person who picks it up and uses it might be evil. But not the gun itself."

"But to a true hanky-stomper," Ben replied, "it's the gun that is evil."

"Well, that just proves my point," the blunt-talking Jersey said. "All liberals are as dumb as rat shit."

Ben shook his head and laughed. "Quite the contrary. Most left-leaning people possess average or above intelligence."

"You'll never convince me of that," Jersey stood her ground. "I read an old magazine the other day, published back in '94 or '95. This guy had been arrested something like forty or fifty times for various offenses. I'm serious, people!" she said, looking at the disbelieving faces staring at her. "This guy's criminal history started when he was about thirteen years old. He'd been arrested for drug-dealing, breaking and entering, rape, assault and battery, child molestation, assault with a deadly weapon, attempted murder, conspiracy to commit murder—all kinds of stuff. He had fifteen DWI convictions against him, from various states, and yet he still had a valid driver's license from some state and until he got drunk and ran over and killed some lady, he was free to drive and walk the streets. And this writer was moaning about the harsh sentence this sorry bastard received. The writer had to be liberal, right, General?"

"I'm sure he was."

"And you're telling me that liberals are rational people, and have good sense?"

Ben smiled. "I'm sure the writer of the article blamed the individual's life of crime on something that happened during childhood."

"Oh, yeah. When he was thirteen, his father grounded him for a week as punishment for doing something, or not doing something. That night, the guy beat his father's head in with a fireplace poker while his dad was asleep. And do you know how much jail time that punk got?"

"Probably none."

"That's right. Now, I don't believe that a thirteen-year-old should be put to death," Jersey said. "But I do believe that he should have been institutionalized until he was rehabilitated."

"I agree with you," Ben said. "But the catch is this: most psychiatrists were liberal, most judges were liberal, many lawyers were liberal, most social workers were liberal. Ninety-nine percent of TV anchors and newspaper reporters were liberal. Talk show hosts were liberal. Yet a full fifty percent of Americans were moderate or conservative in their views. We had little representation in Washington and practically no support in the news media."

"How could that be?" Cooper asked. "I thought the American system was built on full representation for all its citizens."

"Theoretically, it was. Looked real good on paper. Didn't work worth a shit in reality. It would come as a great surprise to Blanton, but I agree with him on one very important point: many Americans were simply too goddamn stupid to govern themselves. And behind all of Blanton's fancy rhetoric, that is the main reason he's coming after us. He knows the Rebels are the cream of the crop. The hardest working, the most intelligence, the best, of the best. We've got a good toe-hold in this nation, and he knows he can't allow us to flourish. He's gathering the rabble around him. He's pulling together and arming the whiners, the complainers, the do-nothings, those who want something for nothing. He's building a second army out of those who want government in every aspect of their lives. But rabble have helped bring down stronger armies than ours."

"You think we're really in for a long haul on this one, don't you, sir?" Cooper asked.

"Yes, I do, Coop." He smiled. "As the leader of one nation put it a few years back: the mother of all battles."

"Kill the father," Cooper said softly.

Every eye turned to Cooper, including Ben's. "What are you saying, Coop?"

"Kill Blanton. Some of the scouts are still in place."

Ben walked to a boarded-up window and stared out for a time. Then he slowly shook his head and turned around. "I can't do that, Coop. I can fight his army. I could depose him in a bloodless coup. But I could never kill a president of the United States. There is just too much American in me for that." He frowned. "At least I hope that situation never confronts me."

"Bad idea, Coop," Jersey said. "We're all Americans. Don't ever forget that."

"It was just a thought," Coop said.

"If it makes you feel better, Coop," Ben said. "I had already thought of it." He smiled. "But I'm not above sending people in on a snatch and grab."

Revere was ready for a push against the Rebel positions, all along the line. The Rebels had backed up and dug in along Highway 2, stretching from Montana to US 51 South in Wisconsin. It was indeed a very thin line of resistance.

"But no artillery along that line," recon reported back to Revere.

"No. Raines wouldn't have them there. They're some twenty-odd miles back. And from all reports, their artillery has more range than ours." Revere moved to the radio. "I want everybody buttoned up for an ambush. And you can bet one is coming. So be ready. Move out."

This time the divisions moved out cautiously, with everybody buttoned up, which is exactly what Ben had figured they would do. In tanks, Bradley Fighting Vehicles, and other types of armored personnel carriers, including recently armored trucks, all buttoned up against attack, vision is quite impaired.

Revere's recon was good, and they had scouted the area, of course. But during the more than week's lull, Rebels from all the nine front-line battalions had plenty of time to dig in deep and secure.

In a move that Revere was sure Ben would not

expect, he had ordered his divisions split up, taking as many roads as possible on their way south. Bad decision. Ben had anticipated that and had teams out, ready to blow the bridges on the old county roads, front and back, and then scatter, leaving many of Revere's people stranded.

Revere had known the hottest action would be in Ben Raines's sector, and he had moved his CP there. When the first reports began coming in, he was livid with rage.

". . . Cut off from main force," came the broken radio transmissions from a dozen units. "Under heavy Rebel attack. Can't hold. No place to run. We . . ." Silence.

"Goddamnit!" Revere fumed. "How did he know? Nobody in my own command knew except me until the last possible minute. That son of a bitch!"

Ben had been called worse over the years.

Revere had lost several thousand troops, quite a lot of equipment, an immeasurable amount of morale among his people, and had not taken one inch of ground. His forces had been thrown back at every attack point. Those FIB troops who had made it through the artillery barrage found themselves cut off and looking smack into the faces of extremely unfriendly Rebels. Knowing that Raines's Rebels would ask for surrender only one time and demand a response very quickly, the FIB troops threw down their weapons and put their hands in the air. Those in Ben's sector were taken to him immediately.

Blanton was shocked by the latest turn of events.

His aides expected him to throw a temper tantrum, but he was surprisingly calm. He walked slowly back to his office in the old resort hotel and closed the door. His wife mouthed a few choice words, threw a couple of lamps against the wall, and joined her husband.

Back in Ben's battle zone, a small group of very frightened prisoners, officers and sergeants, were brought to see him. All fully expected to be shot.

Ben pointed to chairs. "Sit," he said. They sat. "Are you hungry, thirsty?"

The six men and two women shook their heads, not knowing how to take this man that they all had been brainwashed into believing was the 21st century's rendition of Attila the Hun and Adolph Hitler.

"Why are you people fighting me?" Ben asked.

"Because you're the antichrist," a woman blurted.

Ben laughed and the members of his team laughed with him. "I think my chaplains would be very much surprised to hear that. While I am not an overly religious man, I do attend services occasionally and I have been known to pray from time to time. Come on, people. You have to have a better reason than that. Now, come on, tell me the real reason why the Rebel form of government is so repugnant to you."

"You want to destroy this nation and burn the Constitution," a man said.

Ben shook his head. "Is that what Blanton has been force-feeding you people?"

"You have concentration camps," another man said. This one wore a major's insignia.

Ben smiled. "Where are they?"

"In the area you call Base Camp One."

Ben shook his head. "People, the Rebels don't have concentration camps or anything that even remotely resembles them. We have one very small prison in Base Camp One, but it is nothing like the prisons this nation had before the war. We stress rehabilitation and our people work very hard to restore the prisoner's sense of dignity."

"Is that where you are going to put us?" the second woman asked.

"I'm not going to put you in prison. Any of you. What I am going to do is offer you a bath, food, civilian clothes, and a chance to start over. But I would like to ask you just one question: who the hell is Paul Revere?"

"Commanding General of the Army of the Forces of Independence and Brotherhood," the major said.

"I know that. But where did he come from?"

"We are required only to give you our name, rank, and service number," the major said.

"Get them out of here and let them bathe and change clothes and have some food," Ben said to a Rebel officer.

"Our last meal?" one of the women asked.

"Oh, lady," Ben said wearily. "I'm not going to shoot you. The only way any of you will get hurt is if you try to grab some Rebel's weapon. I don't care if you get up and run out of this office and go back to your own lines. I really don't. Run, if you want to." He looked at Corrie. "Pass the word that these people are free to return to their own lines." To the prisoners: "But if I were you, I'd take my offer of a bath and a change of clothes and some food.

138

Our rations are really not bad and our medical facilities are top-rate. Wander around, talk to people. I think you'll find that we're not monsters or raving lunatics like that nut Blanton has so cleverly painted us." He stood up and walked to the office door and opened it. "Go on. Leave. You won't be harmed. Talk to the people in camp. I think you'll find that we are really just plain, ordinary folks. We just have this little hang-up about living free and safe and everybody pulling their weight, that's all."

One of the women, a sergeant, was the first to stand up and move toward the open door. She paused, looking up at Ben. "The mess is in the gym," Ben told her. "That's about three hundred yards to your right. The evening meal should be ready. Fried chicken, mashed potatoes, corn on the cob, some sort of dessert, and iced tea or coffee." The lady had incredibly pale blue eyes and was quite lovely. She filled out her BDUs very nicely.

"Maybe we were wrong," she said softly. "Maybe we have been fed false information about you and the Rebels."

"Denise!" the major said sharply.

Denise looked at the major. "I want to see for myself, Major. I want to see if we've been fed lies and half-truths."

"You know these people are experts at brainwashing, Denise. And don't eat the food. It's probably drugged."

Ben got a good laugh out of that. "Major, it's a mess line. We'll all be eating the same thing."

The major glowered at Ben.

Ben ignored him and held out his arm to Denise. "May I walk with you, miss?"

139

Cooper and Beth winked at each other.

"Certainly, General," Denise said.

"Here we go again," Jersey muttered, rolling her eyes.

"What about me?" Cooper hollered.

"See to the needs of the prisoners," Ben told him.

"I really would like a bath and a change of clothes," Denise said, as they strolled along the old road.

"I'll walk you over to the quartermaster and see that you're outfitted . . . in civilian clothing."

Denise smiled a very pretty smile. Ben figured her to be in her early to mid-thirties. Sort of a honey-blonde, the hair cut short.

"Major Nelson is a staunch supporter of President Blanton and his philosophies, General."

"I never would have guessed," Ben said drily.

"You'd really turn us loose?"

"That's my plan. If you want to go, that is."

Denise looked around her as they walked. Rebels were walking about, sitting down chatting, catching a few winks of sleep, cleaning weapons. No one seemed the least bit concerned that enemy troops, which outnumbered them fifteen or twenty to one, were only twenty-five miles away.

"Why would I not want to return to my unit and my friends, General?" Denise asked.

"Because what they are doing is wrong, and what I'm doing is right, that's why."

"You're going to have to convince me of that."

"I plan on giving it my best shot."

## Fourteen

"This is the best food I've had in months!" Denise said, returning with a second helping of everything.

The lady had a healthy appetite. Ben said, "Unfortunately, our field rations aren't nearly this good. We've been eating rations taken from Herr Jesus Hoffman's goose-steppers for several months. Tell me, if Blanton is so concerned about liberty and justice and truth and all that, why didn't he pitch in and help us out fighting the Nazis?"

She looked at him and blinked. "What about Herr Hoffman? What Nazis?"

Ben sugared his coffee and smiled. "Just like I thought. He kept that news from the troops. I would imagine he hoped that Hoffman would defeat us and kill me. He better be glad that didn't happen. Hoffman's people would have shoved a flag pole up his liberal ass and left him to rot."

Ben brought Denise up to date about the year-long battle with the New Army of Liberation.

She was appalled at the thought of a massive Nazi army on United States soil. "And your Rebels whipped them?"

"Thoroughly."

"I swear to you, we knew nothing about that, General."

"Oh, I believe you. Does that tell you anything about your leaders?"

"Unfortunately, yes. Why do you hate liberals so?"

"Somehow, I can't believe you are a true liberal, Denise."

"That doesn't answer my question."

"I don't hate liberals, Denise. I just don't want to live under their form of government. I'd like for you to see Base Camp One. See how we live."

"Blanton says it's a terrible place. There are daily hangings and shootings."

"Denise, there hasn't been a hanging or a shooting down there in so long I can't even remember the last one. A black man, General Cecil Jefferys, a close friend of mine, is administrator of Base Camp One. You're sitting here amid people of all nationalities, all faiths. Does that tell you anything about how right-wing we're supposed to be?"

She smiled. "All right, General. So Blanton has exaggerated the situation somewhat."

"*Somewhat!* I don't think the man is playing with a full deck."

"Would you believe there are those of us who feel the same way?"

"Of course, if you have any sense you couldn't think otherwise."

"When he was elected to the White House, Homer Blanton was a good, decent man who only wanted to do the right thing."

"For everybody, which isn't possible. He also was

and probably still is a liar and a coward. Did the strain get to him, Denise?"

"I don't know. I've never seen the man in person. He stays in that huge resort hotel in New York State and . . ." She bit back the words. "I guess I've given away his location, right?"

"No. There are lots of resort hotels in that area. Oh, hell, Denise. We know where he is. I could send a K-team in anytime I want to."

"K-team?"

"Kill-team."

"Are you going to?"

"I have no plans to do so . . . at the present time," he added. "Finish your supper. I want you to hear something."

"Indoctrination speech?" she asked with a smile.

"No. I assure you, we don't give those. A person has to work to join us, Denise. It's like respect. It can't be handed out like candy. It has to be earned."

"Your right-wing philosophy is showing, General Raines."

"I do let it boil over occasionally."

Back at the CP, Corrie got General Tom Thomas on the horn.

"Tom? Ben Raines here."

"'Lo, Ben. It's been a long time."

"Quite a few years. Tom, give this up. You're not going to beat me."

"I don't like your politics, Ben. You're too far to the right for my tastes."

"Like them or not, Tom, you're still not going to beat me. All you're going to do is spill a lot of blood—most of it on your side—and kill a lot of men and women—most of them your people. Blanton is a sick man, Tom. The strain got to him. My God, look at the people he's surrounded himself with: the most liberal people that ever sat in the house and senate. Is that what you want for the nation?"

"Not necessarily, Ben. All that can be worked out later."

"I hope you don't believe that, Tom. You know from past history that if you give a liberal an inch, that inch soon turns into a mile. Look what happened with gun control."

"It's no use, Ben. You've divided this nation and a divided nation cannot stand. You know that. You've got some good things going on down there at Base Camp One, but many of your ideas are just too radical. Even for an old soldier like me."

"All right, Tom. If that's the way you see it. Answer this, if you will: who in the hell is Paul Revere?"

"I think he's a South African, Ben. I'm just not sure. But he's a top soldier."

"Thank you. Will you at least think about what I said?"

"You have to be stopped, Ben. This nation must be united."

"With Blanton at the helm? And all those crybabies with him? No way, Tom. No way."

Static greeted his words. General Thomas had broken off.

Ben looked at Denise. "I tried. At least I can say I tried."

The next day, Major Wilson and three men were allowed to return to their units. Denise and three others elected to stay with the Rebels.

"You should have shot them," Jersey told Ben sourly. Ben laughed and walked back inside his CP.

Denise cut her eyes to the petite young woman with the hard, dark eyes. "You believe that strongly in what you're doing?"

"Yeah. I sure do."

"Because of General Raines?"

Jersey thought about that for a moment. "He's part of it. Sure. It used to be, most people thought, that if something happened to the general, the movement would fall apart. But that was tested a few months ago, and the movement just got stronger and more determined to survive, and to win. The Rebel movement will never be defeated. I've seen Rebels crawl through their own blood, holding their guts in with one hand and a gun in the other, just to kill one more of the enemy before they died. Do Blanton's people have that kind of dedication?"

Denise smiled and shook her head. "No. They don't."

"You know why?"

"No."

Several dozen Rebels had gathered around, including those with Denise who had chosen to stay. The Rebels smiled, for they knew that when Jersey elected to voice an opinion, she really let the hammer down.

" 'Cause you were with a bunch of losers, that's why. Blanton put together a lot of mercenaries to form the core of his army. But ninety percent of the others are those types of people who, back when the world was whole, wanted something for nothing. Give me this and give me that and I got a right to do this, that, and the other thing. I demand this, that, and the other thing. Without having to work for it. Blanton's shit, he's surrounded himself with advisors who are full of shit, and he's got shit for an army. Revere's attacked twice and lost several thousand people and a lot of equipment. We haven't even had one Rebel wounded. That ought to tell you something about the quality of men and women who support Ben Raines. Oh, we'll lose people before it's over. We might lose half our force, or more. But we will never surrender. And as long as there is just one man or woman willing to pick up a gun and fight, the Rebel movement will never die. Never!''

The fight had turned into a stalemate, with Revere reluctant to commit his forces past the line they had established until the gangs of thugs and punks and street slime Blanton had recruited could get into place behind the Rebels. What he and Blanton seemed unable to realize was that the Rebels had no intention of allowing anything like that to happen.

Helicopter gunships and PUFFs were roaming the skies miles behind the lines. Whenever groups were spotted, they were challenged by ground troops or radio. If they turned out to be hostile, they were wiped out to the last person. It was brutal, ruthless, merciless. It was Rebel warfare. No gentleman's rules, no Geneva convention. The only rules were those of Ben Raines, and they were simple: Kill the enemy.

Even Revere was shaken by the coldness of the

Rebels in dealing with their enemies. Nine battalions of Rebels had stopped three full divisions cold.

Blanton and those with him were sickened by the field reports. None of them had any experience with war. They did not realize the callousness needed to win battles.

Not even Revere and his top soldiers were as ruthless in war as Ben Raines.

Contrary to what Ben believed, Homer Blanton was not suffering from any type of mental illness. He was a smart man, and a good man in his own right. He was just about three bricks shy of a load when it came to common sense.

While Ben Raines realized fully that the philosophies of the Rebels would not work for a large percentage of the American people, Homer Blanton came into office convinced that his philosophies would and should work for all. And even after a great world war and the collapse of every government around the globe, he still believed that.

Homer Blanton was about to come face to face with reality, in the form of Ben Raines.

"General Raines on the radio, sir," a Blanton aide came rushing into the room. "He wants to speak to you."

"I have nothing to say to that war-mongering bastard," Blanton pouted. Blanton was a real good pouter. And 'Ol' pooter' had been replaced by saltier descriptions.

"Is that what you want me to tell him, sir?" the aide was very nervous about the prospect of having to call General Ben Raines a bastard.

"No," Blanton's better judgment took control. "I'll speak with him." He walked to his communications room and took the mic. "President Blanton here."

"You want to sit down and talk with me, Blanton?" Ben asked.

"It's a trick!" Vice President Harriet Hooter squalled. "Those savages will come here and rape and ravage us all."

"Horrors!" Rita Rivers bellowed. "A fate worse than death!" This from a woman who'd once taken on an entire platoon of Marines from San Diego. For ten dollars each.

The president glanced at the two women, both of whom looked as though they'd recently been thoroughly whipped with an ugly stick. "Not likely," he muttered under his breath. He lifted the mic. "Are you serious, Raines?"

"As serious as a crutch, Blanton."

"He's losing the war!" Blanton shouted to the room full of people. "He's losing the war and wants to make a deal. My God, I'll show him how tough I can be." To Ben: "No deals, Raines. You're finished and you know it. I will accept your unconditional surrender, however."

Twenty-five hundred miles away, Ben looked at the speaker as if not believing what he'd just heard. He slowly shook his head and keyed the mic. "Blanton, what the hell are you talking about?"

"Your surrender, you ninny!"

"Blanton, listen to me, I have no intention whatsoever of surrendering to you or to anybody else. Now once and for all, is that understood?"

"Then why did you radio me? I'm confused."

Ben had a dandy comeback for that last remark but decided to let it slide. "Would you like for us, that is you and I, or is it you and me? Never mind. Would you like to sit down together, like gentlemen, and talk for a couple of hours?"

"About what?"

Ben laid down the mic and rubbed his temples with his fingertips. He was getting a headache. He sighed and picked up the mic. "About ways to end this fighting."

"Ah-hah! So you *are* losing the war!"

"No, Blanton," Ben said wearily, "I am not losing the war. You're losing the war. You are getting men and women killed needlessly. Listen to me, Blanton. Twice your troops have assaulted our lines. Twice we have thrown them back and inflicted heavy losses upon them, both in personnel and equipment. Your army hasn't gained an inch of ground that we occupy. Don't you read the reports sent in by your field commanders?"

"Of course, I do!" Blanton snapped. "But I don't think the situation is as bad as you, or they, profess it to be. The generals may have exaggerated somewhat. Generals do that, you know?"

"Do you want to talk or not, Blanton?"

"I don't believe I have anything further to discuss with you, Raines."

"You are a goddamn fool," Ben muttered. He keyed the mic. "I gave you your chance, Blanton." He smiled and tossed the mic to Corrie. "I think in a few hours the Pres is going to change his mind. Get your field equipment together. We're going head-hunting."

"When?" she asked.

"Right now!"

# Fifteen

Ben ordered one company from each of the nine battalions on the line to be made up of the most experienced men and women and to make ready for a night excursion into Revere's territory. It was to be one of the strangest forays yet for the Rebels. Their orders were not to kill unless absolutely necessary, but to capture as many prisoners as possible and return with them to Rebel lines. Ben wanted to send Blanton a message and he felt this was one of the better, and bloodless, ways to do it.

The Rebels were moving moments after full dark. Moving northward like ghosts in the night. The editor of the newspaper at Base Camp One, a former big city editor who had thrown in with the Rebels several years back, had written extensively about the Rebel army. He had ended his article with this: "They are nice men and women. Polite and soft-spoken. After meeting and chatting with them, your first and last impression is that these are the types of people you would want as your neighbors. Many are family men and women; many are deeply religious. But under all of that, this reporter has to conclude that the men and women of the Rebel Army are the best mountain climbers, the best parachutists, the best at surviving in any situation, the best trackers, the best dog-sledders, the best skiers, and in any combat situation, the most murderous ambushers and cut-throats the world has ever seen. I am proud to call them my friends and I hold them in the highest regard."

Blanton's troops were about to find out just how accurate that editorial was.

A young FIB sergeant relaxed in his foxhole. He had just finished carefully eyeballing his perimeter and was satisfied no enemy was near. Then a hard hand clamped over his mouth and he felt the coldness of sharpened steel against his throat. A low voice said, "If you move, you're dead. Don't try to shake your head. If you do, you won't have a head."

Another dark shape took his weapons and quickly fashioned a gag over his mouth. The knife was removed from his throat and the young sergeant almost cried with relief. He had been sure he was going to piss all over himself. In the very dim light he watched a silenced .22 caliber autoloader taken from leather. The Rebel showed him the gun. He nodded his head in understanding.

"You make the slightest noise, you're dead. You got that?"

The FIB sergeant again nodded his head.

"Move out. South. Stay low and quiet. Go."

The Rebels worked for several hours, then silently gathered and herded their prisoners south across the designated strip of No Man's Land and then onto Rebel-held soil.

From Montana to Wisconsin, the Rebels collected

over a thousand prisoners that night. The only injury on either side was when a prisoner twisted his ankle. He was left behind, miles south of where he'd been taken prisoner.

By midnight, radio messages began pouring in to CPs from one end of the zone to another. General Paul Revere went into a towering rage. In New York State, President Blanton was awakened and sat in his PJs and robe at his desk. He was too stunned to speak for a moment.

When he finally found his voice, he asked, "And not a shot was fired?"

"Not a shot, sir."

"And how many troops were taken?"

"Latest reports say well over a thousand."

Blanton looked at the aide. "Go ahead. I know there is more. Tell me."

"Ah . . . at each sentry post and CP where personnel were taken, the Rebels left behind a, ah . . . well, a rubber duckie."

"A what?"

"They left behind a little rubber duckie. You know, the kind you play with in your bathtub."

"I don't play with goddamn rubber duckies in my bath, goddamnit!"

"Well, I didn't mean you, sir. I meant . . ."

"I know what you meant. I . . ."

He was interrupted by a knock on the door. A security guard stepped into the room, his face pale.

"What the hell do you want?" Blanton demanded.

"One of the sentries is here, sir. With a message from General Raines."

"How the hell did he get a message from General Raines?"

"It was handed to him out in the woods."

"Ye Gods!" the president yelled. "You mean the Rebels are here?"

"Apparently they've been here for some time, sir. Shall I show the guard in?"

"By all means," Blanton said, rubbing his face.

The soldier was nervous. Very nervous as he stood in front of Blanton's desk.

"Where is your weapon, soldier?" Blanton asked.

"Ah . . . she took it."

"She?"

"Yes, sir. It was a woman dressed in cammies, sir. Black beret. She just . . . well, materialized right out of the woods and put me on the ground."

Blanton sighed. Shook his head. "You are supposed to be one of the best-trained soldiers Revere has. Yet you heard nothing?"

"I didn't hear a sound, sir. Not until she judoed my ass and put me on the ground. That's when she gave me the message."

"What message?"

"Well, sir, part of the message is, 'General Ben Raines, commander of the Rebel Army, respectfully requests a face to face meeting with President Blanton. Or the next time, it'll be your butt that gets grabbed.' "

"Meaning me?" Blanton asked.

"I guess so, sir."

"What else?"

"If you will agree to a cease-fire, General Raines will do the same, and you and the General can work out the details of the meeting."

The President looked at the wall clock. It was five o'clock in the morning, EST. Three o'clock MST. VP Harriet Hooter came rushing into the room. She wore no makeup and had not brushed her hair. Blanton wondered if she'd parked her broom in the hallway.

"Is it true?" she hollered. "Have the Rebel hordes descended upon us?"

Rita Rivers came charging into the room right behind her. She looked even worse than Hooter. "Have the racist, right-wing Rebels defeated our armies?" she yelled.

Blanton almost lost it. He struggled mightily. He stared at the former drug dealer and road whore turned U.S. Representative and in a carefully controlled voice, said, "No, Ms. Rivers. Our armies have not been defeated. But I have decided to have a meeting with General Raines."

Hooter and Rivers both flopped on the floor in a dead faint.

Moments after Ben had radioed Cecil at Base Camp One, telling him about the upcoming meeting with Blanton, Cecil began sending out teams of special operations people to New York State. They would parachute in to beef up the scouts already in place. Cecil did not trust Homer Blanton any more than he felt he could tame a rattlesnake. By the time Ben arrived at the meeting, Cecil would have more than five hundred of the most highly trained men and women in the world in place in case of a double-cross.

"General Cecil Jefferys on the radio, sir," a Blanton aide told Homer, sitting at his desk having one of his carefully hoarded bottles of RC Cola and a Twinkie. Nine o'clock in the morning. "He's radioing from the Rebels' Base Camp One."

"I know who he is," Blanton said sourly. He walked to the communications room and picked up the mic. "This is your President, Jefferys."

"You're not my president," Cecil told him. "I didn't vote for you."

Hundreds of miles away, Blanton grimaced. He was getting really, really tired of hearing that. "What do you want, Jefferys?"

Harriet Hooter came flapping into the room. "Parachutists!" she yelled. "Paratroopers are landing all over the place. We're under attack! Do something."

Blanton almost told her to go stand on the porch of the hotel and stare at the Rebel soldiers. One look at her face and they'd surely surrender. And take Rita Rivers with her. There might be some Rebel men with extremely lousy taste in women and Rivers could pick up a few bucks. Instead, Blanton keyed the mic. "We have reports of paratroopers landing near us, Jefferys. You know anything about that?"

"That's why I radioed, Blanton," Cecil said. "Those troops are Ben's security . . . in case you have a double-cross in mind."

"I gave General Raines my word, Jefferys!" Blanton flared. "And that is . . ."

"Pure crap as far as I'm concerned. I'd rather kiss a rabid skunk than take the word of a liberal."

"You are a very insulting man," Blanton said.

"Just a truthful one, Blanton. Now you listen to

155

me. Don't even think of a double-cross when dealing with Ben Raines. If Ben gave his word there would be no trouble from his end, he'll stand by that. But he'll be ready for a double-cross from you."

"Why, for God's sake?"

Cecil chuckled. "Blanton, you've got a short memory. Every time we've dealt with the liberal branch of the democratic party—of which you were and are a member—they've double-crossed us . . . or tried to. Don't even consider it this time. Warn your people to walk as though they're walking on eggs around Ben. I'm offering this as a friendly piece of advice, not as a threat."

"All right, General," Blanton's tone softened. "I will take it as such."

"Nice talking so cordially with you, Mister President."

"Very nice chatting with you, General Jefferys."

Ben listened as President Blanton gave General Revere his orders. "There will be a cease-fire with absolutely no hostilities between Revere and the Rebels commencing immediately. Is that clear?"

"Yes, sir, Mister President," Revere said, but Ben could tell he was speaking through clenched teeth and did not like the orders at all.

"Corrie," Ben said, "get General Revere on the horn."

"General Revere? Ben Raines here. How about us sitting down and jawing some?"

"I have nothing to say to you, General Raines," Revere said, a definite edge to his voice, "that cannot be discussed over the air. What have you done with those prisoners you took?"

"They are well and safe. They are being transported back to Base Camp One for processing and will be turned loose a few at a time. I know your voice, General Revere. We've met somewhere down the line."

"Do you have anything else you want to say to me, Raines?"

"Nope. Have a good day, General."

Revere broke off.

"You know him, General?" Corrie asked.

"Yes. I'm sure I do. I just can't put a face to the voice." He turned to Cooper. "Coop, where was Denise assigned?"

"To supply, sir. You said to keep her out of combat and personnel."

"Go get her, please. And have Lieutenant Kolwalski come over here. She's a really good artist."

Denise and Kolwalski went to work, with Denise describing General Revere to the artist. After the work was done, Ben sat for a long time, staring at the charcoal drawn image on the large white paper.

"You know him, General?" Jersey asked.

Ben nodded his head. "Nick Stafford. He hasn't changed much at all. We were both special forces types as the Vietnam war was winding down, both of us working for the CIA. Back then it was called sheep-dipping. Nick went bad. Raped some very young girls. I turned him in. I heard he broke out of the stockade before he could be returned to the States. Now he turns up as General Paul Revere. Nick always did have a strange sense of humor. But he was a top-notch soldier."

"You think Blanton knows all that?"

Ben shook his head. "I doubt it. All that was a long time ago. And for some reason I can't explain, I don't think it would be wise to warn the president of it. I've got a bad feeling about General Nick Stafford/Paul Revere."

"You think this Nick Stafford might be playing both ends against the middle?" Jersey asked.

Ben held nothing back from his personal team. His team was the first to know of any major decisions. "I wouldn't put it past him. Beth, have you finished the report on the prisoner interrogation?"

"Just about. Many of the officers in Blanton's army came to him with General Revere. They form the nucleus. We have also learned that Blanton is training at least one more division—and possibly two—up in Canada. Just as you thought, the new division, or divisions, are made up almost exclusively of Americans who hate the Rebel movement. Punks, thugs, criminals, trash of all colors—whiners, complainers."

"That should be an extremely interesting army," Ben said sarcastically.

"They won't have much in the way of discipline," Corrie remarked. "That's something those types of people lack."

"Yeah, but sheer numbers could do a lot of damage to us," Cooper injected. "We're short in every battalion and stretched thin."

"You're right about that, Coop," Ben agreed. "If Revere ever learns of the holes in our lines . . ." Ben let that trail off. Everybody in the room knew that would be disastrous. "All right, people. Let's pack up and go meet President Blanton."

"What a thrill," Jersey said. "I'm practically swooning from all the excitement."

"When it gets overwhelming," Cooper said, standing up and getting ready to bolt for the door, "fall in my direction, darlin'."

Jersey chased him out the door, threatening dire consequences when she caught up with him.

"Far better it is to dare mighty things, to win glorious triumphs, even though checkered by failure, than to take rank with those poor spirits who neither enjoy much nor suffer much, because they live in the gray twilight that knows not victory nor defeat."

—Theodore Roosevelt

Book Two

# *One*

Ben's team made bets as to how they would arrive at the old resort hotel. Beth won. They were going to parachute in. It was by far the fastest way to get to the ground, for the nearest functional airstrip was many miles away. Another reason was that Ben simply did not trust Blanton.

"Shit!" Jersey said. Although she had jumped many times, she still was not overly thrilled about hurling her body out of a moving airplane at five thousand feet.

"Tiger-stripe," Ben told his people. "Look sharp. Carry enough ammo for a sustained fire-fight. We may be jumping into a real stem-winder. I just don't trust that socialist bastard or those wimpy hanky-stompers he's got around him."

Ike had flown in and would assume command in Ben's absence. "If Blanton and I can reach some agreement to end this fighting, I fully expect Revere to go on the offensive as soon as he gets word of it. And you can bet he's got informants among Blanton's general staff. Stay on middle-alert, Ike."

The flight across country was uneventful. The

planes set down at a Rebel outpost in Kentucky for refueling and then it was on to New York State the next morning. Blanton and company were standing on the porch of the resort hotel when Ben and his people came floating down.

"Oh, I just knew Ben Raines would do something terribly macho!" Harriet Hooter sniffed. "How utterly theatrical."

"Honky, racist son of a bitch!" Rita Rivers said.

The troops of Blanton were very much in evidence, and they stood silently around the huge old hotel, watching the Rebels land. Their commanders had met with the teams of special ops people Cecil had sent in, and Blanton's troops were very careful to keep their weapons at sling and their hands still.

"I just know we're going to be ravaged," Representative Fox said, standing behind the First Lady, who was standing behind her husband for the first time in twenty years—who was standing behind a post.

Blush Lightheart was wearing a bulletproof vest, motorcycle goggles, and a helmet. He looked like a bigger idiot than he really was. He wished he could have found a gun, but since he was one of those who had twittered and sobbed and peed their panties and finally passed legislation outlawing all guns—except those in the hands of punks, thugs, street slime and other worthless dickheads—weapons were sort of hard to find. Unless one knew where to look. And Blush didn't.

"President Blanton," Ben said, stepping up onto the stairs leading to the porch. "Nice day, isn't it?"

"General Raines," Blanton acknowledged, stepping away from the post. Those behind him moved

166

with him. It resembled a short conga line . . . with Blush out of step.

"You there!" Rita hollered, waving at two black Rebels. "Lay down your arms and stop being the lackeys of this racist pig." She pointed at Ben.

One of the black Rebels winked at Ben. "You want me to eliminate her now, General?"

"Oh, my God!" Rita shrieked, and jumped behind Blush.

"Great stars and garters!" Blush squalled. "Get away from me, bitch!" Both of them bolted for the front door and got all jammed up together.

Ben laughed so hard he sat down on the steps. He took out a handkerchief and wiped his eyes, looking up at Blanton, who was slightly embarrassed. "Is this a fair representation of your Forces of Independence and Brotherhood?"

That stung Blanton. "I suppose a certain type of person would find fear amusing."

"Fear? Fear of what?" Ben stood and walked up to the landing. He towered over Blanton. "No law-abiding person has any reason to fear a member of the Rebel Forces."

Rita and Blush were still hung up in the doorway, with Rita doing some pretty fancy cussing and calling Blush some very uncomplimentary names concerning his sexual preferences.

"Yep," Ben said, moving to a wicker chair and leaning his Thompson against the porch railing. He jerked a thumb toward Rita. "That's what I call true brotherhood and understanding."

Blanton sighed audibly.

\* \* \*

After some semblance of order was restored, Blanton and Ben met privately in Blanton's office. They sat for a moment, looking at each other.

Blanton finally broke the silence. "I never in my life would have thought this day possible."

"Why? We both want basically the same thing: order and stability."

"But the roads we take to those ends are quite different."

"I put people to work, Homer. If they don't want to work, they get the hell out of any Rebel-controlled area. And I won't tolerate crime. Now how far apart does that make us?"

Blanton was noncommittal.

"And where in the hell do you get off calling me the Great Satan, a shit-head, and a baby-killer, and my people malcontents?"

"I will admit that leaflet was a bit overdone."

"Thank you. And we don't rape and pillage either."

"Rita and Harriet will be sorry to hear that," Homer muttered.

"Beg your pardon?"

"Oh! Nothing. Talking to myself. It's a bad habit I have."

"I do the same thing."

"Really? General . . ."

"Call me Ben."

"Thank you. Ben . . ." He leaned forward, putting his elbows on the desk. "Do you think we could coexist, our two societies, peacefully?"

"I don't see why not. I'd rather see us come together instead of having two separate nations within a nation." He smiled. "As a matter of fact, I was working on a book about that very thing when the nation started coming apart, and then the Great War came. Two countries carved out of the United States. One extremely liberal, the other conservative."

"How did the book end?"

"I never got a chance to finish it. Your federal agents seized the manuscript."

Blanton sighed. "I made a lot of mistakes, Ben."

"You sure as hell did. But you're a big enough man to admit it now, and that's good."

"I tried to do too much for too many, far too soon."

"Yes, you did. Do you see now that this nation cannot be all things to all people, all the time?"

Blanton smiled. "We will never agree on that, Ben."

"Probably not. But at least we're talking, and that beats the hell out of fighting."

"Do you blame me for the Great War, Ben?"

Ben shook his head. "Oh, no. Not at all. And I don't think historians will either. No reason to. When you took office, the world was changing so rapidly it was breathtaking. Major world events were happening with such speed that no one could keep up. The entire world was rushing toward self-destruct. And it did."

Jersey entered the room over the loud protestations of a Blanton aide. She ignored him until he clamped one hand on her shoulder. Jersey spun around and stuck the muzzle of her M-16 under the man's chin. "You have a deathwish, partner?"

"Ah . . . no," the aide managed to say.

"Then don't ever put your goddamn hands on me again. You understand?"

"Yes, ma'am."

Ben stood up. "What's wrong, Jersey?"

"Something weird's going on, General. About half of Blanton's guards have pulled out. And they did it real quick."

"Pulled out?" Blanton asked, getting to his feet. "Why?"

"You tell me," Jersey said menacingly.

"I swear to God I don't have a clue as to what's going on."

That was another opening for a great comeback for Ben, but he let it slide.

Blanton turned to the aide who had made the mistake of putting hands on Jersey. "Fred, where is Bobby?"

"I don't know, sir. I haven't seen him since before General Raines arrival."

"Find him."

"Yes, sir."

"It's a trick, I tell you!" the voice of Harriet Hooter came screeching and bouncing off the hall walls. "Raines is pulling something nasty and evil and totally Republican."

"Spoken like a true liberal," Ben muttered.

Blanton glanced at him and smiled. "Come on, Ben. Let's see what's happening around here. I'm sure there is some reasonable explanation for my guards' disappearance."

"Nick Stafford."

"Who?"

"The man who now calls himself General Paul Revere. His real name is Nick Stafford. We served together briefly in 'Nam." Ben brought the president up to date on Nick Stafford.

"My God!" Blanton said.

The sounds of gunfire reached those in the old resort hotel. "Rebels are under attack!" Corrie called.

Fred, the aide, came rushing up. "Our people are under attack, sir."

"Kill that double-crossing, no good Republican bastard!" Harriet hollered, pointing at Ben.

Jersey gave the woman the bird.

"How dare you!" Harriet said. "You camp follower. You cheap little road whore."

Jersey took a step toward the former representative, fully intending to clean her clock. Ben grabbed her by the seat of the pants. "No contest, Jersey. Just consider the source and forget it."

"Our people are under attack," Blush rushed up. "But not by the Rebels."

"Head for cover!" Ben shouted, giving Blanton a push toward the doors. "Nick's trying to take us all out. I should have guessed it."

The old resort hotel suddenly exploded and the floor beneath Ben's boots opened up and swallowed him. The last thing he remembered was being conked on the head by what felt like a sledge hammer. He was plunged into darkness.


Ben came out of the darkness into more darkness. His head throbbed and he couldn't move his legs. He could hear no sounds at all. He blinked a couple of times and his vision began to clear. There was some light, but not much. He looked at the luminous hands of his watch. Eight o'clock. He'd been out for hours. Something was cutting painfully into his back and it took him a moment to figure out it was his Thompson. At least he still had that. He lay still for a couple of moments, while his vision cleared even more and his brain began to work at one hundred percent.

Revere's people must have planted explosives all over the damn hotel, Ben concluded. Then just before the charges went off, they split for the woods and got into a fire-fight with Blanton's loyal people and Ben's Rebels.

Ben wriggled around and freed one boot from the debris, then the other. He still couldn't see for shit so he moved very carefully, not wanting to bring tons of the old hotel down on him. He got to his feet and found his cigarette lighter, sparking it into flame. He ached all over, but could find no serious wounds. Standing in one spot, he slowly did a full circle. The floor was still attached to one side of the wall, the other side blown free and hanging at an angle. He was in the cellar. He moved to the concrete foundation and found a door. It was either locked or jammed shut. He kicked it open and stepped into a long corridor. He did not have the foggiest notion where it led, but wherever it went was a damn sight better than where he was, so he started walking.

He stumbled over a body and nearly fell down. He knelt down and saw it was one of Blanton's aides. The man's chest had been crushed by a heavy timber. Ben walked on. He came to another door and opened it, exposing a stairway. He could see stars above him. Very cautiously, moving silently, his Thompson at the ready, Ben slowly climbed the stairs, finally stepping out onto what had been the porch.

There were bodies everywhere. Ben made his way through the rubble and to the ground. He turned, looking back. The old resort hotel had been flattened except for the north wall, which still stood.

Ben began inspecting the bodies. It had been a hell of a fire-fight, for sure. He found Rebel dead, guards and troops loyal to Blanton dead, and troops wearing red armbands dead. Ben assumed those were Revere's people. He took a flashlight from one of his Rebels but did not flash the beam, not wanting to advertise his location just yet. He took twin canteens, field rations, and a back pack from other dead Rebels and, moving cautiously, made his way away from the hotel grounds. He could do nothing in the night except get himself shot, so he found a place in the shrubbery and spread the ground sheet and laid down, pulling the blanket over him. Since there was nothing he could do until light, he went to sleep.

He awakened several times during the night, but heard nothing out of the ordinary. Up at his usual time, long before dawn, Ben shivered in the cold, but did not light a fire. He breakfasted on field rations and sipped water from a canteen, waiting for dawn. It seemed very slow in coming.

He quickly field-stripped his Colt .45 auto-loader, and found it unharmed. He had left his Desert Eagle .50 behind for his trip. Ben still preferred the old service auto-loader, considering it to be a fine old workhorse.

As dawn began to silver the sky, Ben could better see the terrible carnage that sprawled silently all around the ruins of the hotel. There appeared to be hundreds of bodies. It was eerie, for they were all dead. As Ben walked amid the horror, he could see why. All of his people and the people loyal to Blanton had been delivered the coup de grâce: a bullet to the head. After inspecting the bodies, Ben concluded that Revere's forces had carried off most of their wounded.

Ben began gathering up weapons, ammo, field rations, and first aid kits and hiding them in the woods around the hotel grounds. He had no idea where his personal team was; only that they were not among the dead around the hotel. He did not know if they had been captured, were miles away fighting Revere's troops, or believing him dead, trying to make their way back to Rebel-controlled territory. They had good reason to believe him dead, for several of his team and several of Blanton's people had seen the floor open up beneath his boots and the walls cave in on him.

Ben hooked grenades on his battle harness, loaded up five more clips for his Thompson, filled a pack with ration packets, horseshoed ground sheets and blankets, and started walking down the side of the road he assumed led to a main highway of some sort. Damn thing had to either dead end or lead to something.

He had traveled about half a mile when he heard the sound of voices. Ben took to the brush and began slowly making his way toward the voices.

When he saw who the voices belonged to, he suppressed a groan—VP Harriet Hooter, and Representatives Blush Lightheart and Rita Rivers. Senators Hanrahan, Arnold, and Ditto. Of course, there was not a gun among the bunch. Naturally. He couldn't think of any bunch he disliked more than this one.

Ben stood up. "Quiet down!" he said. "You're making enough noise to wake up Rip Van Winkle." He walked into the camp and shook his head at the sight. It was a miserable-looking bunch of people. Not a one of them had had enough presence of mind to grab up from the dead a food packet, canteen, first aid kit, gun, or grenades.

"We thought you were dead, General Raines," Senator Hanrahan broke the startled silence.

"Well, I'm not. Come on, follow me. We're going back to the hotel."

"Whatever on earth for?" Blush asked.

"To get you people outfitted for the field. You'll all die of exposure dressed as you are. It's threatening rain now. You've got to have tarps and blankets and ground sheets. We'll get the clothing off the dead. Let's go."

"Off the *dead!*" Harriet hollered. "How grotesque!"

"Move your ass, lady," Ben told her. "Before the bodies start the second stage of stiffening and start to stink."

"I refuse!" Rita Rivers said.

"Then stay here and die. I don't give a damn one way or the other." Ben turned and started walking toward the hotel. He did not look back. He knew they'd all follow him, and they all did, bitching and complaining all the way. Until Ben threatened to shoot the next person who broke noise discipline. That shut them up.

"Green is simply not my color," Blush bitched,

holding up a cammie BDU shirt. "Yukk," he said, looking at the blood stain.

"Put it on and find some britches and boots that fit you. All of you. Move, goddamnit!"

"You don't have to use so much profanity, General," Hanrahan said. "There are ladies present."

Ben had disliked Hanrahan from the moment he'd heard the man speak, some years back. That dislike had grown over the years. Hanrahan took one look into Ben's eyes, and averted his gaze and closed his mouth.

"Wise decision, Senator," Ben said. "Very wise."

# Two

Ben got his reluctant commandos outfitted and ready to move. Almost to a person, male and female alike, they handled the M-16s Ben shoved at them like they were fondling live snakes.

"I haven't the vaguest idea how to operate this evil thing," Harriet said.

"The person behind the gun may be evil, Ms. Hooter," Ben told her. "But since the weapon is not capable of thought or reason, it is impossible for the gun to be evil. Move out."

Before Harriet could come back with one of her usual liberal—and totally out of touch with reality—comments, Blush Lightheart said, "I have never fired an M-16, but I was quite proficient with a hunting rifle in my youth. I never liked to kill animals but I did become a good shot."

"Good," Ben replied. "I want you to get up here and lead this . . ." For a moment he was at a loss for words. ". . . dubious gathering. I'll range ahead about a hundred yards."

"You want *me* to *lead*?"

"Yes. I'll signal when I want you to move out. When I signal you to get down, get down fast."

Rita Rivers immediately started boogeying. Which was a pretty good trick, since she was carrying about forty pounds of gear.

Ben cast his eyes toward the heavens for a moment and then moved out. About a hundred yards away, he motioned for the rest to follow.

"Forward, troops!" Blush ordered.

Ben hoped with all his might he did not meet with any type of resistance until he could hook up with some his own people.

"My feet hurt," Harriet complained.

"My back hurts," Hanrahan bitched.

"I think I have herniated myself," Arnold announced.

"Silence in the ranks," Blush said.

Ben heard the faint drone of a plane and motioned the group off the side of the road and into the brush. The single-engine plane was flying low and slow, with spotters on each side, behind the pilot.

"Keep your faces down," Ben ordered.

"Why?" Hooter asked.

"Because the paleness can be easily seen." He looked at Rita. "Excluding you, of course."

"Honky, racist son of a bitch," she replied.

"I'm certain that remark was not meant as a racial slur," Blush objected. "The general was merely stating a fact."

"Oh, shut up," Rita told him.

"Tut-tut," Senator Hanrahan said. "Shame on both of you."

The plane flew on and Ben got the group up.

178

"Stay close to the brush," he told them, as he studied a map. "We should intersect with Highway 86 just up ahead. That will lead us to Lake Placid—if anything is left of the town."

"Not very much," Blush told him. "It's been looted and stripped down to a shell."

"By poor unfortunate people who were oppressed for years and were only trying to survive in this still racist and sexist society," Hooter immediately piped up. "Ruled by people with guns!" she added.

"Right on, sister!" Rita hollered.

"Move out," Ben said wearily.

Ben didn't attempt to push the group hard, allowing them frequent rest stops. Hanrahan was well past middle age and the rest were about Ben's age, but not nearly in the physical shape he maintained.

During one of the rest stops, Ben began questioning the group. "Did anybody see what happened to Blanton?"

No one did.

"How about my personal team?"

Nothing.

"I was knocked unconscious for a time," Hanrahan said. "The blast knocked me down."

"I ran outside and was immediately set upon by this huge brute of a man who seemed intent on ravaging my body," Rita said coyly.

"No one but Godzilla would want to ravage your body," Blush told her.

Rita flipped him the bird.

No one knew anything. The blast had knocked them all to the floor and most scrambled to their feet and ran outside and into the woods. They had wandered about until linking up.

Ben remembered shoving Blanton away just as the floor opened up under him so there was a chance he was still alive.

While they rested, Ben eased away from the bedraggled-looking bunch, took out a small hand-held scanner, and began searching the bands. His worst fears were soon confirmed as he picked up chatter from Revere's troops. A group of Rebels had been taken prisoner and were being held at Saranac Lake. Blanton and the First Lady were presumed alive and a search was on for them. Ben Raines was confirmed dead. Ben smiled at that. "Not just yet," he muttered.

Senator Ditto walked over and sat down beside Ben. "General, I know you don't like me; perhaps with good reason. But for the time being we are all in the same boat . . ."

"Wrong," Ben said. "We are not in the same boat. I could walk away from this group and easily survive. Within a week I could have a resistance force gathered and be fighting Revere. You people are a stone around my neck. None of you, with the possible exception of Blush, know anything about guns, or survival, or rigging booby-traps, living off the land, or tactics of staying alive. You goddamn sorry bastards and bitches castrated this nation with your wimpy legislation. You ruined the intelligence community, tied the hands of law enforcement, disarmed the people, and bankrupted us with taxes. Fuck you, Ditto. I have a good mind to take Blush with me and just walk off and leave the rest of you for the jackals."

The group had gathered around and all heard Ben's heated words.

"You'd take a fag and leave us?" Rita said. "What are you, queer?"

"I wish," Blush muttered. He raised his voice. "I can tell you with absolute certainty that General Raines is not gay. Believe me, we know who is and who isn't."

"Thank you," Ben said.

"Well, for heaven's sake," Blush replied. "It wasn't meant as any type of compliment!"

"Are you going to leave us for the jackals, General?" Senator Hanrahan asked.

"No. I couldn't do that. I just want you all to stop your whining and complaining and do what I tell you to do when I tell you to do it."

"I am senior here, General," Hanrahan said. "And I speak for the entire group. We will do whatever you tell us to do. We might not like it, but we will do it."

The rest of the group nodded their heads.

Ben looked at them and had to work to suppress a smile. "Fine. You are now all guerrilla fighters." He reached out and took Rita's M-16. "We will now have a short course on the use of the M-16 rifle."


Ben found a shady and well-hidden glen just outside of Lake Placid and left the group there, warning them not to move or raise their voices. He'd be back.

"You promise?" Harriet asked.

"I promise," Ben assured her. " 'Til death do us

part," he added. Or until I find some safe place to leave your ass, he thought.

"I shall protect the group with my life," Blush said. "A lonely soldier on his vigilant watch."

"That's lovely, Blush," Harriet said, patting his hand.

Ben left before the shit got too deep.


Ben reconnoitered the town carefully before entering. It appeared to be a dead town, with much of it in ruins. Then a slight movement in the smashed-out window of an old home on the edge of town caught his eye. He waited and watched. The movement came again and this time Ben could see who and what it was. A man wearing BDUs. Ben began working his way toward the house, staying low, skirting the house widely and coming up behind it. He spotted a ton-and-a-half truck parked in the garage. He was careful not to brush up against the house when he reached it. He could hear male voices.

"I hate this crap, man. This town is spooky."

"Relax. This is easy duty. At least we're not sleepin' on the ground and being shot at."

"You do have a point. But it's weird just us in the whole damn town."

"Yeah. To tell you the truth, man, I'd rather be over there where the Reb prisoners is being held humpin' some of them good lookin' Reb gals."

"I like it when they put up a fight. I like to slap 'em around."

Ben stepped in through the back door and gave the would-be rapists a taste of .45 caliber justice.

The heavy slugs made a big mess out of both the men. Ben picked up their radio and headed for the truck. Ten minutes later he pulled off the highway and into the shady glen.

"I thought I heard shooting," Hanrahan said, as Ben got out of the truck.

"You did." Ben inspected the bed of the truck. Rocket launchers, plenty of rockets, and cases of field rations. "Get in," he told the group. "And stay low."

"Where are we going?" Harriet asked.

"To get as close to where my people are being held as possible. Then I'm going into town to raise some hell."

"Alone?" Blush asked.

"Yep. Come on, people—move!" He didn't tell them that this could well be their last journey. A single rocket could send them all over the place, in bits and pieces. He figured what they didn't know wouldn't hurt them. At least not for very long.

Ben found a gravel road that more or less headed in the general direction he wanted to go and stayed with it. Hanrahan was very tired and looked awful. His color was bad. Ben made him ride in the cab with him.

"Do you know where we're going, General?" he asked.

"Call me Ben. Oh, yeah. I know where we're going. I just don't know where we are at the moment."

The older man stared at Ben for a few seconds and then chuckled. "I could find myself liking you, Ben."

"Don't," Ben said shortly. "Because I don't like one hundred percent liberals."

"One hundred percent liberal, eh? So you admit you have some liberal in you?"

"Sure. I'm a tree-hugger and an animal lover. To some degree I'm an environmentalist. The Rebels have had teams working all over this nation trying to see to the needs of children and deserving adults. We've set up a monetary system. I've got some of the best minds in the nation down at Base Camp One working around the clock on ways to harness the power of the sun. And they're doing it, Senator. I had trained scientists shutting down all the nuclear power plants around the nation, eliminating the danger of a melt-down. My people have been busy collecting books and art and preserving them for future generations. We have newspapers from all over the nation on microfilm, so those who follow us will have some understanding as to what went wrong. Of course, we already know what went wrong; I'm sitting beside one of the reasons. We have the best doctors staffing the finest hospitals offering the people the most up-to-date medical care. The Rebels have successfully fought armies that sought to occupy this nation and enslave Americans; and we've done that at a huge loss of life. There are people of all faiths and all nationalities and all races in the Rebel Army. We work together without bickering and without bigotry. We have a workable society in place, with all systems fully functional. And what have you goddamn liberals been doing since the Great War? Nothing. Except putting together an army to try to defeat the Rebels. Pissing and moaning and making flowery speeches to each other. OK. Now it's your turn, Senator. Tell me why I should like you."

Senator Hanrahan sat for several miles in silence. He sighed a lot. "Our intelligence about your society was wrong," he finally said. "I should have seen through General Revere—should have known he was plotting a takeover. I spent too many years on the intelligence oversight committee."

"You sure did. Fucking it up."

Hanrahan shook his head. "You know by now, of course, he had spies in Base Camp One."

"He doesn't anymore. Just before I flew to the meeting with Blanton we flushed them out and shot them."

"After a trial, I hope."

"A very short one."

"We will never agree with your system of justice."

"That's your problem, Senator. It works for us, and that's all that matters. We don't pat criminals on the head and mope about feeling sorry for them and making up excuses and rationalizations about why they did what they did. The law is the law, and in our society it is enforced to the letter. Every human being holds the key to their own destiny. It's start-over time, Senator. Everybody gets a fresh start. Many of the men and women who make up the Rebel Army were once criminals. You didn't know that, did you? Oh, yeah. I offered them a fresh start. A one time only amnesty. It will never be offered again."

"We heard you had done that. We didn't believe it."

Ben shrugged his shoulders in complete indifference to what Hanrahan and his cohorts believed as they bounced along the old gravel and dirt road.

"If our president is alive . . ."

"He's your president, not mine," Ben corrected.

"If he is still alive, will you make any attempt to work with him?"

"No. We have long had plans to enlarge the Rebel-controlled areas. Effective immediately, Base Camp One will take in Texas, Oklahoma, Louisiana, Arkansas, Mississippi, Tennessee, North and South Carolina, Alabama, Georgia, and Florida. You people can have what's left."

"Good Lord, man!" Hanrahan almost shouted the words. "You can't be serious."

"As serious as a crutch, Senator."

"You are a bold one, Ben Raines. But you're forgetting we have quite an army. There are hundreds of thousands of people out there who are opposed to your form of government."

"I have never been called timid. As far as your army goes—an army made up of losers and whiners and complainers—you won't have it long. I intend to squash it like a roach. And Blanton *is* alive. He's being held up here with my Rebels. I heard it on short-wave."

"Thank God! What about the First Lady?"

"I don't know."

"Do you have a workable plan for freeing your Rebels, General Raines?"

Ben smiled. "I always have a workable plan, Senator. That's why I'm general of the most powerful army on the face of the earth, and you're unemployed."

# *Three*

Ben left the group in a secure area, well south and slightly east of the town. Loaded down with rockets, C-4, timers and detonators, and ammo, he headed into town. He left his Thompson behind and carried an M-16 because of the weight of the weapon and ammo. He stayed off the roads and stuck to the woods and meadows until he came to the edge of town. Once there, he began to circle until he found where the prisoners were being held. It was on the outskirts of town in what appeared to be some sort of playing field; baseball or football, Ben couldn't tell. Using his binoculars, Ben studied the situation. It could have been worse, he concluded. As it was, the area was only loosely guarded, and as the night drew closer, the area would be shrouded in darkness, for Ben felt sure that power had not been restored this soon. He ate some crackers and washed them down with water from his canteen. He had spotted several dozen of his Rebels among the crowd, including Jersey, Beth, Cooper, and Corrie. Now how would he get them out?

Ben napped for a time, as he alternately slept and

pondered the prisoner situation. Then he smiled. "Hell, why not?" he muttered.

When it was full dusk, Ben readied some hunks of C-4 and worked his way close to the prisoners. He planted explosives on truck gas tanks, set the timers, then as quickly as possible moved away from that area. He was carrying six rockets for the Armbrust launcher, all of them HE fragmentation anti-personnel rockets. When the trucks blew, he was going to make life pretty damned miserable for a lot of Revere's troops, and quite a bunch of them had gathered on the opposite end of the field, away from the prisoners.

The C-4 blew and Ben fired the first rocket. The explosion sent bits and pieces of Revere's soldiers flying all over the sound end of the field.

"Jersey!" Ben yelled. "Straight north, people. Let's go!"

He quickly readied another rocket and let it fly, then tossed the Armbrust to a Rebel who had jumped the low fence and landed by his side. "You have four pickles left, son," he told the young man. "Make them count."

"Yes, sir!" the Rebel grinned.

Ben started letting the lead fly from his M-16. Some of the Rebels had jumped their guards during the first few seconds of noise and bloody confusion, and had seized their weapons, turning them on their captors. In less than half a minute, the old playing field was in the hands of the Rebels and those troops loyal to President Blanton. Flames from exploded and burning vehicles were dancing upward, and the smoke soon cut visibility down to nearly nothing.

Revere's troops never had a chance once the war dance started. All Rebels were extensively trained in hand to hand combat and they put that training to good use against their poorly trained and very startled captors.

Ben's team gathered around him as the flames leaped and crackled and the smoke swirled. "Where's Blanton and his wife?" Ben asked.

"We don't know," Beth said. "Last we heard they were being held somewhere in the town."

"How many troops are we up against?"

"Couple of battalions," Jersey said.

Ben looked at her face. She had a black eye, a busted lip, and several swollen and bruised places. "Who'd you tangle with, Short-stuff?"

"Couple of guys tried to rape me. They finally decided it wasn't worth the effort."

Corrie had taken a radio from one of the dead and was monitoring it. "The colonel in charge of this lash-up is ordering his people to regroup and defend the town," she told Ben.

"He's a fool," Ben said. "Get the troops around me."

Cooper stepped away and started shouting. Jersey said, "We're pretty much cut off here. We can't expect any help. The way I heard it was a timed push. Revere threw everything he had against our people out west at the same time the assault against the hotel was carried out."

"We'll make out. Everybody armed? OK. Let's take the town."

Raines's Rebels were not accustomed to being taken prisoner, and they were pissed-off. Those troops loyal to Blanton exchanged silent glances and fell in beside the Rebels, looking to Ben for command.

"We need their equipment," Ben said, as he led the walk toward the ruins of the old town. "Let's take as much of it intact as we can."

"A Colonel Rush on the horn, General," Corrie said.

Ben took the mic. "This is General Raines. What do you want?"

"Raines, you assault this town and I hang President Blanton and his wife."

"And then I take you alive with the guarantee that it will take you a minimum of three very long and very painful days to die, Colonel. And I'll turn the women that your troops raped loose on them. Think about that."

The colonel had obviously heard that the Rebels could be extremely harsh at times. It did not take him long to make up his mind.

"He's ordering his people to fall back," Corrie told Ben. "Blanton and his wife and the staff members taken prisoner are all right. He's leaving them behind. Revere's people are in retreat."

"Chicken-shits," Jersey muttered.


Neither Blanton, his wife, or the members of his staff were hurt, except for their pride, which had been severely bruised.

"I am extremely grateful to you and your people, General Raines," the president said.

"Save it," Ben told him. "We've just learned that a full regiment of troops loyal to Revere is moving at us from the north; from the training base in Canada—some of the thugs and punks and gang members you recruited. We've got to get the hell out of here. Mount them up, people."

The reunion between Blanton, Hooter, Hanrahan, and the others was tearful, and at Ben's sharply given command, very short. He ordered a few of his people back to the hotel to retrieve all the equipment they could get into the trucks and told another group to head for the center of the mountain range and set up camp there.

"My people don't take orders from you, General," Blanton told him.

"That's fine with me," Ben said. "You're on your own." Ben turned and walked away.

Blush looked at Blanton and said, "You, sir, are a fool!" He shouted after Ben, "Wait, General. I'm going with you."

Rita Rivers, who was still slightly irritated because none of Revere's troops had ravaged her said, "Good riddance."

"General Raines is an arrogant and insufferable ass!" Harriet Hooter said.

"But we need him to stay alive," the first lady said. "Come on, Homer. Put pride aside and let's go."

"Yes, dear," the pres said.

It took the convoy all night to reach their destination. Corrie quickly set up communications and Ben got in touch with Cecil.

"We're all right," he assured his long-time friend. "Just tired and sleepy. I've sent personnel over to Fort Drum to retrieve those supplies and equipment we cached up there. How's it looking out west?"

"It could be better, but Ike is holding so far. Revere's troops are poorly trained. And our long-range artillery is helping to save the bacon. Blanton and company?"

"They're with me. Reluctantly."

Cecil laughed over the miles. "I'd love to hear some of the debates you and Blanton are going to have."

"Oh, he's not a bad guy, Cec. Just a typical liberal with his head up his ass, that's all."

"How did he receive the news about the expansion of our territory?"

"I'm not sure Senator Hanrahan has told him yet! Doesn't make any difference. There isn't a damn thing he can do about it."

Several of Blanton's staff were standing around in the old home Ben had chosen for his CP. They frowned at Ben's remarks but made no comment. For the moment, General Raines was correct. For the moment.

The reports General Revere was receiving were sketchy, but he got the message. Rebels had attacked the holding area and had freed those captured Rebels and the troops loyal to Blanton. The message was more than a little vague about just how Blanton was freed. Blanton really made no difference anyway. He was a paper president running a paper government. The only thing that really bothered him was the news that Ben Raines was still alive. For a couple of days he had really felt up-beat. Then the news that Raines was still alive mentally knocked him to his knees.

Revere sat down behind a battered and scarred old desk. He had to come up with a plan to bust through the Rebel lines and then he could do an end-around. But he couldn't shift his people and concentrate them for one big massive push. As soon as he did, that damnable ex-Navy SEAL, Ike McGowan, would swing his east and west battalions around and then Revere would be boxed.

Revere sighed. He knew perfectly well what this war would turn into: a damn guerrilla war. And there were no finer guerrilla fighters in all the world than Raines's Rebels.

This war, Revere concluded, could drag on for years.

The next morning, Blanton sent one of his aides with a demand that Ben grant him an audience.

Ben looked at the man. "Well, why in the hell didn't he just come over and knock on the damn door? Sonny, there isn't much pomp and, circumstance with us. Tell him to come on. But make it quick. We're liable to be fighting at any time. That enemy regiment is pushing hard."

Blanton came right over and got to the point. "General, what is this I hear about you splitting from the Union?"

Ben leaned back in his chair. "Homer, there is no Union. Why can't you understand that? It's over. Done. Finished. We've got to rebuild from the ashes. I'm only taking eleven states. You've got the rest."

Blanton took a deep breath and started quoting

the Declaration of Independence. Ben waved him silent.

"You're awfully fond of spouting Jefferson, Blanton. So let me quote some Jefferson to you. How about 'I hold it, that a little rebellion, now and then, is a good thing, and as necessary in the political world as storms in the physical.' Sit down, Homer. And listen to me."

Blanton sat.

"You spout the Jefferson that suits your ends, so I'll spout mine. How about, 'The basis of our government being the opinion of the people, the very first object should be to keep that right.'"

Blanton remained silent. Since he was a minority elected president, there was damn little he could say about quotes from Jefferson's letter to Colonel Edward Carrington.

"And how about this from Jefferson's first inaugural address. I'll take it slightly out of context, as you did: 'A wise and frugal government shall not take from the mouths of men the bread they have earned.' That's not exact, Homer, but it's close."

"You've twisted that all around, General!"

"Shut up!" Ben shouted, pointing a finger at the man. "Don't make me angry, Blanton. You wouldn't like me much if you made me angry. I'll give you one more Jefferson quote that in all your time in the White House you never once uttered. 'No free man shall ever be debarred the use of arms.'" Ben smiled. "You are familiar with that one, aren't you?"

Blanton said nothing.

"Or how about this one: 'What country can preserve its liberties, if its rulers are not warned from time to time, that the people preserve the spirit of resistance. Let them take arms.' I never heard you mention that one, either."

"What is the point of all this, General?"

"Very simple, Homer. Very basic. The Rebels are armed. We're going to stay armed. We are going to carve a new nation out of eleven states. And the reasons we're going to do that are simple. Never again will the government be allowed to disarm its law-abiding citizens. Never again will asinine and frivolous lawsuits be allowed to clog up our courts. Never again will a law-abiding citizen be jailed or sued for protecting what is theirs, be it self, loved ones, property, or pets. Never again will law-abiding citizens be afraid to walk the streets their tax dollars helped to build and maintain."

"Are you quite through?" Blanton asked, a stiffness to his words.

"No. You listen. We can work together, Homer. Our nations can exist side by side. We can sign mutual defense treaties. We can trade with each other. We can have the same currency. We can have open borders. We can do all that, or you can fight me and you'll lose. Now I'm through."

"You'll fight fellow Americans?"

"I'll fight anybody who stands in the way of the right of law-abiding citizens to enjoy liberty, freedom, and the right to live without fear of thugs and punks and two-bit, liberal, would-be dictators."

"You'll destroy this nation!" Blanton shouted the words.

"Where in the hell have you been for the last few years, Blanton? Under a rock? The nation is destroyed. It's in ruins except for the areas controlled by the Rebels. Doesn't that tell you anything?"

"You dare to call *me* a dictator? What in God's name are you, General?"

"I was first appointed by the people and then I was elected, Blanton. In free and open elections. Held on a Sunday, by the way, to make it easier for everybody to vote. You'll never understand our system of government, Blanton. It's too simple, too basic for liberals to comprehend. If the Rebel way is so harsh, so brutal, so restrictive, why then do we have several dozen communes of hippies living willingly, freely, and openly within our controlled areas? True, good, peaceful, back-to-the-earth-type hippies. You want to go visit with some of them when this war is over?"

"No. We're well aware of those communes. We've monitored signals from someone called Thermopolis. Obviously a false name. What is his real name?"

"I don't know. I don't care. Why should I care? It's none of my business."

Blanton stood up. "I'm going to pull together what is left of the armed forces and leave you, General."

"That's the best news I've heard in weeks. Providing you take Harriet Hooter and Rita Rivers with you."

Blanton walked to the door. There, he paused and turned around. "We shall meet again, General. In open combat. And we'll win, for God is on our side."

Ben smiled. "Yeah, I've heard that before, too."

Blanton stalked away and Jersey strolled in. "Corrie says that regiment is about a day and a half away. Two days at the most. We've got about a hundred and fifty Rebels here, tops. How are we going to fight a regiment, General?"

"Like porcupines make love, Jersey. Carefully."

# *Four*

Blanton and his people pulled out with only Lightheart reluctant to go. Ben's respect for the man had grown. Lightheart appeared to have more sense than anyone else who served President Blanton. Ben put the presidential party out of his mind and turned to his own people, gathering around him. Ben had requested air drops from Cecil and the supplies had been delivered that morning. Ben had immediately sent out teams to start mining the only road in and to set up ambush points.

"We're the mouse against the elephant," he said, pointing to their location on a map. "So the first order of business is to cut that elephant down to size." He tapped the map with a stick. "When they reach this point, they're going to be real cautious. So we're going to let them come on. We want them in deep and relaxed before we spring the trap. Revere can't pull troops from the front to assist them, and Ike can't send anyone to help us. So we're on our own. We're going to hit and then run like hell. We'll regroup here." He again tapped the map. "I don't want any prisoners," he said flatly. "Disarm any who try to surrender and turn them loose or shoot them. I don't care. That's up to you. Just remember this: we are not only fighting Revere and his people, we are also facing a battle with troops loyal to Blanton. Speaking quite frankly, this is probably the most fucked-up situation we've faced in a long time. I don't like fighting people who are flying the American flag. It's very repugnant to me. But I cannot reason with Blanton; I can't reach any sort of compromise with him, so there it is, and here we are. Squad leaders start moving your teams out. Good luck and God bless."

Ben pulled his small team around him. Cooper asked, "Which side you reckon God is on in this thing, General?"

"I think he's neutral, Coop. I think He sat back a long time ago, long before any of you were born, and put Earth on the back burner." He paused, smiled, and looked heavenward. "Well, He didn't strike me dead so I guess we're not totally out of favor." The team laughed at that. When the laughter had subsided, Ben said, "Let's go, folks."

The small teams of Rebels were spread out and dug in along a mile-long stretch of road. Each team was armed with rocket launchers—with every member of the team carrying four rounds—Big Thumpers, and automatic weapons. Each squad leader made certain every member knew the escape routes and where to rendezvous. They very carefully dug in and waited.

The colonel leading the advancing regiment sent recon in first. The recon moved carefully and cautiously. But they seldom investigated more than twenty or so yards on either side of the old highway.

Bad mistake. As soon as the recon teams had passed, the Rebels slipped out of their hidey-holes and reset the Claymores and placed C-4 at preselected sites. Then they slipped back to their holes and waited.

The first tanks of the long column appeared and the Rebels let them rumble past, allowing them to roll deeper and deeper into the trap. Ben and his team were located at the south end of the mile-long corridor of death, with a handful of Rebel scouts a few hundred yards past that point. When the enemy recon passed Ben's location, they paused to radio in the all-clear. Five seconds later they were dead, felled by silenced .22s. Their bodies were quickly dragged off the road and tossed into the brush just as the first tank drew up to Ben's location.

"Now!" Ben said, and Cooper fired the Armbrust. The rocket slammed into the side of the tank and turned the inside into a fiery death for the crew. Beth took out the second tank and Jersey finished the third one. Up and down the mile-long stretch of highway, explosions shattered the quiet and a rattled regimental commander screamed orders to get the hell out of there.

But it was too late and too confusing. The tanks and trucks got all jammed up in their haste to get away and it became a turkey shoot for the Rebels and a massacre for the enemy troops. Then the Rebels vanished, running all out east and west. When they reached a preselected heading, they cut south, heading for the rendezvous spot. They left behind them a mile-long section of smoking, burning, and exploding hell. The Rebels headed for the ruins of a tiny town at the intersection of Highways 28 and 30.

They had not suffered a single person lost due to death or wounds.

While Ben and his people regrouped, the regimental commander of Revere's troops had to hold up and lose a full day clearing the road and seeing to the wounded and burying the dead. Blanton and his troops had crossed over into Vermont and set up in the Green Mountains. His more experienced and worldly and less liberal commanders monitored the antics of Ben Raines and his Rebels by radio and exchanged glances. None of them were looking forward to tangling with the Rebels. But how to convince President Blanton that declaring war on the Rebels was going to be a bloody and terrible mistake? They were soldiers, and they would do as their commander in chief ordered. But they knew in their hearts they would never defeat the Rebels. To do that, they would have to wipe them out to the last person, and that was impossible. The commanders met and selected General Taylor to meet with Blanton.

"Mister President," Taylor said. "It's time to put past political differences behind you and give serious thought to joining forces with the Rebels and defeating General Revere. When that is done, then you and General Raines can sit down and work something out."

Blanton shook his head. "No. I won't do that. I will not allow that man to flaunt the constitution."

Taylor sighed. "Mister President, I've got to convince you of something. Ben Raines couldn't, but maybe I can. Those thousands of people rushing to join us are worthless. They're losers—before the Great War, and afterwards. Believe me. My people have interviewed those types for months . . . *years!* They want something for nothing. They're scared to death of Ben Raines because they can't live under very simple and very basic Rebel rule—"

"Of course, they can't," Blanton cut him short. "No one wants to live under a dictatorship."

General Taylor sighed. "Mister President, I am sworn by oath to serve you. I will not break that oath. I will stand by you. But you are very wrong about General Raines. The Rebels don't live under a dictatorship. They are the freest people on the face of the earth."

"Oh, that's nonsense!" Harriet Hooter stuck her mouth into it. "How can everybody be free when everybody is armed to the teeth with those horrible, nasty guns?"

General Taylor cut his eyes. He couldn't stand the woman, but she was a friend of the president. "Ms. Hooter, that is precisely the reason they are free."

"Nonsense!" was her reply. "Horrible, nasty Republicans."

General Taylor stood up. "Mister President, I would much rather have General Raines for an ally than an enemy."

"That is possible only if General Raines and his followers will swear allegiance to the flag of the United States of America and agree to relinquish the territory they now claim and rejoin the Union."

"That, sir, is something that will never happen."

"Then the war will be long and costly, but we

shall eventually crush them in battle," said the president. "For God is on our side."

"Shit!" said the general, then left the room.


General Revere and his people were stopped cold and could not advance an inch. He sent commando teams sweeping around both ends of the Rebel lines. He stopped sending them when none of the previous teams reported back. There was no turning back for Revere; he was committed and was fully aware of what would happen to him should he lose. Neither President Blanton nor Ben Raines would hesitate a second in ordering him shot on the spot.

General Taylor had ordered Revere's supply lines severed. In a week or so, that would begin to tell. Revere had to make a decision, and had to make it soon. There was just no way he could fight on three fronts. He had sent messages out to the warlords he knew leaned toward his way of thinking, but so far, no replies had come in. If they would just swing over to his side . . .

"General," an aide broke into his thoughts. "The spokesman for all the warlords, Al Rogers, just called in. He and all the others have agreed to fight with us."

"All right!" Revere jumped to his boots. "Get all my people in here, Jimmy. We've got to move fast."


"Something weird's going on, General," Corrie called to Ben. "Colonel Taylor has been ordered back. Base Camp One reports massive movements of warlords and their people. Thousands of well-armed people. Intelligence seems to think that gangs of all colors have apparently put aside their differences and agreed to fight against the common enemy."

"Us," Ben said.

"Right."

"Well, you can bet they've thrown in with Revere. Get me Ike on the horn."

"Go, Eagle," Ike said.

"Ike, you heard from Cec?"

"That's ten-four. What's going on?"

"I don't know for sure. But I'll bet you a bottle of whiskey that Revere will be pulling out, or has already begun doing that, and heading in this direction. Those warlords and their people will be throwing up a line right down the middle of the country to block you."

Ike was silent for a moment. "Could be it, Ben. We intercepted a message that General Taylor had cut Revere's supply lines. He'd be hurting in a couple of weeks. If these punks are well-equipped, they could hang me up."

"Expect that, Ike. According to reports, they are very well-equipped. Revere's going to try to take out Blanton and his people, then deal with me. I've got some decisions to make, Ike. I'll get back to you. Eagle out." He looked at Corrie. "Get me home base, Corrie."

"Cec here, Ben. What's up?"

"Let me hear your opinion on what the warlords are doing."

It was the same as Ben thought.

"Ben, you're not going to try to assist Blanton and his people, are you?" Cecil asked.

"With what, Cec? Less than a company? I'm not going to sacrifice my people because of his hard-headedness. I'll try to advise him, but whether he takes that advice is up for grabs. Probably he won't."

"And then?"

"I'm taking my people and getting the hell out of here. Have a battalion start moving north, Cec. Armor, artillery, the whole mobile bag. As many people as you can spare. Stay on the east side of the Mississippi. We'll link up with them somewhere in Indiana."

"Will do, Ben. Cec out."

"Get me Blanton, Corrie." Ben poured a cup of coffee while he waited.

Corrie said, "The president is not available at this time, General."

"Not available? What the hell is he doing, watching for the maple sap to start dripping?"

Corrie ducked her head to hide her grin.

"Can you get me General Taylor?"

"I'll try, sir."

Ben rolled a cigarette and sipped his coffee.

"General Taylor on the horn, sir."

"General Taylor? Ben Raines here." He laid it all out for the man.

"Damn!" the general said, when Ben finished. "I think you're probably right, General Raines. I'll give your suggestions and my recommendation to the president and urge him to take your advice. But . . ."

"Yeah, I know. Good luck to you, General Taylor."

"Luck to you, General Raines."

Ben handed Corrie the mic and said, "Pack it up, people. We're shagging ass out of here."

* * *

They had names like Bad Boy and Bull, Jammin'
Jimmy and Rappin' Sid. Others were called Street
Queen and Glory Girl, Lovely Leroy and Kansas
City Kid. Still others went by the handles of Ass
Kicker Kelly, Moline Max, Cool Man Milo, Toy Boy
Bart, Ross the Rumbler, Dido Duke . . . and so on
and so forth, well past the point of being nauseous.
They were the absolute dregs of a fallen society. In
the past, billions of taxpayer dollars had been spent
(by a democrat-controlled, liberal government) trying to help people such as these. The money might
as well have been flushed down the toilet. The sobbing sisters and hanky-twisters and snit-throwers in
congress just never understood that street punks
and gutter slime respect only one thing: brute force.

One cannot offer these types compassion because
they don't have any, for anything or anybody. They
are the types of people who want something for
nothing. They demand a job but they are unquali-
fied to do anything except mug and rob and assault
and rape and kill. They demand that society foot
the bill to train them for work and then complain
that the jobs they're offered are beneath them. They
demand respect at the point of a gun or a knife.
They come in all colors, all races. They are savage
and ignorant and bigoted and don't have enough
common sense to pour piss out of a boot, and they
are proud of it. When they don't get their way, they
riot and loot and burn and then demand that the
law-abiding, tax-paying citizens pay to rebuild their
neighborhoods.

These types were about to discover that their way

of thinking was totally alien to the Rebel philosophy. These types were about to discover that in the Rebel society, if you contribute nothing to society, that is exactly what you get from it. These types were about to discover that if you threaten a Rebel, you run the risk of getting killed—very quickly.

"You were right," Corrie said, monitoring transmissions as the column rolled south and west out of New York State. "Our scouts report that the punks are throwing up a line on the east side of the Mississippi River. And they are well-equipped."

"Artillery?" Ben asked.

"Yes. But not under their command. Revere's people control that."

Ben was silent for a couple of miles. "While we were fighting Hoffman and his Nazis for all those months, Revere and his people were busy setting all this up. It almost worked. Ike has confirmed that Revere is swinging his people around; shifting them to the east. Revere thinks he's going to put me in a box. Has Cec put that battalion on the road yet?"

"Yes, sir. Pushing hard to link up with us."

"Tell Ike to hold his positions until we are certain of Revere's motives," Ben said. "At my command he is to begin first swinging his westernmost battalions south and east. When the last of Revere's battalions are east of the Great Lakes, Ike will start lining up north to south in the heartland, facing the Mississippi River and the punks."

"Then we'll start harassing the punks from the rear," Cooper said.

"Right," Ben said.

Jersey smiled. "Kick-ass time!"

# *Five*

Ben pushed his people hard, rolling the short convoy as fast as he dared along the old crumbling highways. If they could travel at 45 miles per hour, that was good. Usually it was less than that.

Blanton's agents had done their work well in spreading the "chicken in every pot" (skinless) crap. Sometimes people hidden along the way shot at them, sometimes the people waved and cheered. Residents of the battered nation were pretty evenly divided between the Rebels' form of government and the old unworkable, so-called "democratic" type of government.

"Looks like about half the people are for us and half against us," Beth remarked.

"The old government would have worked if the politicians had adhered to the constitution the way it was written and stopped trying to screw it up," Ben said, during a welcome break. "But it seemed like suddenly every liberal became an expert on the constitution . . . interpreting it the way they wanted it to read."

"How about folks like us?" Cooper asked. "Why didn't we get a say in matters?"

Ben smiled and poured another cup of coffee. "The news media usually branded anyone who believed in using lethal force to protect what was theirs a right-wing lunatic. We didn't have much of a chance to say our piece. Usually when the press did stick a microphone under the nose of a citizen who believed they still had a right to protect what was theirs, it was nearly always some ignorant, bigoted ultra-right-winger with an alligator mouth and a hummingbird ass."

"We're going to have company just about a mile down the road, General," Corrie called. "Some group calling themselves Partners of Peace."

"POP?" Ben said with a smile.

"That's a hell of a lot better than Warriors of Peace," Lt. Bonelli said with a laugh.

When the laughter had subsided, Ben asked, "What frequency are they using?"

"CB."

"Very up to date, aren't they?"

"Channel 19," Corrie added.

"Really professional," Jersey said, stretching out her diminutive frame for a short nap.

"Wake me up in thirty," Ben said, lying down. He was asleep in two minutes.

"Scout it out," Lt. Bonelli said, jerking his thumb toward the road.

They returned just about the time Ben was waking up.

"The interstate is blocked and they're definitely waiting for us," the Rebels told Ben. "And they're well-armed."

The convoy had skirted Youngstown and were staying on I-76, working their way to Indiana.

"Looks like about a hundred of them," the other Rebel said. "Men and women. Flying the American flag."

Ben sighed. "Exactly what I didn't want. This is shaping up to be a full-blown civil war. Blanton's smart. That's what he wants. He's the good guy and we're the bad guys. He's worked for many years setting all this up. I'll give him credit for patience."

"What about POP?" Cooper asked.

Ben stood up and stretched. He reached for his Thompson. "Let's go see what their beef is."

The Rebels could have easily shot their way through, or simply bypassed the area. But neither of those was, at the moment, acceptable to Ben. About five hundred yards from the barricade, Ben halted the convoy and got on the CB.

"You people do not own the highways," he radioed. "Please allow us to pass."

"You are a traitor, Ben Raines," a man's voice came through the speaker. "You have turned your back on the President of the United States. Your reign of terror ends here."

"Are they kidding?" Beth asked.

"I don't think so," Ben said, keying the mic. "I don't know where you got your information, mister, but it's wrong. I offered help to the president. He turned it down."

"We did?" Jersey looked at Ben.

"Sort of," he replied.

No one had to ask what the Rebels should do if the members of POP opened fire. No one fired on the Rebels without retaliation. If the members of

POP had a death wish, they couldn't have found a better group to see that their wishes became reality.

"You lie, Ben Raines," the spokesman for POP said. "Everybody knows you are a liar."

Ben had been called lots of things both before and after the Great War, but being called a liar was something he would not take. Everyone who knew Ben even slightly knew he was honest to a fault. Ben was uncommonly blunt with the truth. "Clear that goddamn road," he radioed. "And do it quickly. That is the only warning you are going to get." He turned to Lt. Bonelli. "Rocket launchers in place?"

Bonelli nodded.

"You go straight to hell, Ben Raines!" the spokesman said. "We are prepared to die for President Blanton."

"Idiots," Ben muttered. "Put two HE's into that barricade" he ordered.

The vehicles that blocked the interstate went up with a swooshing boom as the high explosive rounds impacted against them and ignited the gas tanks. Bodies and parts of bodies were hurled into the air and slammed away from both sides of the road. Those left alive put their feet to work and hit the trail.

"Clear the wreckage," Ben ordered.

Deuce and a halves moved up and pushed the mangled hulks out of the way, clearing one lane. The Rebels mounted up and moved forward. At the smoking site, Ben saw the American flag the members of POP had been flying lying on the grass, just off the shoulder.

"Hold it, Coop." He got out of the Hummer and righted the flag, jamming the pole deep into the ground. He looked at a member of POP, sitting on the ground, holding a rag to his head. The man was not badly hurt, only scared as he looked into the muzzles of dozens of M-16s, all pointing at him.

"Well, go ahead and shoot me, Ben Raines," the man said, a quiver in his voice.

"I have no intention of shooting you," Ben told him. "Unless you try to shoot me or any of my people."

"President Blanton's agents told us you were initiating a scorched earth policy. That you killed everyone who did not agree with you."

"Blanton is a politician and lying is second nature to a politician," Ben replied. "You have a doctor with your group?"

"Yes."

"Fine. Then my medics won't have to waste time checking you out. You just remember this: the next time you threaten a Rebel, you might not get off so lucky. Goodbye."

The Rebels mounted up and moved on, leaving the citizen with the bloody bump on his head sitting on the ground, looking very confused.

As it turned out, the communications network of Blanton's supporters throughout the nation was much more sophisticated than the Rebels first thought. Somebody from POP got on the horn and warned other groups that the Rebels played rough and dirty and didn't bluff worth a damn. Ben's small convoy encountered no more trouble as they rolled through Ohio and into Indiana. As before, some citizens cheered them and others booed and hissed and shook their fists.

Ben started stopping along the way, talking to those who were friendly to the Rebels. He told them of the new nation that was being formed. If they thought they could live under Rebel law, he invited them down.

The exodus started.

The Rebels bypassed the ruins of Indianapolis and started angling south. They linked up with the battalion sent from Base Camp One at the junction of Highway 57 and I-64.

"If that's a battalion, I'm Daffy Duck," Lt. Bonelli said, lowering his binoculars.

"I think Cecil just might have overdone it a bit," Ben said, lowering his binoculars. He had spotted Colonel Dan Gray amid all the vehicles and personnel. "Come on. Let's sort all this out."

"Don't blame me," Dan said, after shaking Ben's hand. "Ike ordered me to join you. We've got approximately two and a half battalions here, and that's not counting artillery and armor."

"What's the latest from Revere?"

"He's definitely moving against President Blanton's troops. Intel reports he's saving us for last. We've been seeing a lot of people, families, moving south. What's that all about?"

"They're heading for the new nation we're carving out."

"What is this new nation going to be called, Ben?"

"The Southern United States of America. The flag will be the stars and stripes. With eleven stars."

Dan smiled. "That's what that new factory down at Base Camp One is so busy working on."

"That's right."

"President Blanton is not going to be happy about this."

"Blanton's happiness or lack of it is not my concern."

"Everything is all jumbled up, Ben," the former SAS man said. "We're getting reports that Canadians are fighting Canadians over the building civil war down here. They're split about fifty-fifty. Looks like about the same here in the Colonies." He said the last with a smile. "General Jefferys is of the opinion that Blanton wants a civil war."

"I agree with that assessment. Why else would the man feign his own death and stay in hiding for years? Why the elaborate network of agents quietly working the nation, and the secret military bases?" Ben shook his head. "He's a slick one, all right."

"Ben, we held off Revere's army with trickery and deceit and experience. There is no way that Blanton's troops can even come close to our proficiency."

"You're right. In a manner of speaking, I agreed to help Blanton. He wanted no part of it. Hell with him. The only one I feel sorry for, believe it or not, is Blush Lightheart."

"Oh, I believe it. You are aware that we do have some homosexuals in our ranks?"

"Of course. They were warned to keep their sexual preferences confined to others of their particular persuasion."

"I wondered if you knew."

"Very little goes on in this army that I am not aware of," Ben said with a smile.

\* \* \*

The convoy pulled out the next morning, heading west into Illinois. Almost two thousand ground troops, with tanks and artillery to back them up. The column stretched for miles, and it put fear into the hearts of those who backed Blanton, and joy in the hearts of those who favored the Rebels' form of government.

Ben knew Blanton had spies everywhere (that much had not changed since his administration when federal agents were spying on everybody they could—including Ben Raines), so there was no point in making any attempt to conceal what the Rebels were up to. That would have been near impossible anyway, considering the size of the columns.

"We'll head south when we reach I-57," Ben told his officers late one afternoon. "We'll start cleaning out Revere's punk army and working north at what's left of Memphis. Dan, get your teams of scouts dressed in civilian clothing and in cars and trucks and motorcycles and get them going. I want comprehensive reports from them. When we get a bit farther south, we're going to have to cut back east and cross the Ohio River and come at them that way. Most of the bridges are blown over the Mississippi. Corrie, have you heard any reports today about Blanton and his troops?"

"Nothing, sir. They've gone silent."

Dan studied Ben's face. "You're worried about the man, aren't you, Ben?"

"Yes," Ben said after a slight hesitation. "He's an American president. I didn't like or trust him years back and I don't like or trust him now. But he's still a living, elected president. And he's a law-abiding, decent American citizen. But I can't be his nanny. Get some sleep, Dan. See you in the morning."

The column was in southern Illinois, just about to cross the Ohio River, when the first reports from the scouts came in. Revere's punk army was stretched out all along the Mississippi, on both sides of the river, and they were extremely well-equipped. The only thing they didn't have to match the Rebels—as far as equipment went—was long range artillery. But they were well-supplied with mortars and appeared to know how to use them.

"Let's find out," Ben said with a hard smile.

Nothing was left of Memphis but burned-out and bombed hulks of buildings. Most of the nation's cities had been destroyed in order to wipe out the cannibalistic Creepies. Rebel units began moving to the west, from the east side of the Missouri bootheel, south down to the outskirts of Memphis.

Rappin' Sid and Cool Cal were the leaders of the gangs whose jobs it was to prevent the eastward advance of Ike's Rebels. Revere just hadn't counted on Ben Raines coming up behind his punk army.

Thirteen and 14 Battalions, under the command of Raul Gomez and Jim Peters had set up across the river in Arkansas and at Ben's orders started pounding the punk positions with long range 155s.

"Holy shit!" Rappin' Sid yelled as the huge shells began raining down on his position. The first few rounds had landed dangerously close to his headquarters and had knocked him out of the chair. He'd been listening to his favorite rap group, The Snot Drippers, perform on tape their greatest hit,

"Give Me Yo' Watch & Wallet or I'll Kill the Bitch That's With You." The song really had not enjoyed much success since ninety-nine percent of the nation's radio stations had refused to play it. But it had become a favorite among certain street gangs . . . which should give one some insight as to the overall mentality of the aforementioned.

Then Ben cut loose with his own 155s from behind Rappin' Sid and Cool Cal's position. The first round landed just behind Cool Cal's HQ, collapsed the rear wall, and knocked the punk out of his chair, sprawling him face down on the littered floor. To make matters worse, he lost his favorite comic book, the one that featured Ghetto Man killing all the cops in the city and screwing all the rich bitches who had refused to go along with redistributing their wealth.

"Good God!" Cal hollered, crawling to his feet just as the second round landed in front of the old home and the concussion blew out all the windows and doors. Cool Cal wound up on his butt in the bathroom, his head resting on the commode seat.

Rappin' Sid grabbed up the radio mic and alerted the next gang north, which was commanded by someone called Little Pecker, up in the Arkansas town of Osceola. "We're under attack from the west and the east. Defend yo' turf, man. Death to Ben Raines and the Rebels!" He grabbed his M-16 and headed out the front door just as another 155 round landed in front of the house. The concussion tore the door off its old hinges. The door slammed into Rappin' Sid and knocked him down the hall. Sid ended up in the kitchen with the muzzle of the M-16 stuck up one side of his nose.

Little Pecker immediately radioed Big Pecker up in Blytheville, who radioed Boo Boo in Caruthersville, who contacted Poke Chop in Portageville.

Ben looked over at Corrie, earphones on her head. She was laughing so hard tears were running down her cheeks. "What got you started?" he asked.

"Little Pecker, Big Pecker, Boo Boo, and Poke Chop," she managed to say.

Ben stared at her for a moment. "Did you suddenly develop a speech impediment?"

She couldn't speak. Just handed him the headset. Ben listened, a smile slowly creeping across his lips. He started laughing. Ben sat down beside Corrie and removed the headset. He shook his head. "I guess I should be ashamed of myself, but I can't help it," he said over the thunder of artillery. "The mightiest army on the face of the earth has been reduced to waging war on someone called Poke Chop."

"It gets worse," Corrie finally managed to speak.

"How?" Ben asked.

"Someone named Super Dick is commanding the gang in Charleston."

# Six

"That trash defending along the river is not going to hold," General Revere was advised.

"Of course, they're not," Paul said. "I didn't expect them to hold. Just buy us some time, that's all. I want Raines and the Rebels to destroy them."

"Clever," the colonel said. "We would have had to contend with them later on anyway."

"That's right. Raines is doing us a favor."

An aide came into the big tent. "General Taylor has broken up his army and sent them out in small units dressed in civilian clothing. The president, First Lady, and staff have gone underground."

"Goddamnit!" Revere cursed. "Do we have any idea where they might be?"

"Not a clue. They just dropped out of sight."

"We know the government built dozens of underground bunkers—from small to huge—before the Great War, and then added hundreds after that, stocked with enough supplies to last for a century. Blanton and his staff could be anywhere. They could be in any one of a dozen or more states. Keep looking. I want them found, and I want them killed."

"How many people do we pull off the line?"

Revere hesitated, then said, "As many as you need. Find President Blanton and staff, and kill them!"


Beth finished decoding the message communications handed her and studied it for a moment, then she walked out of the trailer and over to Ben. "Strange message, General. Does this mean you?"

Ben read the cryptic note. FIND & KILL EAGLE AND CHICKS. He shook his head. "Eagle was the Secret Service name—one of them—for the president. The chicks are probably his wife and staff. Has Corrie had any luck in making contact with Blanton?"

"Negative, sir. Intell thinks they've gone hard underground."

"They may be right. Both before and after the Great War, the government built several hundred bunkers deep underground and stocked them with plenty of food and water and fuel for generators."

"Do you know where they are?" Cooper asked.

Ben smiled. "Most of them."


Deep underground in the mountains of West Virginia, President Homer Blanton sat at the head of the long table and stared at his staff and those senators and representatives who had been with him for years. The arguments had been heated, and everyone was pausing to let tempers cool.

Lightheart stood firm and he picked it up. "Let General Raines and his people have their nation, Homer. They're going to have it anyway—whether we like it or not."

"No!" Harriet Hooter shrieked, and everyone present winced. Her voice was like someone dragging their fingernails across a chalkboard.

"No!" Rita Rivers shouted.

"No!" Benedict hollered.

Senator Hanrahan was unusually silent, as was Ditto and Arnold. Blanton's eyes touched Hanrahan. "You have said nothing for an hour, Senator."

"Give the Rebels their country," Hanrahan said, his words soft. "Or we'll be at war from now until the end of time."

"Have you lost your mind?" Harriet squealed.

"Perhaps I've just found it," the aging senator said. "Ben Raines spoke to me at length, and his words stung. He's very correct in saying that we ignored a large segment of the American population. We over-taxed the good citizens to pay for programs the majority of them didn't want. We had no right to seize private firearms. We just didn't have the right to do that. We went soft on criminals and hard on law-abiding citizens. Oh, we were well-meaning in what we did . . . I guess. Looking back I'm not so that sure we weren't all on a powertrip. We all knew that a straight across the board flat tax was the really fair way to go. But instead we made great flowery speeches and in the end screwed the American people with such a complicated tax system not even tax lawyers agreed on how to interpret it. We . . ."

"I must protest this," Harriet Hooter hollered. "I feel . . ."

Hanrahan looked at her and stepped completely out of character by saying, "Shut your goddamn mouth. For once, just close that great flapping orifice and listen."

Harriet's mouth dropped open so far it would have taken a team of Percherons all working in harness all day to wrench it closed.

"Why, you damned old senile fool!" Rita Rivers shouted, jumping to her feet.

"Shut up!" President Blanton said.

Rita's mouth started working like a fish, but no sounds were coming out.

"And sit down," Blanton added. Rita sat. "Go on," he said to Senator Hanrahan.

Hanrahan shrugged his shoulders. "You've admitted privately that we were wrong, Homer. Time and time again we were wrong. Now I'm admitting it. I think that Ben Raines is a fair man . . ."

Harriet almost had a heart attack at that, and Arnold and Benedict looked stunned.

"People who are offered jobs and refuse to work at them deserve nothing from the government—that is, if we had a government. Face it people, the only stable government in the world, that I am aware of, is the Rebel government. Oh, my, yes, their laws are harsh; Orwellian, to our way of looking at it. But they—the Rebels—don't mind living under those laws. Ben Raines is not asking us to live under his laws. He's just telling us that he and his people are not going to live under ours. He has stated he will discuss a compromise. All right, let's try it. I personally think we can work with General Raines. It's certainly worth a try."

"I'll think about it," Homer Blanton said.


Rappin' Sid and Cool Cal survived the barrage with their sanity and not much else. On both sides of the river, the Rebels had laid down a blanket of deadly walking-in artillery, the 155 rounds systematically destroying everything in their path.

Then Ben sent his ground troops in.

The "troops" of Rappin' Sid and Cool Cal (those who were still alive) had no stomach left for the fight. For thirty-six hours the artillery of the Rebels had rained down on them, and a heavy and unrelenting artillery barrage is the most demoralizing of all combat situations. Most threw down their weapons and surrendered. Those who chose to fight were killed; no mercy, no quarter.

Rappin' Sid and Cool Cal were brought to Ben's CP. They were badly shaken men. Ben stared at them for a long minute, his cold eyes shifting from one to the other.

"Is you gonna off us, man?" Rappin' Sid mush-mouthed.

"Can you speak proper English?" Ben challenged.

"Huh?"

"I said, can you speak proper English?" Ben shouted. "Goddamn, are you deaf as well as ignorant?"

The two ex-gang leaders stood silent.

"I'd guess you both were about twenty when the Great War blew the world apart," Ben said. "Ample time for you to have graduated from high school and have some college or vo-tech. Ample time for you to have found jobs and begin contributing to the society in which you lived. Did you do any of those things?"

Rappin' Sid, who was black, looked at Cool Cal, who was white. Neither of them had ever held a job and they were both high school drop-outs. Rappin' Sid was from Chicago, Cool Cal from St. Louis. Before the Great War they were street punks. They still were. Both of them had police rap sheets half a city block long.

"My daddy beat me," Cool Cal said.

"The teachers picked on me," Rappin' Sid said.

Ben leaned back in his chair and stared at the pair. He thought: Why do I even bother talking with them? It's always the same old story. It's always someone else's fault.

The Rebel ranks were dotted with men and women who had come from broken and dysfunctional homes—men and women who had suffered child abuse and poverty . . . yet who had not turned to a life of crime. They had gone on to live productive lives, making no excuses for their childhood deprivations, placing no blame on society.

Ben stood up and the gang leaders tensed. "Get out of here," Ben told them.

"And do whut?" Cool Cal asked.

"For just once in your miserable lives, try to live decently. Plant gardens. Fix up a home and respect the rights of others around you."

"Ah ain't no mottha-fuckin' farmer," Rappin' Sid said defiantly. Then his eyes widened and his breath became short as he stared into the eyes of Ben Raines. His lips formed a large O. Rappin' Sid sud-

224

denly realized he was looking into the face of death; realized that one more smart-assed crack out of his mouth might well get him a bullet right between the eyes. He could almost hear the hoof-beats of the Pale Rider.

"Shut up," Cool Cal hissed.

Rappin' Sid bobbed his head up and down. "You be right, sir," he said to Ben. "I'm gone like a breeze. You ain't never gonna see me 'gain."

"If I do see you again," Ben told him. "Or you," he cut his eyes to Cal. "And you are doing anything other than living quiet, decent lives, I'll kill you *on the spot!* Do you understand?"

They understood. For the first time in their lives they realized there was no fall-back place. No social workers, no probation officers, no soft-hearted judges and weepy lawyers. No free rides. They were looking sudden death square in the eyes.

Rappin' Sid remembered something his long-suffering mother had once said. "We walk the straight an' narrow, right, sir?"

"That's right."

"I can do that," Cool Cal said quickly.

"Good," Ben told him. "See that you do. You have one minute to clear this camp. Move!"

The last time Ben saw Cool Cal and Rappin' Sid they were picking them up and putting them down, heading east.

"Whoo!" Little Pecker said frantically, when he learned of the fate of Rappin' Sid and Cool Cal and that the Rebels were moving toward his location . . . on both sides of the river. He radioed Big Pecker.

"They's strength in numbers," Big Pecker said. He recalled that line from somewhere. "Pull out and head on up here. Then we'll join up with Boo Boo and figure somethin' out. Git gone, man."

The Rebel scouts reported that a mass exodus was taking place, the gangs pulling out and moving north. The Rebels relentlessly followed them.

Far to the north, Ike had split his battalions and was working both sides of the Mississippi River, working south, putting the gangs in a slowly closing vise.

"Hey, General Man," Bad Boy radioed to Revere. "This plan of yours ain't workin' out worth a shit for us! We're gettin squooze somethin' fierce."

"Hold your ground," Revere ordered.

"Screw you!" Big Foot Freddie radioed. "I didn't join this here chicken-shit outfit to commit suicide."

Hundreds of miles away, in the underground bunker in West Virginia, General Taylor listened to the heated exchanges. "Ben Raines is a brilliant tactician," he said to no one in particular. "I do not look forward to meeting that man in open battle. He's totally unpredictable. You can't read him. He doesn't follow any rule book."

"I'm not sure all our troops will fight him," a staff colonel said softly, standing close to the general.

"I know," Taylor whispered. "Except for that ragtag pack of losers and complainers and whiners that think Blanton is the next best thing to God Almighty."

"Is it true that his own staff is divided?"

"Yes. Senator Hanrahan did a one eighty on the issue. Surprised the hell out of me." He chuckled. "I think it surprised the hell out of *him,* too."

The Rebels chased the punk gangs all the way to the Missouri Bootheel, harassing them every foot of the way. There, under the command of a huge thug who called himself Super Dick, the punks decided to make a stand of it. As far as numbers went, they more than outnumbered the Rebels. But when it came to discipline, they were zip. These were strong-arm types, most of them long on muscle and cruelty, many of them much more intelligent than they appeared, but extremely short on common sense.

"We'll stop 'em, people," Super Dick boasted to the gang leaders. "We're out of the range of them pricks and cunts acrost the river."

Wrong. The Rebels had rocket-assisted projectiles with a range of just about 40,000 yards.

"And we's a hell of a whole lot more smarter than them, too."

Sure.

Thirteen and 14 Battalions got into position just east of Sikeston, Missouri while Ben and his battalions set up just across the river near Wickliffe, Kentucky. They readied their 155s and 203mm howitzers.

Super Dick readied his punk army for a ground attack that didn't come. "Somethin' funky goin' on," he muttered.

Funky arrived in a barrage of nasty surprises for the gang members. On the east side of the river, Ben opened the funkiness by launching a salvo of artillery rounds, each round containing 195 M42 grenades while the batteries of 13 and 14 fired HE and WP rounds.

The few remaining residents of the small Missouri town had fled before the arrival of the gangs. Whether they loved or hated the Rebels, all had a pretty good idea how Ben Raines would deal with the gangs. Many had followed the tactics of the Rebels for years, listening to short wave broadcasts from around the battered country. About half headed south to become a part of the new Southern United States.

The high explosive rounds shattered buildings and sent brick and mortar and lumber flying in all directions. The willie peter set things blazing and the hundreds of exploding M42 grenades turned the small town into a death trap. Frightened gang members went running wild-eyed in all directions. But they soon discovered that there simply was no place to run to escape the deadly hail that rained down upon them.

"Hold your positions!" Super Dick shouted. "This can't last long."

Wrong.

The barrage began at 0700 and the guns finally fell silent three hours later. There was little left of the town except fire, smoke, and ruins. Of the hundreds of gang leaders who had very unwisely gathered in the small Missouri town, only a handful remained alive.

"Goddamn you, Ben Raines!" Super Dick screamed into the mic. "Goddamn you to hell! You don't fight fair!"

"Mop it up," Ben ordered.

# Seven

"You just kilt them all," a badly frightened and trembling gang leader said to Ben. His crotch was stained from the urine his relaxed bladder had emptied into his underwear during the murderous and hours-long artillery barrage. "You kilt hundreds. I never seen nothin' like it. They's blowed off arms and heads and legs and guts . . ." He began crying, the tears cutting traces down his dirty cheeks. "And the blood. Oh, God, the blood!" He sank to his knees and put his face into his hands and wept. The gang leader, who went by the moniker of Lucky Louie, lay on the ground, curled into a fetal position, sobbing uncontrollably.

Even Super Dick was subdued. He had the shakes and could not make them stop. He was twitching like a dry leaf in a breeze. "My old lady was runnin' crost the street when a round hit. She just disappeared, man. She just . . . wasn't no more."

"You have my shallowest and most insincere condolences," Ben said acidly.

Super Dick blinked and slowly shook his big,

shaggy head. "You got to be the hardest son of a bitch I ever seen!"

"Thank you."

"Is you gonna off us?" Little Pecker asked. He'd been looking for Big Pecker but had been unable to find him. If he ever did he'd have to scoop him up with a shovel and a spoon.

"I don't know. But right now I'm going to give you some advice."

"Well, here it comes," Poke Chop sneered the words. "The man gonna give us a lecture about us bein' bad boys."

Dan Gray took one step forward and placed the muzzle of a .45 autoloader against Poke Chop's head. He cocked the .45 and Poke Chop shit his underwear.

"At your orders, General," Dan said.

"JesusGodAlmighty!" Poke Chop shouted. "I got a right to speak my piece."

"You have no rights, punk!" Dan said.

"I cain't take no more of this!" Little Pecker wailed, sinking to his knees on the ground. "I'll do whatever it is you want me to do, General."

"Me, too!" Boo Boo blubbered. "Oh, Lard, Lard, don't kill me. I don't wanna die!"

The Rebels had proven that when very harsh sentences are carried out promptly after being handed down, crime takes a tremendous nosedive. Crime of any type was so rare in any Rebel-controlled zone it was viewed as a phenomenon.

Poke Chop was stinking something awful and the breeze was ripe with it. "Get him out of here, Dan," Ben said. "And convince him to live a life free of crime. Tell him what will happen if he doesn't."

"Right, sir!" He lowered the pistol and prodded Poke Chop in the side. "Move, you misplaced cesspool."

"Don't kill me," Little Pecker begged. "Please don't kill me."

Ben turned to Cooper. "Get them out of here, Cooper. Turn them over to the chemical boys and girls and find out what they know."

"Right, sir."

He looked at Corrie. "Let's get over to the comm truck and find out how Ike is doing.

"Piece of cake, Ben," Ike told him. "These punks are all bluster and hot air. We're blowing great big gaps in the line. I figure at the rate we're going, we'll be linking up in a couple of weeks."

"Sooner than that, Ike. I'm ordering everything we have that will fly into the air. These punks have no SAMs. That's been confirmed. The sooner we get this trash done with, the sooner we can turn our attention to Revere and his people. You will have a new flag in your hands in a few days. Cecil bumped me a few hours ago. Fly it proudly."

"Will do, Ben. Shark out."

The new flag had been flown to Ben that morning, during the bombardment. The pilot had landed at a small strip just east of Ben's position. The new flag of the Southern United States of America was very much the same as the original American flag. Only the stars were different. The Rebel flag flew eleven of them, in a circle. Under the circle of stars were the words that had flown on one of the flags at the Alamo: COME AND TAKE IT.

The pilot had also brought hundreds of tiny sew-on flags for the Rebel uniforms, those were being passed out to the troops now.

Ben walked the encampment. Many of the Rebels were silent as they sewed the new flag onto the right sleeve of their BDUs—silent and very, very proud. The pride they felt was almost a tangible thing.

Ben now wore the old French Foreign Legion lizard cammie uniform, and he was the only Rebel who wore them. He did not wear any other insignia denoting his rank of Commanding General of the Rebel Army. He didn't have to.


President Blanton sat alone in his office deep underground and fingered the small sleeve flag of the new Southern United States of America. He was highly irritated and it showed on his face. The flag had been brought to him only hours before.

"Where did you get this?" he had questioned the young soldier.

"Plane flew over, sir. Dropped a whole bunch of them. I, uh, guess, sir, General Raines knows where we are."

Now, alone, Blanton muttered, "Sure he knows. Bastard used to work for the goddamn CIA." He touched the sleeve flag. "He really did it. He really, officially, broke away from the Union." He looked at the words under the circle of stars. COME AND TAKE IT.

Senator Hanrahan entered the office with the presidential seal embedded in the polished tile floor. Blanton looked at him and lifted the tiny flag.

"I saw it, Mister President," the aging senator said. "Hundreds of them were dropped."

"That son of a bitch Raines!" Blanton cursed, his face turning red. "Flaunting this piece of traitorous shit in my face." He hurled the sleeve flag to the floor. "You know what he is? He's a goddamn seditionist."

Hanrahan sat down. "It's rather hard to be a seditionist when there is no stable government to preach sedition upon, sir."

"*I'm* the goddamn government!" Blanton flared. "*You're* the government. *We* represent the government. We were elected by the people, not Ben Raines."

Blanton pressed a button on his desk and an aide stuck her head into the room. She looked like a college cheerleader. "Get General Taylor in here," he ordered.

When Taylor was seated, Blanton said, "We keep our people hard to ground, General. All of them. Arms and uniforms hidden. We'll let Generals Revere and Raines slug it out and whoever wins will surely be considerably weakened afterward. That's when we strike at the victor with everything we've got. Including gas."

"Tear gas?" the general questioned.

"Nerve gas," Blanton said.

"Now, wait a minute," Hanrahan said. "You wait just a damned minute here, Homer."

"No!" Blanton shouted, slamming a hand on the desk. "I will preserve this Union by any means possible. I am still the Commander in Chief. Correct, General Taylor?"

"That is correct, Mister President. You give the orders, I carry them out."

"Just as long as we understand each other," President Blanton said.

News of what happened in Southern Missouri spread quickly south to north along the Mississippi River. Morale began to sag among the punk army. Less than twenty-four hours later, morale and discipline broke apart after Ben sent helicopter gunships and PUFFs into the gang-controlled area around Cape Girardeau, Missouri. Death from the skies took on a new meaning as the Apache helicopters and the PUFFs roared in and turned the gang-controlled streets into something that resembled an open-air slaughter house. From the skies, the streets and alleys and sidewalks and lawns began to look like Jonestown ten-fold over.

Then the artillery began its roar and pounding. After only one hour of rounds from 105s, 155s, 203s, and 81mm mortars raining down on them, the punks packed it in. Ben ordered a cease-fire and let the gang members stagger out. Trembling, white-faced, and wild-eyed from shock, the gang members came stumbling out of the fire and carnage, hands held high over their heads. Many of them were openly weeping.

Revere had promised them that the Rebels would be easy to fight. That the battles would be short ones with the gangs always victorious. Revere lied.

"What in the name of God are we going to do with all of them?" Dan asked.

"Disarm them and turn them loose," Ben said. "It's all we can do other than shoot them. I'll grant you that many of them probably deserve no better than a bullet, but . . ." He let that trail off.

The gang members were giddy with relief when they learned the Rebels were not going to put them up against a wall. Within minutes they had chosen a committee and several spokespersons and demanded a meeting with Ben Raines.

"This ought to be interesting," Ben said, sitting in the lobby of what used to be a nice motel complex just off the interstate. He laid his big .50 caliber mag Desert Eagle autoloader on the table in front of him and nodded at Cooper. "Show the spokespeople in, Coop."

Four men were shown into the lobby. Two blacks, two whites. They had elected as their spokesman a big, unshaven, beady-eyed and smelly piece of white-trash who swaggered up to the table. "They call me Big Johnny."

"State your business," Ben told him.

"We got us a list of demands, General," he announced.

"Is that right?"

"Shore is. Furst of all, we got to have guns to protect ourselves agin the lawless and to hunt wif."

"To protect yourselves against the lawless?" Ben repeated.

"You deef?" the lout hollered.

Ben smiled and picked up the Desert Eagle, thumbing back the hammer. He pointed it at Big Johnny.

"Whoa!" the man yelled. The muzzle looked like the end of a fire nozzle.

"First of all," Ben told him. "You don't come marching in here and demand anything."

235

"We don't?" Big Johnny whispered.

"You don't."

"Whut does we get?" another asked.

"Who are you?"

"Cretan Shabazz Boognami."

Ben blinked and Jersey giggled.

Boognami cut his eyes to her and said, "You think that's funny, bitch?"

Jersey smiled very sweetly and Cooper backed away from her. "I think it's hysterical. And if you call me a bitch one more time I'm going to stick a grenade up your ass and see just how far shit splatters."

Boognami's eyes widened but he wisely kept his mouth closed.

Ben chuckled as he eased the hammer down on the big pistol and laid it on the table. "And if you think she's kidding, Shabazz, you're making the biggest mistake of your life. Now the four of you listen to me. You're getting your lives, and that's all. I'm making a mistake by doing that, for a lot of you will not even attempt to live a decent and orderly existence. But I warn you of this: there will be no more breaks from me. This is the only one you're getting from the Rebels. I don't care how you eke out an existence, but it better not include preying on the innocent. Now you drag your asses out of here and don't ever let me see you again. Move!"

The grievance committee did a quick about-face and beat a hasty retreat out of the lobby.

"We'll have to fight them again someday," Jersey prophesied.

"Probably," Ben agreed, standing up and holstering his Desert Eagle. "Mop this sector up and let's get on the road."

After the fall of Southern Missouri and Ike's hard push all the way down into Iowa, the entire line of punks collapsed and they went running in all directions. Revere's plan had worked for a little while, but not nearly long enough.

"Head your people east, Ike," Ben radioed.

"We're going in to bail out the president?"

"Do we have a choice, Ike?" Ben answered the question with a question.

"I reckon not," the Mississippi born and reared man said. "But you know he's gonna be about as grateful as a stepped-on rattlesnake."

"I know that, too. But we're going to have to fight Revere no matter what."

"Ben," Ike said. "Let's meet on this matter. There are things I have to say that need to be said face to face, like standing out in the middle of a field."

He didn't want to say anything over the air. "All right, Ike. When you have a spot picked out, bump me on scramble."

The bump came in by flattened out burst transmission a few minutes later.

"So we meet in an Indiana corn field," Ben said with smile.

"A corn field?" Jersey blurted.

"Well, sort of," Ben said with a wink. "We'll be flying in, Corrie. Arrange it, please."

"Wonder what General Ike's got on his mind?" Cooper asked.

"Strong suspicions of a set-up," Ben said, and then walked out of the comm truck. He paused at the door and turned around. "But then, I feel the same way."

# Eight

Ben had all battalion commanders flown in, and had General Cecil Jefferys, administrator of Base Camp One, now soon to be called the Southern United States of America, flown up.

They were meeting by a lake near the old Hoosier National Forest. Ike had already sent people in to secure the area, and security was tight.

Ike didn't waste any time in speaking his mind. "Blanton is using us, Ben. His military advisers have informed him that we'll take a lot of losses tangling with Revere's people. We'll be weak in personnel and low on everything after the fight. He also knows this fight will take months and he'll be using that time to train and beef up his own army, and probably sending spies and sappers into our home base."

"I'm in agreement with all that, Ike. That's the first thing I thought of. So what would you have me do?" He looked around at all the batt coms. "I want input from everybody on this."

"To hell with Blanton," Greenwalt, commander of 11 Batt said. "We don't owe him a damn thing."

"I'll go along with Greenie," Tina Raines, commander of 9 Batt, said.

Buddy Raines, commander of all the special ops people, said, "I've got to go along with Tina on this, Dad."

"You know where I stand, Ben," Ike said.

Mike Richards, head of the Rebels' intelligence network, said, "There are other things to consider here. If we do nothing, once Revere has whipped Blanton's forces—and he will do that—the whiners, losers, and complainers in Blanton's army—which make up about fifty percent of his entire force—will immediately switch sides and join Revere. He'll promise them pie in the sky and everything else those types of I-demand-this and you-owe-me-that people want to hear, and they'll rush to join him. Then we could conceivably be overwhelmed by sheer numbers. There would be so many of them it would be impossible to protect front, rear, and flanks."

"I concur," West, commander of 4 Batt, said.

"Reluctantly, I agree," the Russian, Striganov, commander of 5 Batt, rumbled.

"I reckon I'm with Georgi," Jim Peters, commander of 15 Batt, called the New Texas Rangers, said.

"I know what it's like to be involved in a civil war," Pat O'Shea, the wild Irishman in command of 10 Batt, spoke up. "Uncle fighting nephew, brother fighting brother. Sister against mum. It's horrible." He looked at Dan Gray. "Do you agree, Dan?"

"Yes," Dan Gray, the former SAS man and commander of 3 Batt, spoke softly.

Jackie Malone, commander of 12 Batt, looked at the faces around her. "Does this problem even have a workable solution?"

"None to my liking," Cecil Jefferys said. "Thermopolis?"

The hippie-turned-warrior, in charge of seeing that everything the Rebels in the field needed got to them, and keeping track of where every unit was, shook his shaggy head. "We're damned if we do and damned if we don't. And we're going to be hurt badly either way we go."

Ben said, "How badly, Therm?"

"My people figure that if we manage to whip both armies, that is Revere and Blanton, we will suffer at least a sixty percent loss and perhaps higher than that. We're going to have a thousand-mile plus supply line that will be very vulnerable to attack."

"In short, we're fucked!" Tina Raines said bluntly.

"I should wash your mouth out with soap," Doctor Lamar Chase, Chief of Medicine, said. "However, I concur with your very brief and profane summation. Ben, providing medical treatment will be a nightmare. And we're only just now starting to replenish our supplies. Stay out of this conflict."

"Blanton has nerve gas and plans to use it against us," Mike Richards chilled the group.

"You know that for a fact?" Ben challenged. "You have people that close to the man?"

"Yes, to both your questions. During the affair at the old resort I managed to get one of my people into Blanton's army and he's now in G2."

Ben's face turned hard as marble. "Mike, I want a constant update on Blanton's whereabouts. Cecil, when you get back to Base Camp One, I want some of our nuclear warheads reprogrammed for a Doomsday Strike. And I want Blanton to know all about it. If he uses nerve gas against us, the nukes fly when he surfaces. And let that lying son of a bitch know that one will be programmed to impact with his nose."

"All right, Ben," Cecil said.

The Rebel commanders seated around the three old picnic tables were silent, all watching Ben. They knew that when Ben's face became set with anger and his eyes were like blazing bits of flint, he was unpredictable and could—and had—become terribly savage. Anything that threatened his dream of the Southern United States of America, with true justice and stability and order for all who chose to live there, regardless of race or creed, could turn Ben into an extremely dangerous person.

"There is another alternative that we have not discussed," Rebet, commander of 6 Batt, said.

Ben looked at him.

"Take out Blanton."

General Taylor wore a small smile as he walked into President Blanton's office. He carried a message from General Raines. Rebel communications had finally triangulated Blanton's position and sent them a message by burst.

"You have a message for me from the Rebels, General?"

"Yes. They say if you value your life you will cease broadcasting from this location. If they can triangulate our position, so can Revere."

Blanton flushed deeply, but said nothing.

"The second message is from General Raines, personally. He has ordered the recomputing of a number of missiles located at Base Camp One . . . armed with nuclear warheads. In the event you use any type of deadly gas against any of his people, he will, and I am quoting here: 'Incinerate your ass.'"

Homer jumped to his feet. "He wouldn't dare!"

"Oh, he'd dare, all right," General Taylor said, meeting the president eye for eye. Then the general smiled hugely.

"What the hell do you find so funny?" Homer hollered.

"How Raines knew about your plans to use nerve gas."

Blanton sat down hard. "We've been violated!"

"The word is penetrated," General Taylor said drily.

"Whatever."

"We know who it is."

"Shoot him!"

"Can't. Obviously his work is done. Captain Miller slipped out the back way sometime last night and by now has probably linked up with a Rebel recon patrol."

"My God, General! Are you telling me Rebels are *here?*"

"Oh, they've been here for about a week. They're all around us. They aren't doing anything. Just watching the mountain."

"Why wasn't I informed?"

"What would you do, Mr. President?"

"Engage them in combat and wipe them out!"

The general gave the president a pitying look. He shook his head and left the office, closing the door softly.

The mighty war machine called the Rebels had shut down momentarily. Ben was still undecided as to what to do. Revere was making no hostile moves toward Ben or toward where he might suspect the president to be hiding.

Ben had ordered his people up to his location in Indiana, for when he did make up his mind, he would move quickly. Blanton had not responded to Ben's warning concerning his use of nuclear weapons in retaliation for any nerve gas attack, but Ben knew the man was no fool . . . even if he was a screaming liberal.

His batt coms were fairly evenly split on the issue that faced them. But whatever decision Ben reached, they would follow. That was not in question.

And, as Ben had predicted, the punks and thugs and former street slime that had gathered under Revere's banner and tried to contain the Rebels along the Mississippi River had once more come together. Not as large a force as before, but so much wiser in the ways of the Rebels. They realized they could not go head to head with the Rebels. Not alone. They had to have help. But where would they get it?

They really wanted no part of Revere, for the men who had once more emerged as gang leaders realized that Revere had been using them. With the main force of the Rebels now east of the river, the gang leaders came together for a meeting in Nebraska.

The Rebels were aware of the meeting, but at Ben's orders, took no action. "I'm certain they're up to no good," Ben said. "But I don't know that for sure. Intel says they've harmed no one . . . that they can find. So we'll leave them alone until they make a hostile move."

Blanton's army-in-hiding, although not as large as Revere's forces, had spent their time training, and were shaping up to be a fairly well-organized force. But they had not yet been bloodied, so only time would tell as to their effectiveness.

The lazy summer days crawled by, with each opposing force growing in numbers, training, seeing to equipment, stockpiling supplies for the mother of all battles that each side knew was coming.

To the west lay the army of malcontents and punks and thugs. They had smartened up considerably. Their leaders had sent out teams to search for weapons, and had found them. What they couldn't find, they made. They could have used their abilities toward peaceful ends, but they chose not to do that. They chose, instead, to use their intelligence to forward a life of crime and degradation . . . which only proved what Ben Raines had maintained all along: most criminals will remain a criminal, no matter what society tries to do to change that.

Over half of those former thugs and punks that had elected to join ranks with the Rebels over the years had deserted, unable to adjust to a life of order and discipline and respect for the rights of others. Ben's analysis people had worked out the percentages, and the results were predictable. Three out of four simply would not be rehabilitated into any sort of productive existence.

"So what else is new?" Ben had replied at the conclusion of the study. "I've been saying that for years."

Citizens of the battered and war-torn and ripped-apart country that was once called the United States of America were making hard choices, carefully studying the various factions who were poised at each other's throats, ready to leap into a war that would, in all probability, last for years.

President Homer Blanton promised pie in the sky and something for everybody. His agents laid out the tired old liberal claptrap that they'd been espousing since the early 1960s . . . but whose programs had managed only to plunge the nation deeper and deeper into debt and dissatisfaction, seen the crime rate soar, and in general accomplish nothing. But still there were those who believed it could work. Among this group were people who in general wanted something for nothing; they wanted cradle to grave security from the federal government (which after the Great War did not exist) but at the same time their left hand never really knew what their right hand was doing.

Revere offered a totalitarian form of government, vaguely along the same lines of the Rebel philosophy. But most people saw Revere as no more than a smooth snake-oil salesman—the man who would be a dictator king.

The hordes of punks and thugs promised nothing except total anarchy . . . and they had their supporters. A surprisingly large number of supporters.

Which came as no surprise to Ben. Long before the Great War fire-ballooned the world into turmoil, morals had been taking a terrible beating, public education had turned into an expensive and terribly profane joke, classrooms were out of control and discipline was practically non-existent. Athletic programs seemed to be more important than education. In a vain quest to insure that everybody got the same treatment (something that Ben Raines called the Animal Farm Syndrome), many kids were spending more time being bused halfway around the world than they spent in classrooms. The liberal folly of the seventies, eighties, and nineties left two generations of unhappy, dissatisfied, poorly educated, and confused young people.

Ben Raines and the new Southern United States of America offered those who were willing to work for it, peace, order, education, values, jobs (for those who were qualified), security, and medical care from cradle to grave. Ben's system was not perfect; certainly it had flaws and he would be the first to admit it. It was not for everyone. The few laws the Rebels had on the books were extremely harsh and enforced to the letter. People with a give-me-something-for-nothing, or you-owe-me-something attitude couldn't live under the Rebel form of government. Rebels respected the land and the environment and each other's rights. Those who leaned toward criminal activities soon learned they had no rights. None. The Rebel judicial system was very simple: either you did the crime, or you didn't do it. There was no double-standard in the administration of justice. The law applied to everybody, regardless of race, religion, sex, wealth, social standing, or lack of it.

Ben was once asked to explain the Rebel philosophy. He smiled and said, "After all these years, if you have to ask what it is, my advice to you is to stay out of Rebel-controlled territory. Unless you want to be buried there."

# Nine

President Blanton was the first to break the silence of gunfire. Over the loud objections of General Taylor and the general's staff, Blanton ordered his elite guards to attack and take prisoner the Rebels watching his mountain hideout. Bad mistake. Those Rebels watching the mountain were hand-picked and hand-trained by Dan Gray and Ike McGowan. They were SEAL trained, Ranger trained, Special Forces trained, Marine Force Recon trained, Air Force Commando trained, and SAS trained. They had seen long bitter months (in some cases, years) of brutal warfare, most of them seeing it all around the world, and they weren't about to be taken by green troops, no matter how well trained.

Blanton's elite guards never came back.

"Where are they?" Blanton questioned, after twenty-four hours had passed.

"Probably taken prisoner by the Rebels," Taylor said tightly.

"But those were the best troops I had!"

"Goddamnit!" General Taylor lost his cool. "You're not fucking around with a bunch of candy-asses out there, Mister President. Those Rebel soldiers are hard-line, well-trained, disciplined, dedicated, tough-assed professionals. They've been doing this for years. Just recently, outnumbered ten or so to one, they held off nearly four divisions of Revere's troops. *Four goddamn divisions!* If you wage war against the Rebels, they're going to eat you for lunch, mister!" He paused to take a breath and an aide stuck her head into the room.

"Wonderful news, Mister President! Generals Forrest, Holtz, and Thomas have left Revere and are on the way here. With over a division of troops with them. They are all prepared to swear allegiance to the United States of America and to support you all the way."

"Thank you, Lord, thank you!" Blanton said earnestly, looking heavenward.

"They won't be enough," Taylor said. "Not against the Rebels."

Blanton slammed a hand on the desk. "That's it. By God, that's all. I've had enough of you. You are relieved of duty—immediately!"

"That suits me just fine," Taylor said tightly. "You sanctimonious dipshit!"

General Taylor was gone within the hour, taking two battalions of troops loyal to him with him. On his way out of the mountains, on his way to Ben's location in Indiana, Taylor was amused to find the entire contingent of Blanton's elite guard, limping back to the mountain hideout, minus boots and pants and equipment. The only thing hurt about them was their pride.

* * *

The leaving of the generals did not upset Revere; their taking over a division of troops did. But not for long. The division he'd been holding in reserve was ready to go and counting all the small units he had in hiding all over the country, he was confident he had enough men to overwhelm both Raines's Rebels and Blanton's FIB. Still, he waited to see what Raines was going to do.

Ben shook hands with General Max Taylor and waved the man to a chair. "Any relation to that other Maxwell Taylor?" Ben asked.

"I don't think so. Hell of an outfit you've got, General."

"Call me Ben. Yes, it's a good outfit. General . . ."

"Call me Max."

"Thank you. I won't ask you to fight against Blanton's . . . ah, FIB."

Taylor laughed. "He never did get it. Never could figure out what we were laughing about. Well . . . Blanton's not thinking straight. He's a man obsessed . . . but he's obsessed with doing what he thinks is right." He stared hard at Ben. "Like someone else I just met."

"This nation became too diverse for democracy to work, Max. There were too many dissatisfied taxpayers who felt they had no representation in Washington; and I'm one of them." He pointed toward his troops. "And thousands more just like me camped right out there. It would have worked if the original meaning of the Constitution had been adhered to. But it wasn't."

The career soldier nodded his head. "I know,

Ben. I know. I'm no liberal-lover. The left-leaning members of congress did as much to ruin this nation as the Great War."

The two men were generally in agreement. Ben said, "The troops you brought with you?"

"Top-notch soldiers."

"I'll give you two more battalions, Max. Eleven and 13 Batts. Keep that gang of punks and street slime off my back when the shooting starts."

"You got it."

"You draw up a list of equipment that you need, and don't short yourself on artillery." He smiled. "We have the very best."

Max grinned. "Yeah, I know. You stole it from us!"

General Taylor took the four battalions, backed up by heavy armor and artillery, and moved out. Once across the river, he split his forces and set up four resistance points; not so far apart that one could not quickly reenforce the other in case of attack. By doing that, he closed much of the route the punk army could take. The Great Lakes, especially Lake Michigan, blocked much of the northern route, the Rebel-controlled Southern United States cut off the southern route. That left the punks only a very few bridges over the Mississippi, then they had to cut south to avoid Lake Michigan. They could not take any Canadian route, for that would put them into direct conflict with Revere's forces. So if they wanted to butt heads with Raines's Rebels, they first had to get through the lines that General Taylor had thrown up.

Big Foot Freddie was placed in command of all the gangs, and he was having a hell of a time figuring out how to get across the Mississippi River without first tangling with Taylor's battalions. His recon people—many of whom were ex-servicemen—reported that Taylor had tanks and artillery up the ying-yang. The last thing Big Foot Freddie wanted was to mix it up with a bunch of main battle tanks, for he had nothing in the way of weapons to stop them.

He sat down at his HQ in Nebraska and scratched his head. "Shit!" he summed it all up.

Generals Forrest, Holtz, and Thomas pulled Blanton's army out of hiding and began whipping them into shape. They all had a gut-feeling that the showdown was not far off. Revere had moved his people closer, stretching them out from New York State down into Ohio.

Civilians were getting the hell out of the area in contention. There was a wild exodus of cars and trucks and motorcycles and horse-drawn wagons and buggies heading out in all directions. The mother of all battles was about to give birth.

Ben tried one more time to reach some sort of settlement with Blanton. Corrie got the president on the horn and Ben took the mic.

"Blanton, without our help, Revere is going to eat you for lunch. It's going to take him some time to do it, but he'll get it done. Getting yourself killed is not going to see your lofty ideals bear fruit. I don't particularly care for clichés, but half a loaf is better than no loaf."

"Will you and your Rebels swear allegiance to the United States of America and help me make this nation whole again?"

"No, Blanton, we will not."

"Then we have nothing left to discuss, Raines." Blanton broke off.

Ben had deliberately spoken to Blanton on an open net. There was no need for secrecy now, everybody knew where everybody else was. He handed the mic to Corrie just as she received incoming.

"General Revere, sir."

"Go ahead, Nick."

Hundreds of miles away, Revere/Stafford chuckled. "I wondered when you'd put it together, Ben. How you been, partner?"

"Better than nothing, Nick." He cut his eyes as Denise walked into the CP. She had lost weight and gained a hell of a lot of muscle tone during an accelerated Rebel training course. He nodded at her and she smiled.

"You want to throw in with me, Ben?" Nick asked.

"You know better."

"Yeah, I guess I do, at that. But . . . I had to ask. Ben, you're going to fuck up bad by fighting me. Surely you know that."

"We're both going to get bloody."

"Doesn't have to be, Ben."

"Sure, it does, Nick. You couldn't make it living under Rebel law, and I won't live in a dictatorship, and that's what you have in mind."

"Last chance, ol' buddy. You better think about it."

"I don't have to think about it. But there is something you better understand, Nick. When you come after me, you damn well better finish the job. For if you leave just one Rebel alive, they'll track you down and cut your throat while you're sleeping some night."

There was a long pause before Nick keyed the mic. "Yeah . . . I heard that about you folks. But, Ben . . . I have to take that chance. We all do. You, me, Blanton, and the punk gangs out west. It's showdown time. All bets are down and the dice are hot. So . . . may the best man win."

Ben smiled. "Oh, I will, Nick. I will."


Blanton had listened to the exchange in the comm room. He was so angry he was trembling. He clenched his hands into fists and cussed. "That arrogant bastard!"

"Beg your pardon, Mister President," General Holtz said. "But Raines is not an arrogant man. He is just a very capable one and a brilliant leader."

"He and his Rebels have fought all around the globe, sir," General Thomas said. "And they have never been defeated."

"And I'm not sure we can defeat him," General Forrest said glumly.

"Nonsense!" Homer scoffed. "God is on our side."

The generals all sighed at that.


"Go to middle alert, Corrie," Ben ordered. "Immediately. Everybody in body armor. Berets are stowed except for specials ops people and scouts, and helmets are the headgear from this moment on."

"Yes, sir."

He turned to Denise. "How was your basic training and indoctrination courses?"

"Rough," she answered quickly. "You people don't ever let up, do you?"

"We can't afford to, Denise. We're always outnumbered." He noticed she had been promoted to the rank of lieutenant. "Your assignment?"

"Eight Battalion."

"That's my son's group. Buddy. He runs a good outfit. Just be glad you're not assigned to Thermopolis's unit."

"Thermopolis? Why?"

"A little con artist named Emil Hite and his Great God Blomm."

"I'm confused."

"If you're confused now, I don't want to be around if you ever meet Emil," Cooper said.

Ben laughed and said, "Come on. I'll walk you over to 8 Batt. You look like you need the exercise."

Denise rolled her eyes at that and followed Ben out the door. She was unaware that it was a very long walk over to 8 Batt's billet and that this was the way Ben staked his claim. By the time they reached 8 Batt, every Rebel in camp would have seen the General personally escorting the pretty lieutenant to her unit. Not one male would have the nerve to ask her for a date. And Buddy would get the message as well. She would more than likely be assigned to the comm van and for the most part kept out of harm's way; as much as any Rebel is kept out of danger. Jersey kept a respectable distance behind the pair, her M-16 always ready.

"Hello, Pete!" Ben shouted to a tank commander. "Ready to rock and roll with Revere's boys and girls?"

"You betcha, General." He eyeballed Denise's derrière and dropped down the turret to spread the word.

"Sonny!" Ben called to a young captain. "How's it goin', boy?"

"Everything's copacetic, boss."

"All right." Ben waved to a platoon leader. "Carol. Your gang ready?"

"Chompin' at the bit, Chief."

"Keep your powder dry."

She laughed and waved.

Denise stopped cold in her tracks when she caught sight of a wild-looking band of motorcyclists, all working on their Harleys. Men and women, tattooed and unshaven and uncurried. "What in the name of God is *that?*" she pointed.

Ben laughed. "Oh, that's Leadfoot and Beerbelly and the Sons of Satan. Over there is Wanda and her Sisters. They used to be outlaw bikers who fought against me—briefly. They decided to throw in with us a few years back. Outstanding fighters. Leadfoot!"

The huge man straightened and turned around and grinned. "Yo, boss!"

"Ready to bang some heads, gang?"

"You damn right, General!" Wanda called. She looked at Denise and said, "My, my!"

Denise blushed as they walked on. "She is, ah . . ."

"Yeah. Bi. She was just kidding with you. Believe

me. Anyone of that bunch would fight to the death to protect a fellow Rebel."

"Hey, Little Bit!" a sergeant yelled to Jersey. "How's about you and me takin' a stroll in the bushes tonight?"

"I lost my taste for dirt sandwiches when I was a little girl," Jersey said. "So stick it up your kazoo, Bernie, and spin on it."

Bernie laughed and winked at the general.

"Political correctness is not observed much around here, is it, General?" Denise asked.

"More than you might think, Denise. Jersey and Bernie have known each other for years. And Bernie is a happily married man with four kids. What you just heard is a game they play. Political correctness got all out of hand just before the Great War. It became ridiculous. Believe me, if a stranger said to Jersey what Bernie just said, he would be stretched out on the ground now with a broken jaw from a butt-stroke."

"And Jersey's punishment for that?"

"Punishment? You have to be joking. No punishment. If he politely asked her for a date, she could either accept or politely decline . . . and he wouldn't push the issue. Common sense has taken the place of textbook law in Rebel society, Denise."

"I have a lot to learn," she admitted.

"Oh, not so much as you might think. If you made it this far, you're in. How many in your training class washed out?"

"About half. Now I see what you mean. They couldn't take the *freedom!*"

"That's it, Denise. For generations, Americans had Big Brother telling them what to think, what

258

to do, how to do it, what to eat, what to drink, how to brush their teeth, how to dress, how to drive their cars, what kind of homes to live in, how much insurance they should have, where to send their kids to school, what they could and couldn't be taught, etc., etc., ad nauseam. Then the speech and thought police moved in toward the end. Political correctness and all that. Here, Denise, the individual pretty much is in charge of his or her own destiny. You see, Blanton is fighting for the old democratic party ideology: control of every aspect of your life." He tapped the small red, white, and blue striped flag with the circle of eleven stars sewn on the sleeve of her BDUs. "We're fighting for freedom."

# Ten

Doctor Lamar Chase had flown in and was ramrodding and haranguing his medical personnel when Ben and Denise walked up to Buddy's location.

"Why don't you retire and go sit on your front porch in a rocking chair?" Ben asked him. "And stop yelling at people."

"Why don't you mind your own business," Chase fired back. He looked at Denise, then back to Ben. "Robbing the cradle again, eh, Raines?"

"Old goat," Ben muttered. "He married a woman young enough to be his granddaughter," he said to Denise.

Chase waggled his eyebrows. "Nice work if you can get it."

Denise laughed at both of them and Chase went off, yelling at some of his medics.

"I gather Doctor Chase has been with you a long time?" Denise asked.

"From the very beginning. Just a handful of us got together after the Great War and decided to form our own nation."

"I remember," she said softly. "It wasn't that long ago."

"The government, what there is of it, in one way or the other, has been fighting us ever since. And this time won't be any different. At least fifteen nations around the world are rebuilding, patterning their new governments after the Rebel way. That's got to tell an open-minded, thinking person that we're doing something right. But Blanton either can't, or won't, see it."

Buddy walked up. Denise noticed that the family resemblance was strong. Eyes, hair, square jaw. But while Ben was tall and rangy, Buddy's musculature was heavy, his arms and shoulders packed with muscle. Denise also noticed that the young man's expression was serious.

Ben picked that up immediately. "What's wrong, son?"

"We just got the message a moment ago. Revere's army is on the move against Blanton's forces. They should make initial contact in a week."

"Put all troops on high alert, son."

"Yes, sir. The lieutenant assigned to me?"

"Yes. I'll see you both later on." Ben turned and began walking back to his CP, Jersey right behind him.

"Interesting man, the general," Denise remarked.

Buddy smiled. "That's one way of describing him. Come on, let's get you settled in. Things are about to pop."


Indeed they were. Revere, showing his experience and knowledge as a commander, sent troops of his new division in a probing action against Blanton's army, holding his more experienced and battle-hardened troops in reserve. His plan was to let Blanton's army score a few minor victories against the inexperienced troops and build a false sense of superiority. Then Revere would launch a major offensive using his mercenaries and smash through.

On the same day that Ben learned of Revere's declaration of war, he learned that to the south, an unholy and unusual alliance had been formed, brought together by agents of Revere. The warlords and cult leaders, Al Rogers, Bandar Baroshi, Carl Nations, Jeb Moody, Carlos Medina, and Jake Starr, had combined their forces to fight against Raines's Rebels.

"Shit!" Ben said. "Four fronts. Corrie, get Cecil on the horn." Ben waited for a moment, then took the mic. "Cec, get some of your people on the road and block Jake Starr's movement north. Contain him in Florida."

"Will do, Ben."

"And you keep your butt out of it. You're not yet ready for the field."

"Spoil-sport," Cec muttered. But he knew Ben was right.

"Corrie, have General Taylor shift two of his battalions to stop this Carlos Medina person. That's going to allow some of the punks to slide through, but it can't be helped. They're not even a fair paramilitary group. These others are far more dangerous."

"I'm on it, Boss."

Ike walked in the CP and stood quietly while Ben

gave the orders. When Ben noticed him there, he asked, "What are we going to do, Ben?"

"Take out these warlords first. Then I guess we'll either fight Blanton's people or Revere's troops."

"Or both," Ike said grimly.

"Yeah. Or both. Probably both. Take two battalions and deal with this Jeb Moody, Ike. I'll take Dan and we'll handle Al Rogers and his bunch of kooks. Tina and Pat O'Shea can take care of Carl Nations. We'll give Bandar Ali Shazam Baroshi to Striganov and Rebet. Keep everybody else in reserve. Let's shake our tailfeathers, folks. We've got work to do."

Al Rogers had settled along the Illinois/Indiana border, stretching his people out from Danville in the north down to Lawrenceville in the south. It was not good ambush country. Ben rolled his two battalions, plus armor and artillery, up to the border and sent people in to look the situation over.

"Not good," the scout said, reporting back. "Rogers hasn't evacuated women and kids from Danville. For that matter, none of the towns along the entire route north to south is loaded with women and kids."

"He knows we do our best not to harm noncombatants and kids," Ben said. He smiled and turned to Corrie. "Tonight we move south. Start the Low-Boys and the tankers out now. Head back east, like we've changed our minds, and at 41, cut south. Cross over the Wabash at Mount Carmel and then we'll head north. We'll take Al out one town at a time, working north, pushing them ahead of us, main battle tanks spearheading. Let's go."

Ten MBTs, turrets reversed, hit the outskirts of Lawrenceville at dawn, and scared the be-Jesus out of the residents by simply driving up to the houses and crashing into them, tearing off porches, destroying barns and outhouses, and causing hens to stop laying for at least a week. No one was seriously hurt, but those on the outskirts of the town sure had any lingering constipation problems taken care of.

Before the Great War, Lawrenceville was about six thousand population. Now less than five hundred of Al Rogers's people eked out a living in and around the town. All that changed one quiet summer morning. The followers of Rogers got off a few defiant rounds, but hit nothing except the heavy armor of the tanks, whining away into the dawn. The men began throwing down their weapons and raising their hands into the air.

"The town is ours," Corrie said. "No Rebel injuries or deaths and only a few minor injuries on the other side."

"That's the way I like it," Ben said. "Drive us into town, Cooper."

Ben wasn't sure of the philosophy of Al Rogers's followers. So many groups and gangs, both left and right of center had sprung up during the year-long battle with Hoffman's Nazis, that his intelligence people were hard-pressed to keep up.

As Cooper drove slowly toward the center of town, Ben could see that whatever their beliefs, the men and women weren't faring very well. By the slight odor hanging over the town, he could tell that basic sewer services had not been restored. On the way in, he had seen that the crops planted were not pushing out of the ground as they should have been for this time of the year.

"A few got away," Dan told him as he stepped out of the Hummer. "Heading straight north."

"Take your battalion and armor and continue the push north," Ben told him. Dan nodded and left at a run, hollering for his people to mount up.

The Rebels had separated the citizens by gender, women on one side of the street, men on the other. Young kids were with the women.

"Does anybody know who is in charge of this rabble," Ben asked. A man was quickly shoved out of the line and marched up to Ben.

Ben towered over the man, who was very frightened and trying his best not to show it. "Why have you chosen to fight against me?"

The man would not reply. He just clenched his teeth and shook his head.

Ben grimaced. "All right. To hell with you, then." He turned to an officer. "Take their heavier weapons and ammo. Leave them .22s and shotguns for hunting, Let's go."

"Wait!" the man called as Ben started to walk off. Ben stopped and stared at the man. "It's a free country, General."

"It was briefly. Until the politicians and federal judges and bureaucrats took control. Then the Great War struck us. I don't know what to call it now. Pockets of anarchy all over the place. You really want to live the way you have been? Your kids aren't receiving medical care, the place stinks like an open cesspool."

"Blanton's gonna fix all that. He done promised he would."

Ben smiled. "A chicken in every pot, huh? I don't see any black folks among your group. You have something against black folks?"

"We don't have nothin' to do with niggers," the man said sullenly. "But you must love 'em. I see coons scattered amongst your soldier boys and girls."

"Mount up!" Ben called. "Let's leave these good folks to their beliefs."

"Wait!" the spokesman yelled. "We got sick."

"That's your problem," Ben said, without breaking stride. He was the last one into the Hummer. "Drive, Coop."

"With pleasure," Cooper said, and headed out, leaving the sad-looking group behind.

"They never learn," Ben muttered. "They just never learn."


To the north and east, Blanton's army had been bloodied and they held against Revere's just-tested new short division. No winners, no losers; both sides had fought to a draw. Out west, Big Foot Freddie had tested General Taylor's very weak and stretched-out lines and still the gang leader's troops had the shit kicked out of them. Far to the south, Jake Starr could not penetrate the Rebel lines Cecil had thrown up. Carlos Medina had tried twice to buck the Rebel lines in the southwest and after sustaining heavy losses finally said to hell with it and ordered his people back home.

"See if you can work out some sort of a peace agreement with him," Ben told General Taylor. "Tell him we'll leave him alone if he does the same for us."

Carlos agreed to that and one gang threat was averted. Taylor immediately pulled his people back to face Big Foot Freddie's people.

"Shit!" Freddie said. "That damn spic done give up on us. He turned yeller."

Not yellow at all, Carlos just accurately read the writing on the wall and wisely bowed out. He told his people, "I think we can live with the Rebels. They're willing to try if we do. So let's try."

In Illinois, Ben had smashed all the way up to I-70 and was preparing to move against the town of Paris. Al Rogers was just about finished and the man had sense enough to know that. He called for a meeting with Ben Raines.

There was both defeat and undisguised hatred in Rogers's eyes as Ben sat down at the table opposite him. They were meeting in a classroom in the old high school building.

"Speak your piece, General," Al said broodingly.

"Not much to say, Al. Just stop fighting us and don't throw in with Blanton or Revere or the punk gangs out west."

Al's eyes widened in disbelief. "That's it?"

"That's it. Live the way you want to live. I won't interfere unless you cause trouble for me or my people."

"You know I don't like certain folks."

"I don't care anymore, Al," Ben told him. "If you and your kind want to hate people for the color of their skin or the way they sincerely worship . . . have at it. But if you ever attempt to come into the Southern United States and try it, you'll find yourself dangling from the end of a rope."

"What you're doin' don't seem right, Ben Raines.

The south is gonna be a mixture of white and nigger and spic and Jew. Robert E. Lee is probably spinnin' in his grave."

"I doubt it, Al. I really doubt it. You should read more about the life of Lee before you start making statements like that." Ben stood up. "Our war is over, Al. Make sure it remains that way. Because if I have to come back, I'll kill you." Ben and his team walked out the door and into the clean, fresh air. It was welcome. Al Rogers didn't smell very good. In more ways than one.

"It must be a peace without victory. . . . Victory would mean peace forced upon the loser, a victor's terms imposed upon the vanquished. It would be accepted in humiliation, under duress, at an intolerable sacrifice, and would leave a sting, a resentment, a bitter memory upon which terms of peace would rest, not permanently, but only as upon quicksand. Only a peace between equals can last."

—Woodrow Wilson

# Book Three

# *One*

Ben sat alone in his makeshift office and read and reread those words from Wilson's address to the U.S. Senate. He had found a battered old copy of John Bartlett's *Familiar Quotations* and had thumbed through it. He was thinking of what would happen when this conflict was over. Ben was a dreamer, but a realist at the same time. He knew what his people were capable of. There was no way the punks were going to defeat the Rebels, no way Revere/Stafford was going to defeat the Rebels, and there sure as hell was no way that Blanton's army would defeat the Rebels. The troops of Blanton and Stafford were going to give the Rebels a hard time, a run for the money, but in the end, the Rebels would win. Ben didn't give a damn for the feelings of Paul Revere/Nick Stafford, but in a strange way he liked Homer Blanton, he'd seen a drastic change in the thinking of Senator Hanrahan, and Blush Lightheart was not a bad fellow—for a liberal.

Ben stood and stretched his muscles. He stood for a moment, listening. He frowned and turned out the gas lamp. He picked up his Thompson and walked to the door leading to the outside and cracked it just a bit. He listened intently. Nothing. No night birds singing, no crickets, no squirrels chattering. He gently closed the door and walked swiftly to the front room of the old house.

"Heads up, people," he said softly. "We've got company, and they're real good."

Corrie immediately got on the horn and put everybody on what the Rebels called QFA: quiet full alert.

"Nobody could have slipped through our security," Jersey bitched in a whisper. "That ain't possible."

"Revere's got men with him that are just as good as we are, Jersey," Ben returned the whisper. "Believe it. Some of the gang members have had hard military training in elite outfits. We're not perfect."

Jersey muttered something terribly profane under her breath and Ben smiled in the darkness.

"Now, now!" Cooper chided.

"Kiss my ass, Coop!" Jersey told him, then groaned, knowing what was coming right back at her.

"Any time, any place, dear."

"Screw you!" Jersey popped back, then shook her head, knowing she had just made it worse.

"I could fit you in tomorrow night," Coop replied. Jersey cussed him softly.

"Incoming mortars! Grab some ground!" a Rebel yelled from the outside, just about two seconds before the fluttering round from an old tube exploded.

"Light up the night," Ben ordered. Seconds later, flares blew the skies into light. "Jesus!" Ben said. "The place is crawling with bogies."

Ben spun around as the back door was kicked in

274

and leveled his old .45 caliber Chicago Piano. He held the trigger back, fighting the powerful old Thompson as it struggled to climb up and right. Ben put half a dozen invaders on the floor, on the ground, and dead and dying as the fat slugs tore flesh and shattered bone.

"With me, Jersey," Ben said. "The rest of you hold the front." We've got spies in camp, Ben thought, as he took up position at a window. At least one and quite possibly two of those on guard this evening were in Revere, or Blanton's, pocket. As much as he hated the thought, it had to be.

Then he had no more time to think about that as the action abruptly shifted to a fever pitch.

Those attacking the camp were wearing the same type of BDUs as the Rebels, making it doubly difficult to tell friend from foe. But that was also working against the attackers.

Jersey's M-16 rattled and two more of the unknown enemy went down in a sprawl. "Some of our own people are fighting against us, General," she called.

"That's what I was afraid of, Jersey." Ben leveled the old Thompson and sent a knot of invaders screaming, stumbling and falling as the .45 caliber slugs stitched them hip to head, working left to right. He popped a fresh clip in, his eyes busy in the flare-lit night.

"They're falling back," Corrie called from the other room. "Pursuit?"

"Affirmative. Small teams. Find out where they go."

"Done."

Ben walked to the radio and picked up the mic.

"This is Eagle. All batt coms double the guards and count heads. We've been infiltrated."

"We don't know how many of the dead were actually working for Blanton or Revere," Dan said the next morning at first light. "But what we do know is that forty-five of our regulars are missing. And many of those were on sentry duty last night."

"But we have no way of knowing how many others who are in Blanton or Revere's pocket are still in camp," Buddy added.

"We will before long," Mike Richards said, walking into the room.

Everyone turned to look at the chief of Rebel intell. "How so?" Ben asked.

"We caught three of our people trying to sneak out," Mike said, pouring a cup of coffee, adding sugar. "My people are chemically interrogating them now. We should know something by mid-morning." He looked at Ben. "You were right, Ben. Denise is one of them."

Ben grunted. "Yeah. I figured she was a plant. It was just too easy."

No one in the room spoke for a moment. Buddy broke the silence. "What, ah, do you intend to do with them, Father?"

Ben cut his eyes to him. "Spies are usually shot, son."

Late that afternoon, Ben visited the three spies, all from Blanton. He had placed Denise in Revere's army and the other two were planted several years back in the Rebels. The three were worn and haggard looking from the chemically induced interrogation. But they were still defiant.

Denise stared daggers and hate at him. "I assume we are to be executed?"

"You assume correctly," Ben told her.

"You will *never* defeat us," she said. "The democratic party will rise like a phoenix from the ashes to once more rule this nation and bring order and peace and justice for all."

"Don't forget a chicken in every pot," Ben replied. "Skinless, of course."

She spat at his boots.

"When is the sentence to be carried out, General?" one of the two men asked.

"Tomorrow. Dawn. I have chaplains standing by for you."

"Any chance we can make a deal?" the third man questioned.

"Maybe." Ben glanced at a guard, and the man was taken from the room.

Ben looked at Denise and the other man. "Anything else either of you want to say to me?"

"Go to hell!" Denise told him.

"Long live the party of the people," the man said.

Ben looked at him. "I never really understood that. How can it be the party of the people when at least half the people don't subscribe to your philosophies?"

"Because we know what is best for all," Denise answered the question.

At that most arrogant of statements, Ben left the room.

*** 

Denise and the man were buried side by side in unmarked graves. For a very brief moment, Ben actually contemplated finding a headstone and having the words, WE KNEW WHAT WAS BEST FOR EVERYBODY chiseled into the stone. But he quickly put that thought out of his mind.

The Rebels in the central part of the nation waited and read reports sent in by recon teams in the east. Blanton's troops were very slowly giving up ground to the superior forces of Revere. Fighting was intense at times, and Blanton's army was putting up much more of a fight than either Revere or Ben had thought them capable of doing.

"If that stiff-necked Blanton would ask us for help," Ike remarked to Ben one morning. "Would you still give it?"

"I don't know, Ike. A few weeks ago, I would have. Now, I just don't know. Probably not, since he sent those troops against us." He shook his head. "I just can't figure the man. He's supposed to be such an intelligent person, but he can't see that hundreds of thousands of people are violently opposed to returning to his type of government. He wants a return to the form of government that was slowly bringing this nation to its knees . . . if the Great War hadn't come along and hastened the process. He can't see that there isn't one nation in the entire world that is returning to the form of government they had before the Great War. He's living in the past and I don't know how to jar him out of that."

"Well, if Revere's army won't, nothing will," Buddy offered.

"I'm afraid you might be right, son."


Blanton had been moved south, to a deep bunker a few miles north of the North Carolina line. His troops were beginning to show the signs of weeks of heavy combat without relief, and Homer Blanton finally got it through his head that his people were not going to win this war. But no matter how passionately his generals pleaded with him to do so, he adamantly refused to ask Ben Raines for assistance.

Then the generals began to talk quietly among themselves, as Ben had suspected (and hoped) they would.

"Maybe six weeks if we're lucky," General Holtz said, just back from the front.

"Or unlucky," General Forrest added.

"A month, max," General Thomas said.

"I can't move the president," Holtz said, toying with his coffee cup.

"He hates Ben Raines that much?" Forrest asked.

Holtz shrugged his shoulders. "Hate? No, I don't think he hates him. I think Blanton is a raging liberal whose idea of government is meddling in everybody's business and running their lives from cradle to grave, and Raines is a hard conservative who believes that it's up to the individual to sink or swim on their own, and when you fuck up you pay the consequences."

Thomas smiled. "And never the twain shall meet."

"You got that right."

"So? And?" Forrest asked.

"I swore allegiance to the flag of the United States of America. But we don't *have* a United States. Those spies that Blanton planted deep in the Rebel movement were uncovered and shot."

"How do you know that?"

"Raines intelligence section sent me a message." He reached into his pocket and tossed three sets of dog tags onto the table. What he didn't know was that the owner of the third set was alive and well and being groomed for use as a double agent, if necessary.

"What now?"

"I just can't bring myself to betray the president. I thought about it. Hard. But I can order him physically moved to safer ground . . . if it comes to that."

"It will," Thomas said. "It will."


Ike had dealt swiftly with Jeb Moody, scattering his people all over the place. Tina and Pat O'Shea had brutalized Carl Nations, and the Russian Bear had dealt quite harshly with Shazam. None of the leaders had been killed, but their troops had been demoralized and for the most part, ineffective. When that had been accomplished, Ben had ordered all battalions, with the exception of 13 and 11, who were attached to General Taylor, to start forming an L-shaped line, running straight south along the Ohio/Indiana line. The bottom of the L stretched out eastward from roughly Evansville, Indiana over to the West Virginia line.

All the Rebels knew what General Raines was doing: he just could not bring himself to fire against the American flag. At least, not yet. He was going to Blanton's aid, whether the man wanted it or not.

Corrie got General Holtz on the horn, on scramble, and handed the mic to Ben.

"General? Ben Raines here. We need to talk about defeating Revere. We can settle our differences, if any, at a later date. After Revere is finished."

A deep sigh is difficult to scramble. Depending on the system used, it sometimes comes out sounding like a fart. "I agree with that, General."

"Just let me lay out my plan to you, and I think you'll like it. I give you my word this is not a trap."

"General Raines, I know it isn't a trap. I also know that you are a man of honor. All right, I'm going to catch hell from President Blanton, but let's meet."


General Holtz, commanding General of Blanton's Army, and General Ben Raines of the Rebels met clandestinely in a lonely forest in Kentucky. Each man brought one platoon of troops and their personal aides.

Holtz was shocked and showed it when Ben told him how he had repositioned his Rebels. "But my intell didn't inform me of this!"

"Your intelligence people probably don't know it was done," Ben said calmly. "We can be very quiet about things when we so desire."

Holtz studied the map and nodded his head. "I think I know what you have in mind, General, and if I'm right, it's brilliant. Regardless of what Blanton says, we'll go along."

"Good. When you're in place, we'll force Revere

to fight on four fronts. He doesn't have the people to do that."

The two men smiled and shook hands. "For the record, General Raines, I think our two societies could coexist very nicely together."

"Oh, they will, General Holtz. They will. Just give us time."

# *Two*

"Never!" President Homer Blanton shouted. "I will never agree with this."

"You don't have any say in the matter," General Holtz bluntly informed the president.

"I am President of the United States!" Homer hollered.

"That's right!" VP Hooter sounded off.

"Down with the military! Up with people power!" Rita Rivers stuck her lip into the matter.

General Holtz almost told Rita to get fucked. But he was afraid she might take him up on it. He cut his eyes to Blanton. "Mister President, with all due respect, without assistance from General Raines and his Rebels, we'll be defeated in a matter of weeks, possibly days. Your presidential guard can only protect you for a short time once Revere's people break through our lines. And when Revere takes you and your people prisoner, he'll either shoot you all or hang you. Now, am I finally getting through to you, sir?"

"I urge you to take General Raines's offer," Senator Hanrahan said.

"As do I," Blush Lightheart agreed.

"Ben Raines is nothing but a nasty, filthy, disgusting Republican pig!" VP Hooter dissented.

"And a honky, too," Rita said.

"Revere's troops are on the verge of breaking through our lines," General Holtz said. "We've got to act now. And I will. With or without your approval."

"All right," Blanton said, bitterness in his words. "Tell General Raines I accept his kind offer of assistance."

General Holtz left the room immediately.

"That decision will go down in history as the biggest blunder of your administration," VP Hooter prophesied.

"Oh . . . kiss my ass!" Homer told her.


It didn't take Revere long to discover he was in a box and the lid was about to be nailed down. He sure as hell didn't want to have to fight both Blanton's troops and the Rebels. He ordered an immediate retreat.

"Pull back to the north!" he ordered all commanders. "Get the hell out of this box."

Ben had anticipated that and had ordered his Rebels at the top of the L to swing east. Holtz ordered his people to swing west. Those moves left Revere with only a small escape hole and it was fast closing. Ben added five battalions of his Rebels, with armor and artillery, to Holtz's two regiments, at the bottom of the L, and ordered them to start advancing straight north.

The walls began closing in on Revere and he

could do little except watch as what began as an orderly retreat soon turned into a rout and his soldiers began fleeing north, trying to reach the dwindling hole to safety.

General Revere got out of the trap just in the nick of time and immediately began setting up new lines in southern New York State. He sent planes and dispatched trucks to bring the punk army of Big Foot Freddie to him. But all that move did was to free General Taylor and his troops, and Ben's 11 and 13 Battalions to beef up the eastern front. Jake Starr, facing a solid line of Cecil's Rebels, ordered his people to retreat back into central Florida. From there, they moved over to the east coast and boarded ships. They set a course for New York, or Connecticut, or some damn place. Just get the hell away from Raines's Rebels and somehow link up with Revere. Shazam, Carl Nations, and Jeb Moody and their followers were doing the same thing.

Cecil sent word to Ben that Florida was more or less clear of punks.

The defeat of Revere and his people was remarkably anticlimactic. Those troops caught in the box had sense enough to know that to continue fighting was foolish. They laid down their arms and surrendered.

"Shoot the hard-liners," Ben suggested to General Holtz. "They're easy to spot if you know what you're looking for."

"I can't do that!"

"Then you'd better realize that you're going to have to fight them again someday."

"Suit yourself," Ben told him. He turned to Corrie. "It's over. Let's go home."

* * *

The officers and troops of Blanton's army watched silently as the mighty machine of war called the Rebels began pulling out, heading for the new nation called the Southern United States of America. They had seen the Rebels in action, up close and personal, and they were impressed.

In Charleston, West Virginia, Ben sat in the den of a fine home that was now the temporary White House for Homer Blanton and rolled a cigarette.

"We don't allow smoking in these rooms," Homer told him.

"Get a fan," Ben replied, and lit up.

The two men sat and stared at each other for a moment. Homer broke the silence. "So what happens now, General Raines?"

"That depends entirely upon you, President Blanton. I'm going home to play with my dogs and catch up on my reading. Perhaps . . . return to writing. That's what I started out to do years ago, after the Great War. And I'll take some part in building a new nation. I don't care what you do, just as long as you don't try to interfere with the running of the Southern United States of America."

"Is that a threat, General Raines?"

"You bet your ass it is."

There were just about as many people coming into the new Southern United States as were leaving. Certain types, of all colors, knew they could never live under the simple Rebel rules of almost total self-government, and packed up and left for the dubious umbrella of protection of a more or less so-called democratic form of government. No one who called themselves Rebel was the least bit sorry to see them go.

Since for years Rebels had been seizing all the gold they could find, Ben ordered the money of the Southern United States to be backed by gold. They would not print more money than they had backing for.

"Ben," Cecil said with a smile. "We have *all* the gold."

"Yeah," Ben replied. "That is a fact, isn't it?"

Revere pulled all his troops across the border into what had once been Canada and began rebuilding.

Ben stepped down as President of the Southern United States of America and called for general elections. He threw his backing to Cecil Jefferys and the vote was very nearly unanimous. For the first time in any large, industrialized nation, a black man was elected president.

The first thing Cecil did was to name Ben as commanding general of the armed forces.

In Charleston, West Virginia, Rita Rivers said to Homer, "Well, now. With a black in power, perhaps we can reason with him."

Homer gave her a very sour look. "Cecil Jefferys is more to the right than Ben Raines. And don't kid yourself, Ben Raines is still the power to reckon with down there. Jefferys will see to the administration of the country, Ben Raines will see to the defense of the country. They don't have police, per se, down there. The army polices the country. Any time the army is the police, the head of the army runs the country."

"That's true if the laws are reasonably complex," Senator Benedict said. "As we tried our best to make them before the Great War. So the average person wouldn't have a clue as to what was going on. But the laws on the books down there . . ." He shook his head. "I don't understand it."

"But it works for them," Senator Hanrahan said somberly.

"Everything seems to work for them," Senator Arnold said. "Damned if I can figure it out."

"It works because nearly everyone is of a like mind," Hanrahan said. "But it isn't a democracy."

"It's a damn dictatorship," VP Hooter said.

"Run by a damned racist, honky Republican," Rita Rivers flapped her mouth.

But it works for them, Senator Hanrahan thought.


Indeed it did. By the fall of that year, less than ninety days after Ben had left Blanton in his office in West Virginia, the SUSA was getting factories back into operation and putting people to work . . . those who wanted to work and could do so without complaining and whining and bitching about it.

Hawaii had declared its independence from the United States and signed a treaty with the SUSA. Blanton was furious, but powerless to do anything about it. He had no navy, no air force to speak of, and his army and a few battalions of marines were in hard training for what they knew would be another campaign against Revere . . . sooner or later.

\* \* \*

After several weeks of rest, Ben took his 1 Battalion and headed out to inspect the SUSA, to "spread a little cheer and joy," he said with a smile.

"Right," Cecil said drily, knowing full well what Ben was going to do, and that it was going to be extremely unpleasant for anyone who did not subscribe to the Rebel philosophy . . . and there were many thousands in the eleven states who did not, and would never go along with the Rebels. They had to be either cleaned out with extreme prejudice, put on the road, or talked to . . . firmly.

Moments after Ben had pulled out, Cecil pointed to Striganov and the Russian grinned and left the office, hollering for his XO to get his battalion ready. They were going to bird-dog General Raines.

There were no undesirables within a hundred mile radius of the old Base Camp One; they had either conformed to Rebel ways, or had pulled out, or had gotten themselves killed when facing off against a Rebel security team . . . or in several cases, when making the tragic mistake of getting up into the face of Ben Raines, who was known for having an extremely low boiling-point when it came to human trash . . . of any color.

For several days, Ben had been studying field reports of hot spots within the SUSA . . . and there were literally hundreds of them. His team and battalion had been with him a long time and could read the signs. They were ready to go days before the official word reached them.

Ben headed south, scouts ranging out several miles ahead, and MBTs right behind them. For the first few hours, the Rebels traveled relaxed, for this area had been in Rebel hands for a long time, and the fields, recently harvested of their crops, were neat, the homes well-cared for, the people open and friendly and waving at the long convoy as it passed.

Doors were seldom locked in Rebel-controlled territory, for in the SUSA everybody was a soldier, everybody was well-armed, and crime, of any type, was virtually non-existent. Under Rebel law, a registered citizen could protect his or her property, life, family, or pets by any means at hand, including deadly force, without fear of arrest or civil lawsuit. After the first few rather violent months of birth, the Rebel-controlled territory—known previously as Base Camp One—had settled down, the word quickly spreading, and criminals giving it a wide berth. Now that the territory had been vastly expanded, the SUSA was purging itself of those people with no respect for one another's basic rights.

It was going to take the Rebels several years to do this, but it was something they were determined to do. And Ben Raines was flawed just enough to enjoy doing it. He had never maintained he was perfect.

Those who chose to live a life of semi-lawlessness, those who felt that they had a right to steal, poach, disregard the law, abuse their children and anyone else who had the misfortune to come in contact with them, live a life of ignorance, and in general contribute nothing to their society, had long ago learned not to live too close to any major highway, for the RSPs (Rebel Security Patrols) had a nasty habit of showing up at the most inopportune moments and rousting them out at the point of a gun and then reading them the riot act.

For years, the area outside of Base Camp One

was known as the Zone. Now the Zone was part of the SUSA. And Ben Raines was on the prowl.

Everybody knew that Cecil Jefferys was President of the SUSA. He saw to the political running of the vast new nation and kept things moving at an orderly pace. President Jefferys was everything an administrator should be, and everything the old Washington politicians had never been.

But Ben Raines, now, that was another story. This was Ben Raines's dream come true, and Ben was going to see it flourish. Cecil Jefferys was by nature a wise, prudent, kind, and giving man. Ben Raines, on the other hand, was polite to ladies, kind to animals and children, respected the rights of law-abiding citizens, and hated human trash . . . and made no apologies for it.

Just about a hundred miles south and slightly east of what used to be known as Base Camp One, the son of a huge and thoroughly disagreeable and cretinous individual named Robert Holcombe came to his father.

"That there Ben Raines is on the prowl, Poppa. And he's a-headin' this way."

Holcombe picked his nose and then hawked a wad of snot on the ground. "Wal, we always knowed that law and order prick would come snoopin' around, tryin' to run our bis-ness. Git the boys together, Malvern. We'll settle Raines's hash once and for all and be done with him." He glanced at a hound, heavy with pregnancy. "And kill that goddamn bitch 'fore she births. We got enuff pups runnin' around here."

# *Three*

The area that Robert Holcombe controlled had for years before the Great War been infamous for the quality of its dubious citizenry. It had been known throughout the South as a bastion for rednecks, white trash, incest, illiteracy, lawlessness, terrible cruelty to animals, open, sneering contempt for any type of law enforcement, and in general it was a haven for human slime . . . but the area, strangely enough was dotted with churches, and the majority attended them. The residents interpreted the Bible as they chose, with some rather bizarre statements coming from the mouths of the so-called preachers.

"Ben is heading straight for Deckerville," Striganov radioed back to Cecil.

Cecil smiled, then replied, "I guessed that was where he'd go. He's long wanted the time to clean out that human cesspool."

"Orders, President Jefferys?"

"Let Ben have his fun. Move in only if he gets in too deep."

Georgi's laugh was strong. "Da, President Jefferys. I will find high ground and watch the fun through long lenses."

"Poppa, here come them Rebs and they's a shit-pot full of 'em!" another of Robert's offspring hollered, from his perch atop the old water tower. Naturally, it was no longer functional.

"That don't tell me jack-crap, boy!" Robert bellowed. "Be a little bit more 'pecific."

"They's tanks and big ol' guns and all sorts of shit, Poppa," the young man, called Cletis, squalled.

The first Hummers, driven by scouts, entered the edge of town.

A citizen shook a double-barreled shotgun at the scouts. "Git your nigger-lovin', Jew-lovin', spic-lovin', queer-lookin' asses on outta here!" he hollered. "This yere's our town and we don't want your kind in yere."

"Yeah!" his equally ugly and yellow-toothed wife yelled. She spat at the vehicle.

"Boy, is the general going to have a fine time with these people," the driver of the Hummer said.

"Watch this," the gunner said. He was Kevlared from the waist up. He popped the hatch, stood up behind the roof-mounted .50 caliber machine gun, and swung the heavy .50 in the direction of the shotgun totin', bad-mouthin' citizen.

"Whooo!" the citizen said, and took off up an alley like the devil was after him.

"Wait for me, you son of a bitch!" his wife screamed as she went flapping after him.

"Hey, there, soldier boy!" a large-gutted man yelled. "You cain't come in here a-pointin' them guns at us. You bastard!" He jerked a rifle to his shoulder and the scout stitched him with the .50.

293

The force of the impacting slugs knocked the man spinning for several yards before he tumbled dead to the old street.

The street filled with angry, shouting, cussing, fist-shaking white trash. The shouting and the cussing faded into shocked silence as the street suddenly filled with 60-ton Main Battle Tanks, their 120mm guns lowered dead at the crowd, as were their 7.62 and .50 caliber machine guns. Rebel troops suddenly appeared on and around the tanks, their weapons leveled at the crowds.

"Jesus Gawd!" one man broke the shocked silence.

Women began hurriedly shooing kids off the street and back to their homes, dress tails flapping as they rushed about.

"Is we gonna settle Ben Raines's hash now, Poppa?" Malvern inquired.

"Hish your mouf, boy," Holcombe whispered. "You tryin' to git me kilt? And git yore brother Cletis down offen that tower 'fore he falls off and makes a big mess."

First Ben's personal platoon came out of the crowd of Rebels, followed by Ben and his team, Jersey's eyes shifting constantly. She'd faced rednecks and white trash before, and knew they were capable of doing some awfully stupid things. She had yet to meet one she trusted.

There were approximately three hundred to three hundred fifty armed men facing the Rebels. Ben said, "The first one of this rabble to fire a shot, kill everyone within range."

"Jesus Lard!" Holcombe hollered, jumping out to face the crowd. He waved in arms. "Don't nobody git no itchy fingers. Lardy, Lardy, Lardy!"

A scout came up and whispered in Ben's ear. Ben's eyes narrowed in fury. He nodded his head. The scout took off at a run, followed by a doctor and two medics.

"You, ah, got you some sorta medical emergency, General?" Holcombe dared to speak.

Ben walked up to the man and grimaced. Holcombe's body odor was fierce. "That once fine mansion up on the hill, overlooking the highway . . . that's where you and yours, ah, den-up, isn't it?"

"Yes, sir, that's right! At airs the finest house in this county, by golly. But it shore is hard to keep up. Why, I reckon if I had me a dozen niggers a-steppin' and a-fetchin' it still would be some job. Why . . ."

"Shut up," Ben told him.

Holcombe shut his mouth, but his eyes mirrored raw hate.

"There is a very old, and worn-out Labrador bitch back there. And some goddamn, sorry, pus-brain has shot her . . ."

Malvern wished he could suddenly be transported to the moon. Everybody knew the Rebels took very good care of their pets. And everybody knew that Ben Raines especially liked dogs.

Oh, shit! Malvern thought.

"That poor old girl, badly wounded, gave birth to her puppies, and badly hurt, managed to perform all the necessary after-birth functions and is trying to nurse those puppies. Did you shoot that old girl, Holcombe?"

"How come it is you knows my name, General?"

"I know everything about you, Holcombe. For years the Rebels have been gathering up police records and floppy discs and computer tapes and accessing hard disc drives from police departments all over the nation. You answer my question, you miserable excuse for a human being. Did you shoot that dog?"

"Naw. I din."

"She was on your place. So who did?"

"She's jist a goddamn ol' wore out bitch, General. Why make sich a big thing out of it?"

Ben jammed the muzzle of his Thompson under Holcombe's chin. Holcombe paled under his summer tan. "I will ask you one more time, and then I will blow your goddamn brains out."

"I din shoot the bitch!" Holcombe shouted. "I din do it. Malvern thar did."

"At whose orders?"

"Mine! I tole him to do hit."

"Why? Did she bite someone? Was she rabid? Why?"

"Hell, we shoot dogs all the time around here. We fight 'em for sport. Hit's good fun. We . . ." Holcombe suddenly realized he was saying all the wrong things to Ben Raines.

Ben lowered the muzzle of the Thompson and pushed Holcombe back toward the crowd. A Rebel doctor approached him and whispered for about a minute. Ben nodded his head.

"The dog didn't die, did she?" Malvern blurted.

"That wasn't about the dog," Ben said. He looked at Robert Holcombe. "Your sanitary facilities are non-existent. You have no medical facilities. Your children are poorly nourished. You have no schools. The list of things you don't have, but should have had you the least bit of discipline, dignity, pride, and concern for your children and for those less fortunate, is depressingly long. In short, you are not the kind of people I choose to have residing in the new Southern United States of America. You will leave."

"Haw?" Holcombe said. "Say whut?"

"I will put it in words you might better understand: carry your white-trash asses out!"

"Where?" Holcombe asked.

"North, east, or west. Make your choice. But get out."

"And if we don't?"

"Then you all shall be buried right here."

"You'd . . . *kill* us?" Holcombe stammered.

"Believe it."

"But there yere's our home!"

"Not anymore. You have two hours to pack up and get out. In one hundred twenty minutes I will start shelling this town." He turned to a Rebel sergeant. "Round up all the animals you can and transport them to safety. The four-legged kind," he added. Ben turned around and walked through the maze of tanks and Rebels.

The Rebel tanks and those not involved in the gathering up of cats and dogs and horses and mules and goats and sheep slowly backed up until they were clear of the town. Ben began positioning his tanks and mortar crews on the high ground.

"Poppa," Malvern said. "Do he mean all that?"

"Yeah," Robert said. "He means it. We'll leave. We ain't got no choice. But we'll link up with President Blanton's people. He don't have hard feelin's for poor folks like us. He's a good Democrat. He knows we cain't hep whut we is. It's the fault of rich

297

folks and sich. So-ciety made us whut we is. 'Tain't our fault. Folks like us got to have government hep. You 'member that, boy. Always look to the government. They'll take care of us. And don't never trust no Republican."

"Poppa?"

"Yeah, boy?"

"Whut's a Republican?"


Ben watched as the long line of vehicles began moving out . . . north.

"They'll link up with Blanton's people," Jersey said.

"Sure," Ben said. "We'll fight them someday."

"They'll spread the word that this has happened all because of a dog," Beth said. "They never grasp the big picture."

"Let them spread it," Ben said as the last vehicle pulled out of sight. "Burn the town. Corrie, alert the combat engineers to come in here with dozers, as soon as they can, and scrap this place clean."

"Yes, sir."

Ben looked at Coop. "How is the old dog?"

"She died."


"This can't be tolerated," Homer Blanton said to his staff. He had just read the reports of Ben purging the SUSA of any he deemed undesirable. "Those poor, poor people. I just feel terrible about this."

Rita Rivers, for once, kept her lip buttoned on the subject. She knew that the majority of people

General Raines was running out were the worst of racists. It had never been pointed out to Rita—and she would have denied it vehemently—that she was also a racist.

"We have to take them in," Homer said. "Set up camps to house them."

"Yes, sir," an aide said.

The military exchanged glances. They knew only too well the types of people Ben was running out of the SUSA. He was keeping the best and the brightest and handing them the dredges.

"Smart," General Holtz muttered.

"Beg your pardon?" Homer looked up.

"Nothing, Mister President," the general replied. "Nothing at all." Which is exactly what Raines is shoving across the borders, he summed it up.


The word spread very quickly throughout the SUSA, and rather than face the scorn and the guns of the Rebels, many people packed up and pulled out. President Blanton would take care of them. He promised he would. And they could live in filth and squalor if they wanted to and he wouldn't interfere. Not like that goddamned Ben Raines.

Cooper pointed to a large billboard. The original message had been painted over with the words: KILL BEN RAINES.

"It's so nice to be loved," Ben said. "Makes me feel good all over."

"How come we're not hitting much resistance?" Jersey questioned.

"Blanton is welcoming all the crap and crud into his fold, " Ben told her. "Making the same mistakes as before. The people who are leaving our sectors know that instead of making them work for what they receive, Blanton will just give it to them. Food, housing, medical care . . . the whole ball of wax. For nothing."

"And their kids?" Corrie asked.

"They will grow up expecting something for nothing. It's a terrible, vicious cycle. And the only way it can be broken is by what we're doing: slapping these people right in the face with hard jolts of reality. You can't force someone to learn at the point of a gun. You have to first ask them to learn. We've given these people in our sectors years to clean up their act. If they haven't done it by now, they're not going to do it—ever. I don't want these types of leeches around good, decent, hard-working citizens. They are a corrupting influence."

"I've heard you and Thermopolis argue this before," Beth said.

"Yeah," Ben smiled. "But he's doing it half-heartedly. He's playing devil's advocate. He just likes to argue." Ben laughed. "And so do I."

Those types of people who refused, for whatever reason, to respect the rights of others, who enjoyed lawlessness, who preyed on the weak, who expected the government to take care of them, who took away from society more than they gave . . . seemed to just melt away at the approach of Ben and his Rebels. They were flooding across the borders, north, east, and west. Blanton's administration, now in full operation—as full as possible, under the circumstances—was almost from the beginning overwhelmed by, as VP Hooter put it, "the wretched refugees from the dictatorship of a Republican madman."

Since a few blacks were beginning to cross the borders, fleeing the Rebel occupation, Rita Rivers could now stick her mouth into the debate. And she did. Often. To anyone who would listen. She formed an organization and called it, Citizens Opposed to the Oppression of Negroes.

The two black members of the newly formed U.S. Supreme Court, each with an inordinate sense of fairness, and also possessing a wild sense of humor, pointed out to Rita that it might be best if she came up with a new name for her group.

## *Four*

Conditions outside of the SUSA continued to worsen under Blanton's open-arms policies with no restrictions, while conditions inside the newly formed nation continued to improve. Bullshit artists, con-men, people who delighted in cheating others out of possessions, loud-mouths, trouble-makers . . . began pouring out of the SUSA. Many times the Rebels ran them out with only the clothes on their backs. And they immediately ran whining to agents of Blanton's struggling government, complaining of the harsh treatment at the hands of the Rebels.

"Those poor unfortunate people," VP Hooter said. "We simply must find some way to crush that terrible regime of Ben Raines."

Blanton stared at her for a moment. "I'm open to suggestion," he said, very very drily.

Hooter shut her mouth and left the new Oval Office.

Conditions were bad in those states that Blanton more or less governed, but it need not have been a hopeless situation. Blanton could have put together a bipartisan government and eased up on his left-wing ultra liberal form of governing. But he didn't. Within weeks of his new emergence, many moderate Democrats—including many of those who had voted for him years back—began to seriously question his policies.

The nation was still reeling from years of anarchy—the cities were in ruins, those factories still standing were no more than piles of rust. Gangs, from a few in number to hundreds strong, still roamed the countryside. Highways were cracked and pot-holed (they were that way even before the Great War, but money that could have been used to maintain the nation's arteries went to fund "great" art projects like putting Christ in a bucket of piss, sculptures of two horses fucking; building huge sports arenas where semi-literate, near neanderthals—if they had not been playing football or basketball and making millions would have probably ended up as muscle for the mafia, holding up convenience stores, or selling dope on a street corner—could blunder around, crashing into each other under the guise of sport while the nation's libraries were closing for lack of funds; and throwing wide the nation's borders for everybody who wanted a free ride from cradle to grave—at taxpayer expense, and hundreds of other congressional pet projects that finally bankrupted the nation), and good, decent, hardworking, law-abiding people were starving to death. So considering all that, what was the first official legislation President Grits-for-Brains signed into law?

Gun control.

* * *

Ben and his Rebels were in southern Alabama when Cecil bumped him, informing him of Blanton's first official act since emerging as president.

"He's in trouble already," Ben said, after reading the communique. "After all the nation has gone through, if that dimwit sends agents out to seize privately-owned firearms, a large majority of the citizens will resist." He paused, then smiled, his eyes brightening with mischief. He poured a cup of coffee and sat down, chuckling softly

"Uh-oh," Jersey said, watching the expression on Ben's face. "The boss is cooking something up."

Cooper looked at Ben. "You're right, Jersey."

Beth said, "This is going to be very interesting. You can bet on that."

Corrie anticipated Ben and made ready to bump President Jefferys.

"Corrie," Ben said. "Get me Cecil on scramble."


A presidential aide laid the paper on Blanton's desk and then backed up. Blanton picked up the paper and scanned it. He wadded up the paper and hurled it across the room.

"That goddamn son of a bitch!" Homer Blanton said. Ol' Pooter had officially been replaced.

TO ALL DECENT, HARDWORKING, AND LONG-SUFFERING AMERICANS OF ALL RACES AND CREEDS: THE SOUTHERN UNITED STATES OF AMERICA IS SEEKING QUALIFIED MEN AND WOMEN TO REBUILD THE COUNTRY. IF YOUR DESIRE IS TO LIVE AND WORK AND RAISE

YOUR CHILDREN IN A CRIME-FREE, DRUG-FREE, GANG-FREE ENVIRONMENT, AND YOU ARE WILLING TO WORK HARD AND RESPECT THE RIGHTS OF OTHERS, CONSIDER RELOCATING TO THE SUSA. IN THE SUSA, EVERY INDIVIDUAL HAS THE RIGHT TO PROTECT WHAT IS THEIRS FROM THUGS AND PUNKS—AND THAT RIGHT INCLUDES THE USE OF DEADLY FORCE. IN THE SUSA, THE RIGHTS OF THE LAW-ABIDING CITIZEN COME FIRST. OUR EDUCATIONAL SYSTEM IS THE FINEST IN THE WORLD. OUR MEDICAL CARE IS EXCELLENT, AND AVAILABLE TO ALL. WE HAVE JOBS WAITING TO BE FILLED. IF YOU ARE WEARY OF THE MEALY-MOUTHED, HANKY-STOMPING, WISHY-WASHY WAYS OF THE LIBERAL DEMOCRATIC PARTY, WHY NOT GIVE US A TRY?

"I hate that son of a bitch!" Blanton said, after retrieving the notice and rereading it.

"Honky, racist, nasty, filthy Republican!" Rita Rivers said.

"I think we should assassinate him," VP Harriet Hooter said.

"Say!" Senator Arnold said. "That's not a bad idea."

"I agree," Senator Benidict spoke up.

"What would Thomas Jefferson do in this situation," Blanton mused aloud.

For one thing, he wouldn't seize personal firearms, Homer.

*  *  *

Ben and team pulled up just on the outskirts of a small southern Alabama town. By now, Striganov was traveling with Ben and battalion. Ben had halted his people and radioed the Russian to join them. He knew Striganov was acting on Cecil's orders and could not refuse them . . . even if he had wanted to.

Striganov lowered his binoculars. "They are flying the old battle flag of the Southern Confederacy. The stars and bars."

"No law against it," Ben said. "But if they're holding people against their will, using them as slave labor, or have a closed society . . . then I suppose we'll have to do something about that."

Striganov cut his eyes to Ben. "It was my understanding that your government passed laws against the flying of the Stars and Bars some time before the Great War."

"They did. One of many very stupid laws pushed through by liberals. As soon as they did, I went out and bought a confederate flag and flag pole. Flew it every day. So did about ten million other people. Northerners, Southerners, Westerners, and Easterners. People who before the law was passed would have never flown a Rebel flag. White Southerners have as much right to be proud of their heritage as black people do to be proud of theirs. It's just a piece of cloth."

The Russian's eyes twinkled. "I think that on this day, perhaps only moments from now, your philosophy is about to be tested, Ben."

Ben wasn't daunted. "Years ago, the courts ruled

on the right of a private club to exclude whomever they chose. If that town is all white, and wishes to remain so, that is their right, so long as people of color who pass through are not harmed in any way, or denied emergency medical treatment or services such as food, lodging, or things of that nature. We'll soon know. Here comes a couple of vehicles."

The two cars stopped and four men got out. They held their hands up to show they were unarmed. "Welcome to Danville, General Raines," the man in the lead said. "We've been expecting you. I'm the mayor, Joe Story. These men are members of the town council. We know that you've sent Rebel teams all around the town; we watched them being positioned. And we know that some of your artillery has us zeroed in. I won't deny that we are well-armed, but we would be very foolish to start trouble with you. And we won't. As long as you don't start it with us. All we ask is that you hear us out. Will you do that?"

"Certainly," Ben said.

"Fine," Joe said with a smile. "Bring as many of your troops into town as you like. We've prepared refreshments and sandwiches."

"Take over, Georgi." Ben turned to his team and personal platoon. "Let's go, people."

What Ben saw impressed him. The town was immaculate. The houses neat and freshly painted. Lawns mowed. Stores open. Gardens well-tended. Children clean, happy at play, and obviously well-cared for.

"Pure white," Beth said, looking around her.

"Yeah. I see it," Ben replied.

From the back seat, Corrie said, "That's 10-4, Far-eyes. Recon reports no people of color anywhere in the county," she said to Ben.

"This is going to be very interesting," Ben muttered.

The town had been a county seat, and tables had been set up on the courthouse lawn. Plates of fried chicken, bowls of mashed potatoes and gravy, fresh corn on the cob, and gallons of iced tea were awaiting the Rebels.

"Do you want a food taster before you eat, General?" Joe asked with a smile.

"Oh, I don't think so," Ben said, filling a plate. "Should anything happen to us, in one hour your town would no longer exist, and every living thing in it would be dead."

"You do bring it all down to the basics, don't you, General?"

Seated, Ben began eating while Joe Story talked. "We came here from all over the nation, General. Right after the Great War. Nearly every state is represented here. We wanted to build a community that was free of gang violence, free of drugs and crime. Where we could teach our kids the way kids used to be taught, without social promotion based on color." He paused to take a sip of iced tea, for the day was warm.

"Good fried chicken," Ben said. "My mother used to fry it like this. Go on, Mister Story. I'm listening."

"The bottom line is this, General: we don't believe in the mixing of the races. Black people occasionally travel through here. To the best of my knowledge, no person of color has ever been abused. Nigger is a word that is forbidden in this

308

community. Black people have been helped if they needed it, and then told to move on."

"And if they don't move on?" Ben asked, buttering an ear of corn.

"We've never been confronted with that situation."

"And if you ever are?"

"Speaking frankly, we'll move them. Or bury them."

"What is your objection to people of color, Mister Story?"

"Not all people of color, General. Just *some* people of color. Their values are different. They worship differently than whites." He smiled. "Most whites."

"And those whites who don't worship the way you think they should . . . you have any of those in this community?"

"No, we do not, General." Before Ben could say anything else, Story asked, "What church do you attend, General?"

"I don't have a regular church, Mister Story. Haven't since I was a kid." Ben smiled. "But I don't condemn others for their manner of worshipping God."

"Let's skim off the grease and get right to it, General" Story said. "I'm speaking for every member of this community. Black people are not going to live here. Not now, not ever. We will not allow our children to be corrupted by their lack of morals, their terrible music, and their inferiority to the white race."

Ben pushed the plate from him. He had lost his

appetite. He agreed with Story only in that there were undesirable people among every race.

"There are several all-black towns north of here, General," Story said. "And you know it. You allowed them to flourish. Are you going to deny us the same right?"

Ben was silent for a time. There was some truth in what the man had said. "They are not all black, Mister Story. There are some whites living in those communities."

"Nigger-lovers!" Story blurted.

Ben smiled sourly. "I thought that word was forbidden in your society?"

"We slip occasionally."

"We're all human," Ben replied.

"You going to fight us, General?" Story asked.

Ben stared at the man. He was sweating, and he was scared. But he was also determined to stand his ground and defend his position. Ben could read that in the man's eyes. "No," Ben said softly. "Not now. Probably someday, but not here. For despite all your assurances, Mister Story, if you stay here, some day some of your people will slip up and do harm to a person of color. It's only a matter of time before that happens. There has always been right and wrong on both sides of the color issue. Many people just can't seem to strike a happy balance between black and white. We have, in the Rebels. But you're not really Rebel material. You couldn't make it in our army. And you're not going to make it in the Southern United States of America, either. There are a number of things that I could do. Cut you off from all aid and assistance from the Central Government. Throw a blockade around this den of

310

hate. But that would be a waste of my time. I can tell that it would be just a matter of time before this community collapses under the sheer weight of your hatred. So while we talked, I took action."

Story lost his cool. "You goddamn nigger-lovin' son of a bitch!" he cursed Ben. "I thought you were on the side of the white people."

"I am on the side of all people, regardless of color, who wish to live and work and get along with each other . . . and who agree to abide by Rebel law. I'm not going to have pockets of hate in the SUSA."

"You going to kill all the women and babies, General Raines?" Story sneered the question.

"Mission accomplished, General," Corrie said, and Joe Story looked at her strangely.

Ben smiled. "Oh, no. I won't have to. Your little town has now been completely infiltrated by Rebel troops. While we talked, two battalions of my troops quietly occupied Danville. We have seized your armory and your heavier weapons. I was curious as to the lack of men in the town. Your militia has been found, disarmed, and is now under guard. You and your followers can now pack up and get out."

"What!" Joe blurted, jumping up and looking around him. The streets around the courthouse were ringed with Rebels. He heard a rumbling and his eyes widened as Main Battle Tanks began rolling into town. He snatched up a hand-held CB from the table and pressed the talk button. "Jimmy! Come in, Jimmy."

Only silence replied.

"Ross!" Story called. "Come in, Ross!"

"Ross is preoccupied," a voice strange to him crackled through the tiny speaker. "This is Sergeant Davis. Could I help you?"

Joe Story sat down in the chair and looked at Ben. Ben sipped his tea and smiled. "Give me a situation report, Corrie."

"No injuries, sir. Occupation of the town is complete. No known pockets of resistance."

"Shit!" Joe Story said, his shoulders slumped in defeat.

Ben stood up. "It's been very enlightning chatting with you, Mister Story. Now you'd better start packing up. You have quite a long drive ahead of you."

# Five

Ben and his battalions followed Joe Story and his people north until Ben was certain the hate-group was indeed leaving the SUSA. Then Ben ordered the column to cut slightly west. He wanted to have a chat with a very militant black who had set up his own bastion of hate and filled it with white-hating blacks.

He wasn't looking forward to dealing with the man who called himself Moi Sambura. Ben had driven Moi out of one section of the country a couple of years back, and felt sure the man had been killed in the battle. Wrong. Moi surfaced in another location and once more began spewing hate. He had closed off his section of the country and killed any white who dared defy his orders to leave. Ben had run out of patience with the man. Moi Sambura's days were numbered.

"This the same guy we kicked ass on awhile back?" Jersey asked.

"Same one. Charles Washington."

"He must be a hard-headed dude," Cooper said. "Or just plain stupid."

"He's not stupid, Coop. He holds a Ph.D. from a very prestigious university. He just hates whites."

"Why?" Corrie asked.

"I don't know. Something truly terrible might have been done to him by whites. And as I told him before, if that is the case, I am sorry. But the past is done. It's time for a new beginning. I've given him more chances than I have ever given anyone else. That's over. And after we deal with Moi, we give Wink Payne another visit."

"You mean that ignorant redneck is still alive, too?" the usually quiet Beth asked.

"Yep. Intell found that out about three weeks ago. And not too far from Moi. Those two have a really weird love/hate relationship. I personally wish they would square off and kill each other."

"Let's finish the job this time, Boss," Jersey suggested.

"I plan to do just that, Jersey."

Moi and Wink had moved into the Talladega National Forest, with Moi and his people occupying the eastern part and Wink and his fruitcakes settling in the western part, with Highway 5 and a small river separating them.

With twenty miles to go before reaching Moi's position, Ben halted the columns and told Corrie to get Moi on the horn.

"The old and very young have been transported to safety," Moi told Ben curtly. "This time, the battle is to the death, Ben Raines."

"You're a fool!" Ben replied. "What the hell does it take to get through to you?"

"Come meet your destiny," Moi told him, then broke off.

"As you wish," Ben muttered. He ordered Striganov to swing around and get in position opposite Wink. "Leave the northern routes open in case they want to run. Wink will do just that; I'm thinking Moi will stand to the death this time. We'll open fire simultaneously."

Ben began placing his artillery for maximum accuracy. It was the middle of the afternoon when Corrie received word that the Russian was in place.

"Do we give them a last chance to surrender?" she asked.

"No," Ben said softly. "Commence firing."

Dozens of artillery pieces and heavy 81mm mortars opened up, hurling out death and fire and destruction. The rolling thunder continued all afternoon and into the night. Ben and Georgi had staggered their artillery; when cool-down was necessary, other pieces were moved up so the deadly barrage never stopped, giving those on the receiving end no relief from warfare's deadliest elements.

Rebel artillery saturated the area with everything at their disposal. The fires from within the war zone lit up the night skies. When Ben finally ordered a halt to the artillery barrage he called in PUFFs and helicopter gunships to add the next touch to this deadly game. It was midnight when he ordered a stand-down and without another word, walked to his tent, pulled off his boots, and laid down on the cot for a few hours of rest.

Ben was up long before dawn and the platoon leaders were waiting for him. A cup of coffee was handed to him. He took a sip and said, "Mop-up commences at 0600. First platoon, A company will go in with me."

Ben's 1 Battalion was known throughout the Rebel Army as the roughest, meanest, nastiest fighters of them all. First Platoon went beyond that. They were all hand-picked and carefully trained by Ike and Dan Gray. They had thousands of hours of combat behind them and fought with the cunning of a wolf and the savagery of a wolverine. They usually took no prisoners.

This time there were few prisoners to even consider taking. For reasons that would remain known only to Moi and Wink and God and the Devil, the two men had bunched their people up. Ben had no earthly idea why they had done it. But the artillery barrage had very nearly wiped them out.

"Must have been fifty or sixty people here," Cooper called, looking at what remained of a huge bunker that had taken several direct hits from a 155.

Ben walked over and looked into the blood-splattered and limb-littered cratered ground. It was not a pretty sight. "Bring some prisoners over here and hand them shovels. They can fill up these holes."

The Rebels were accustomed to Ben's callousness. The prisoners were not. "They were human beings," an older man, a follower of Moi Sambura, pointed out to Ben.

"They were idiots," Ben said, and walked off.

There was no sign of Moi, but Wink Payne had been found and brought to Ben. Ben needed only one glance at Wink to know the man was finished as a leader. He was jerking and twitching and slobber was leaking out of his mouth. The hideous and seemingly endless barrage had shredded the man's nerves. Ben had personally witnessed battle-hardened combat soldiers lie on the ground and scream

316

themselves hoarse under sustained artillery barrages. For there is no place to run, no place to hide, and nothing to do except wait for death to touch you.

Wink tried to talk, but only jabber came from his mouth. He waved his hands and babbled. A Rebel doctor standing beside the man looked at Ben and shook his head.

Ben glanced at a small group of Wink's followers, dirty and blood-splattered and badly shaken. "Take your glorious leader and get the hell out of here. Out of the Southern United States of America." He pointed north. "That way. There is no place for any of you here."

Two of the men stepped forward and took Wink's arms, leading him away. Wink Payne, self-proclaimed most holy and exalted leader of the Order of the Bedsheet was still babbling as he was led off. He had shit his underwear.


The crushing defeat of Moi and Wink just about finished any racist and separatist movement in the SUSA. Most of those so inclined packed up and got the hell away from the SUSA. Ben was fully aware that there would always be pockets of hate scattered throughout the SUSA. He couldn't stamp them all out. They would gather in secret to spew their venom to anyone who would listen. But for now, Cecil had asked Ben to return. The former CEOs and chairmen of the boards of a number of large corporations had surfaced from years of hiding and were asking if they could come into the SUSA and start over. But they were a little confused about the laws in the Southern United States of America. They seemed, so *simple*. Surely they were misreading them?

The CEOs and chairmen and presidents of several dozen companies once on the Fortune 500 were a little in awe of Ben Raines as he strolled into the large conference room. They were expecting a man in a three-piece business suit. What they got was a rugged-looking middle-aged man in old French Foreign Legion lizard BDUs.

Ben laid his Thompson on the table and said, "What's the problem, ladies and gentlemen?"

Cecil smiled and leaned back in his chair. He would enjoy this show.

"Charles Hays, General Raines," a man spoke. "IMB. The best and brightest appear to have all moved into this area. We'd like to have a hand in the rebuilding of this nation. But we just don't understand your laws."

"What is it you don't understand?" Ben asked, sitting down and pouring a glass of ice water. "Hell, a third-grader understands our laws. They're taught in school, beginning in the first grade. Along with values and morals."

"Ms. Cynthia Barnhart, General. RayTon Corporation. But they are your values and morals," the woman stated.

Ben cut his eyes to her. "It's the only game in town, lady."

She arched an eyebrow and sat back in the comfortable chair. Her eyes widened as Jersey nonchalantly strolled in and took a seat along the back wall, where she could keep an eye on everybody in the room.

"This is a private meeting," she told Jersey.

"Stick it in a sock, lady," Jersey replied.

"General Raines," Cynthia said. "I am not accustomed to being spoken to in such a manner . . . by subordinates."

"I'm not your subordinate, lady," Jersey fired back. "And if you continue talking down to me, I'll kick your hoity-toity ass all over this room."

Many of the men and women in the room struggled to hide their smiles. Cynthia Barnhart had been a one hundred percent bitch before the Great War, and the ensuing years had done nothing to temper that. But this lovely, shapely, diminutive, and somewhat savage-looking Rebel soldier wasn't about to be intimidated.

Ben stepped in quickly. "Let me explain something right now. You all may be the movers and shakers of the newly-emerging business world, but that doesn't make you a goddamn bit better than a tractor mechanic or a short-order cook or a private in the army or anybody else. Respect is not handed out on a platter here. It must be earned. A secretary is just that. He or she is not your personal *gofer*. You want a cup of coffee, get it yourself—or hire someone to do that."

"Well, I never!" Cynthia flounced about in her chair.

"You ought to, lady," Jersey said with a wicked grin. "Every now and then. It takes the edge off."

Ben smiled very thinly at the president of RayTon Corporation. He slowly shook his head. "You won't make it here, lady. You might as well leave now. You're just a bit on the pretentious side to fit in well. You'd always be looking down that aristocratic nose at someone, and someone, like Jersey over there, would spread it out all over your face."

"Then she would be put in jail!" the woman said, with considerable heat behind the words.

Ben again shook his head. "Doubtful. Not here and not for several reasons. To borrow a title, lady, this is a brave new world. Almost nothing is the same as before the Great War. It's mainly the little things, ladies and gentlemen."

"Art Grenville, General," a distinguished-looking man said. "American/General Motor Company. Explain those little things."

Ben smiled and his hawk-like features softened. He rose and poured a cup of coffee and returned to his chair. Everybody looked at Jersey, who had not moved to fetch her general coffee.

"She's my bodyguard, not my servant," Ben cleared that up. "Little things, Mister Grenville. Well . . . we're removing every trace of bureaucracy that we possibly can, in order to make life simpler for the citizens of the Southern United States of America. Once a person completes a very basic driving test—which is not necessary if you drove yourself here; that would be a bit superfluous, wouldn't you say—a license is issued. It's a SUSA license, valid in all states. A new license is issued only if one changes address. Every three years a driver gets his or her eyes tested. Once a person passes sixty, every year. We have none of those silly written exams because all traffic signs are universal here. When an income tax is enacted here, it will be a flat tax that everybody understands and that will be a burden on no one. In all probability, we will never have to have a personal income tax. You see, for years we've been sending teams of Rebels all over the world. They've been gathering up all the gold, all the silver, all the diamonds and precious and semi-precious stones. All the famous paintings and other various types of art. All the great works of literature. We have valuable coin and stamp collections that would boggle your mind. In addition, we have stockpiled massive amounts of uranium, lithium, titanium . . . you name it, we've got it. We quite literally have, if converted into cash, untold trillions and trillions of dollars in our coffers. We have enough engines and car and truck bodies and spare parts and tires in climate controlled bunkers to last us for approximately five hundred years. We have planes, ships, massive amounts of artillery and tanks, millions of small arms, and billions of rounds of ammunition. We have all the oil. We heat our homes by a very advanced technique using solar energy. Yeah, it works. We don't need nuclear power. We don't have to pay police, because the home guard is the police. Everybody in the SUSA is a soldier to some degree or another. I expect that by this time next year, we will be able to mass over one million men and women, trained and ready to fight to protect their homeland."

Ben paused to sip his coffee. "This is not a democracy, people. Not as you know it. We do have a president. The people voted him in. The people were asked if they wanted something along the lines of a House of Representatives and Senate. Ninety-eight percent of them said no. That ought to tell you what we think of your system of government."

"Hays Smith, General," a man said. "Telecommunications and Technology Corporation. Pardon my bluntness, but without a house and senate, how the hell do you enact laws?"

Ben chuckled. "I appreciate your bluntness. It's refreshing. The laws are already in place. And while they are not set in stone, it's close. Any new law has to be voted on by the people. And under our system of government, fifty-one percent does not constitute a clear majority. It takes sixty percent to constitute a majority in any election . . . on any issue. I don't anticipate many new laws being put on the books. Everybody seems to be happy the way things are."

"Because you all are of a like mind," Cynthia said.

"Exactly, Ms. Barnhart."

A man raised his index finger and Ben nodded. "Joel Greenburg, General. MicroComp, Inc. Like Hays Smith, I'll be blunt. This is a very restrictive society, is it not?"

"In some areas, yes," Ben admitted. "When it comes to crime, of any sort, we don't tolerate it. We're growing now, and suffering growing pains as we expand into all eleven states. But I assure you, that will soon end when those so inclined toward crime learn—and they will learn, believe me—that citizens of the SUSA are free to use deadly force to protect what is theirs . . . without fear of arrest or civil lawsuit."

"What are your restrictions on guns, General?" Joel asked.

"None. We're all armed."

Ben held up a hand to stop any further questions. "Let's have some lunch and then I'd like to take you all on a short tour. Look around and ask questions of the people. I think you'll be surprised."

"Or shocked," Cynthia added.

"Probably," Ben agreed.

# *Six*

President Blanton was shocked right down to his socks when he learned that some of the nation's largest corporations were planning to rebuild in the SUSA. That was something he had not even·considered. He looked across his desk at Cynthia Barnhart, one of the few that once headed Fortune 500 companies who had met with Ben Raines and decided not to move to the SUSA. What he did not know was that her decision not to relocate was purely personal. She hated Ben Raines and despised his smart-aleck little bodyguard. That bitch had no manners and no respect for her betters. Someday, Cynthia had silently vowed, she'd see that trashy little Indian-looking squaw grovel at her feet.

Dream on, Cynthia. Groveling was something that Jersey did not do well.

Blanton stared at Cynthia. The woman had once been a TV soap star of some importance and Homer just loved TV and movie stars. They were so . . . well, *with it.*

"And the others?" he asked the woman.

"Most are relocating to the SUSA. They seem to

like the prospect of living under a right-wing dictatorship."

To call the SUSA a right-wing dictatorship was about as far off-base as comparing an eagle to a parakeet. But a lot of people, including Homer Blanton, really believed it was a dictatorship. In many respects the SUSA was right-wing . . . but it was far from being a dictatorship.

Cynthia left the Oval Office to return to her office at the State Department. She'd just been appointed to the position of Secretary of State, a post she was certainly qualified to hold, of course. Homer was busy looking for a one-eyed, club-footed, speech-impaired, syphilitic of aborigine ancestry to fill the post of Secretary of Health and Human Services. One must be fair to all, right? One of his first appointments had gone to a former gangster, rap star who called himself Camel Puke. Camel had been appointed Secretary of Education. Which was only fair, since Camel had none. His press secretary—a ditz named Goo Goo MacGruff—had antagonized the rapidly emerging press corps to the point of open hostility. The newly appointed head of the FBI, Lance Loveless, who had been kicked out of the Virginia Highway Patrol's training academy because he could not bear the thought of having to shoot one of those nasty, horrible pistols, was pressuring the pres to call for an immediate ban on guns of all sorts. Anything that went bang or boom, as Lance put it. Blanton's appointment to the newly created, brand-new, by-golly, gee-whiz position of Secretary of GHE—Good Health For Everybody—was a former basketball hero turned coach called Hubba-Hubba who was eight-and-a-half feet tall, drafted into the NBA out of a Mississippi junior high school, and insisted upon coming to work in short pants, without a jock strap.

Homer just could not understand why his regime was not going well.

It's the caliber of people you pick, stupid.


Fall rolled quietly into winter and in the Southern United States of America, conditions were going so smoothly it was very nearly boring. Combat engineers were taking the ruined cities one at a time and demolishing what was left, then clearing away the rubble and bulldozing the area flat. The Rebels got in some target practice because the ruins still held a goodly number of Night People, and the Creeps did not look favorably on having their homes destroyed.

"Why don't they just move out of our area and into Blanton's part of the country?" Jersey questioned. "Since he loves all sorts of weirdos."

"That's a good idea, Jersey," Ben replied. "Corrie, get me Blanton on the horn."

She smiled. "He's not speaking to you, General. He says that since what you did by breaking away from the Union is illegal, and the Southern United States of America is not real, then you must not exist."

Ben looked at her. "He really said that?"

"Yes. According to Goo Goo."

Ben and team were returning from what had once been Birmingham. No trace of the city now existed. It was as if some giant hand had reached down from the heavens and ripped the ruins from the face of the earth and flung them into another galaxy.

Cities in the SUSA were rapidly becoming a thing of the past. The citizens had voted not to have them. From this day forward, smaller communities would be stressed. They were much more personal and friendly, schools were more conducive to learning, smaller towns much better to live in, and easier to defend.

Railroads were being rebuilt and people were happily discovering and using the much less stressful and relaxing mode of travel.

But outside of the SUSA, matters were going to hell in a handbasket. While unemployment was practically zero in the SUSA, unemployment was running rampant elsewhere. Blanton just could not get his regime running; which came as no surprise to anyone with any sense.

"It's the same old tired democratic party philosophy of attempting to do all things for all people all the time," Ben said to a visiting journalist who asked for his opinion on the difficulty the other states were having. "I don't know why in the hell they can't see that it just doesn't work. God knows, they've been trying to make it work for decades."

"Blanton swears that this new nation of yours will someday rejoin the Union."

"First of all, it isn't my nation," Ben corrected with a smile. "It belongs to the people who inhabit it. That's where both the Democratic and Republican parties got off the track years ago. They forgot the country belongs to the people, and the people have a constitutional right to overthrow or amend it if they so desire."

"Will you ever rejoin the Union, General?"

"No. Not as long as one Rebel is alive and can pick up a gun and fight. We'll fight to the last person and we shall never surrender."

"Hard words, General."

"Hard times, my friend."


Even though Blanton had certainly appointed some real squirrels to rather high positions in his newly formed government, somehow he had managed to get some good people in among the kooks and flakes and banana cream pies. His Secretary of Defense, Dick Penny, was one of them. Dick managed to gain an audience with Blanton, after having to run a gauntlet of what appeared to be teenyboppers staffing the new White House. He stopped by a young man who was standing in the hall, snapping his fingers, his eyes glazed. There was an earplug in one ear.

"Pardon me," Dick said. "Are you Secret Service?" He had to repeat the question three times.

"No, man," he was told. "I'm the assistant communications director. I'm on my break. I'm just groovin'. Everything is out of sight. Don't get uptight. It ain't cool to fight. It's right at night. You know what I mean?"

Dick stared at the young man for a moment, then slowly shook his head. "I'm sorry I asked. Excuse me." He walked on. He stopped by the Secret Service guard in front of the doors to the Oval Office. He recognized this man from the old days. "Don, is that hollow head down the hall representative of what's going on around here?"

"I'm afraid so, Mister Penny. You couldn't get me reassigned, could you? Like maybe to Guam. That would be wonderful."

"I'll try."

"Thank you. Go right in. But be ready for anything. Big Mama just left and they had a fight. She threw a vase at him."

"Did she hit him?"

"Unfortunately, no."

"Pity," Dick muttered and walked in. The president was standing by the window, looking out at the first snowfall of the season.

Blanton turned to face the man. His face was grim. "Dick, what would you say if I told you I was considering declaring war on Ben Raines and his breakaway states?"

Dick Penny sat down. Quickly. He felt faint. Lightheaded. He stared at the president for a moment while he recovered. "Mister President, with all due respect, sir, I think that would be one of the dumbest goddamn things you have ever considered." And you have a history of doing some extremely stupid things, he added silently.

"Thank you for your candor, Dick. But I think I will declare war on the Southern United States of America. Just . . ." He waved a hand. "Wipe them out. Boom. Bang. Kablooy."

"Ka . . . blooy?"

"Right. Drop a big bomb on them. Blow them all up. Pow!"

"We don't have a bomb that big, sir."

"Well . . . hell! Build one!"

"A bomb big enough to blow up eleven states without doing damage to us?" Dick shouted.

"That's impossible. Sir, Ben Raines has nuclear capability. You try something like this and he'll put a guided missile right up your nose!"

Blanton sat down. "You really think he'd do that?"

"Hell, yes, I think he'd do it. He told you he would. Ben Raines doesn't bluff."

"Then we'll use conventional weapons and infantry to wipe them out down there."

Dick longed for a good stiff drink. But he knew Big Mama didn't approve of alcohol. Somehow, he had to get the facts of life through to Blanton. "Homer, listen to me. Our latest intel shows that Ben Raines has over twenty battalions of the most skilled fighting men and women on the face of the earth. He has ten other battalions held in reserve. And his battalions in no way resemble our conventional battalions. Every person that swore allegiance to the SUSA is a soldier. Approximately half a million men and women. All armed. Heavily. All trained. Extensively. All the equipment we have we had to build from scratch because Ben Raines and his Rebels *stole* every goddamn tank and plane and gun and truck and ship and boat in this entire nation. He has an Air Force. We don't. He has a Navy. We don't. He has a Coast Guard. We don't. Everything we have is poised to fight off the war with General Revere . . . which we know is coming this spring. And you want to pick a fight with Ben Raines and the Rebels, who have never been defeated? Homer, have you lost your damn mind?"

"Bad idea, huh, Dick?"

"Terrible."

"Well, it was just a thought."

"Don't think it again. Ever!"

After taking his leave from the pres, Dick slowly walked down the long hallway, thinking: is the man losing it? Has the strain finally gotten to him? Or was that just frustration talking back there? Perhaps a combination of both, Dick concluded. Although he admitted that Blanton's seeming lack of basic common sense scared him at times.

He passed by the young man in the hall, who was still grooving, popping his fingers and his gum.

"Hang in there, *dude,*" Dick said.

"Yo, man," the assistant communications director replied, his eyes still glazed from the impact of the music he had plugged into his ear. "Outta sight!"

Dick walked on. Too many young people working around here; with too many idealistic ideas. It's going to end in tragedy unless Blanton comes to his senses and pulls in some older and calmer heads to advise him.

And it's going to end in tragedy a hell of a lot quicker if he ever declares war on Ben Raines.

He stood for a moment at the front entrance and looked past the wrought-iron fence at the crowds of people, all of them protesting about one thing or the other. Food, jobs, housing, medical aid, lack of heat. Dick shook his head in disbelief. There were coal trains loaded with thousands of tons of coal still stuck on railroad tracks, the coal there for the taking, and these yoyos were too goddamn lazy to go get it. There were thousands of long-abandoned homes all over the nation and these people were too goddamn lazy to occupy them and fix them up from the millions of board feet of lumber lying about, theirs for the taking. During the years of hiding after the Great War, Dick and his family had planted huge gardens, he and his wife and children home-canning the vegetables for consumption later. Why in the hell didn't these protesters do the same?

"We want money, We want money, We want money!" came the chant.

"Money?" Dick muttered. "From what? The nation is flat broke."

He chose to exit out the back way. Same thing. Protesters all over the damn place.

"We can clear you a way through, Mister Secretary," a Marine guard told him.

"Thank you," Dick said, his voice just audible over the angry chanting and shouting and cursing from the rapidly growing, unruly mob.

"Rabble," Dick muttered.

"Beg your pardon, sir?" the Marine asked.

"Oh . . . nothing. Just talking to myself. It's a bad habit of mine."

"I do the same thing," the Marine admitted.

Dick managed to get his ten year old car started and work his way through the demanding mob. They pounded on the hood and screamed obscenities at him.

"It isn't worth it," Dick said aloud, once clear of the mob. "It just by God isn't worth it."

He drove to his home in the suburbs and told his wife to pack up and get the kids. They were leaving.

"Where are we going?" she asked.

"To the Southern United States of America. I want to see if Ben Raines has a job for a middle-aged ex-government employee."

# Seven

The Rebels never stopped working during the unusually harsh and long winter that fell upon the nation. Road-building and heavy construction came to a virtual halt, but everything else continued, in many cases, around the clock. Ben knew fully well that Revere was going to launch a springtime offensive against Blanton, and he knew, with a warrior's senses, that Blanton's forces were going to be defeated. It was only logical to assume that once the other thirty-eight states were in the control of Revere, the SUSA would be next. And that would be the mother of all battles.

And Ben had made up his mind on another matter: this time, he would not come to the aid of Blanton. If Blanton and his people sought asylum inside the SUSA, that would be granted. But the Rebels were staying out of the fight . . . unless Blanton agreed to recognize the SUSA as a separate and sovereign nation.

Ben had ordered many of the bridges and overpasses leading into the SUSA blown, and blockaded many of the secondary highways, thereby cutting down the routes any enemy could use getting into the new nation.

Cecil had welcomed Dick Penny and family, and immediately put him to work in the SUSA's fledgling state department, naming the man Secretary of State.

Dick had never met Ben Raines, but during the first few seconds of their first meeting, he realized why the man had been able to accomplish so much. Ben Raines exuded power and confidence. His very presence filled a room. And Dick Penny also sensed, quite correctly, that Ben was a very dangerous man.

But Ben was smiles and handshakes on that first, all important meeting . . . for a few seconds. Then he waved Dick to a chair and got right down to business.

"Is Blanton going to make war on us, Dick?"

"He very much would like to, General," Dick leveled with him.. "But I think I talked him out of it."

"It's going to be a moot point later on this spring, anyway," Ben said, with a shrug of his shoulders. "Because Nick Stafford is going to roll right over him. The man who goes by the name of General Revere."

"Yes. You . . . we . . . are not going to back President Blanton?"

"No," Ben said firmly. "Not the committing of troops. Not unless he recognizes us as a legal and separate nation."

"He's not a bad person, General."

"Oh, I know that. He's fairly likeable . . . for a liberal democrat. Hanrahan, Lightheart . . . they're all right. But I'm not going to commit my people to aid a political party whose views I am diametrically opposed to." He shook his head. "Not a second time. Not unless my conditions are met."

Cecil had warned Secretary Penny of Ben's decision, and the man offered no argument on the subject. He was well aware that Ben Raines had offered to sign a defense pact with Blanton—in return for Blanton recognizing the SUSA as a separate nation—and that Blanton had tossed it right back in his face. Another incredibly stupid act on the man's part.

"You and your wife and family getting settled in, Dick?" Ben asked, and Dick knew then the matter of Blanton's fate was indeed closed.

"Oh, yes. Thank you. But we're all having somewhat of a difficult time adjusting to the land of peace and plenty after what we've been living in for years. Both of us still go from door to door before retiring for the evening, to see if they are locked."

"It's a hard habit to break, and you're not alone. A lot of people still lock their doors at night."

"Do you, General?"

Ben smiled. "No. But I have several dogs and they've very good at alerting me. And," he sighed, "my area is patrolled quite heavily at all times."

"That's the price of fame, General," Dick said.

Ben laughed and stood up. "No, Dick. That's the price one pays for having two or three million people wanting to kill you."


Winter began loosening its icy grip on the nation and Blanton's military leaders braced for General Revere's assault. All winter long Revere had been positioning his troops and tanks and artillery and

Blanton's generals had watched with an increasing feeling of doom. There was no way their smaller and inexperienced army was going to stop Revere and his hard core of mercenaries. The best they could hope for was a delaying tactic, during which time Homer Blanton and staff could be spirited off to safety.

"No!" Blanton said, most emphatically. "I will not ask for asylum in the SUSA. That is absolutely, positively out of the question. I will not go groveling to Ben Raines. Besides, the SUSA does not officially exist. I do not recognize that breakaway nation."

"Homer," one of his top people said, struggling to keep his temper in check. "I know it's difficult for you, but will you stop being such an asshole." That got Blanton's attention. "This Revere/Stafford person will not attack the SUSA. Not until they deal with us. And they will. The Rebels are just too strong a force. You've got to be a big enough man to put pride and stubbornness aside and think about the good of the country."

"Asshole?" Blanton whispered. "You think I'm an asshole, Willie?"

"At times, yes."

"I could not bear the thought of living under a dictatorship," VP Hooter said.

"Horseshit!" Senator Hanrahan spoke up. "What do you think we held the American people under for years before the Great War?"

"It was not a dictatorship, Senator," Homer said.

"The hell it wasn't. We taxed them to the breaking point to pay for programs the majority didn't want, and when they objected and finally spoke up about it, refusing to pay more than what they felt

336

was their fair share, we seized their possessions and/or put them in prison. During your administration—and I accept my part of the blame for it—the dictatorial powers of the IRS bankrupted and made homeless untold thousands of decent, hardworking American citizens. You issued orders—and the congress went along with it—to spy on the people, bug their phones and personal computers, stifle freedom of speech, and you stuffed unwanted programs and legislation down their throats, and in effect told the majority of American citizens that if they didn't like it, that was just too goddamn bad. And you have the audacity to sit there and proclaim that you didn't run your own petty and oftentimes petulant little dictatorship. I say again: horseshit!"

"What's changed you so, Senator," the president asked. "What's happened to you?"

"I'm an old man, Homer. A worn-out old liberal who is tired of dodging the growing number of potholes in a political road that we should have abandoned several decades ago. I'm not saying that Ben Raines is one hundred percent correct. No political philosophy ever is. Ours certainly wasn't, and if you haven't seen that by now—and you obviously haven't—then I feel sorry for you." He stood up and walked to the door of the room. "I'm leaving, Homer. And I'm taking several of your key staff people and senators and representatives with me. We're going down to join Ben Raines. And if you have the sense God gave a goose, you'll do the same. Goodbye, Homer."

Senator Hanrahan opened the door, walked out, and did not look back.

"We'll fight the mongrel hordes descending

upon us!" Rita Rivers bellowed, jumping up and marching around the room, hollering at the top of her voice. She sang a verse of "God Bless America." In rap. Kate Smith was probably spinning in her grave.

"Oh, no!" Blush Lightheart said, covering his ears.

"Right on, sister!" VP Hooter hollered, jumping up to march around the room.

"Wait a minute, Senator Hanrahan!" Blush hollered. "I'm coming with you." He ran out of the room.

"We'll fight them and defeat them!" Rita squalled. "Damn filthy honky republicans. The democratic liberal way is the only right and true and just way. Power to the people. Together we'll carry the banner of liberalism into battle and be victorious over the nasty, filthy republican right. Our slogan will be a chicken in every pot."

The President of the United States took his hands from over his ears and looked at the woman. He sighed and said, "Oh . . . fuck you, Rita!"

"Now?" she asked.


Cecil walked into Ben's office. Ben was doing paperwork and he was frowning. He hated any and all types of paperwork. Cecil was wearing a smile that a charge of C-4 would not have been able to remove. Ben looked up at his old friend. "Want to tell me the joke, Cec?"

"We won, Ben?"

"Won what?"

He held up a paper. "Blanton has agreed to sign

treaties with us. He will officially recognize the SUSA as a separate and sovereign nation."

Ben took the paper and put on his reading glasses, quickly scanning the document. He sighed and removed his glasses, laying the paper aside. "It's a desperation move, Cec. You know that. He wants us to fight his wars for him. That's all this amounts to. He's a goddamn liberal democrat. He'll never keep his word after the smoke clears."

"I beg to differ, sir," the voice came from the open doorway.

Ben looked up to see Hanrahan and Lightheart standing there. He smiled and stood up, shaking hands with the men. "Did you two bring this document?"

"Yes, we did, Ben," Blush said. "And Blanton means every word of it. But there is more. He has agreed to give you total command of our army. The generals agreed to that. Once Revere is defeated, our two nations will exist side by side. We will sign a mutually agreed upon non-aggression pact and work out a free trade agreement. The United Nations is reconvening. They have agreed to the recognition of the SUSA as a separate nation. You've won, Ben. You've won."

There was joy in the SUSA, but it was tempered with the knowledge that a hard battle lay between them and full acceptance as a nation. Many Rebels would die. But freedom has never come cheaply. Members of the Rebel Army reached for their weapons and made ready for war.

Cecil and his staff and Ben and his team flew

into Charleston, West Virginia and were escorted to the White House. Cecil and Homer shook hands warmly. Ben did not offer his hand to Homer Blanton and the President of the United States did not offer his hand to Ben Raines. The two men didn't like each other, didn't trust each other, and that was that.

Rita Rivers and VP Hooter glared daggers at Ben, and he pointedly ignored them.

Ben turned to the large group in the room and said, "I would like for President Jefferys and I to meet privately with President Blanton and VP Hooter."

"Now see here!" Rita protested.

"Please, Ms. Rivers," Blanton quieted her. "All of you. Leave the four of us alone."

Blanton rang for coffee and when that was served and the door closed behind the aide, he looked at Ben. "It's your call, General."

"President Blanton," Ben said, after taking a sip of coffee. "You and I will probably never get along. I think you sense that as strongly as I do. But I really feel that you, and Vice President Hooter, do not truly understand the philosophies of the Rebel government. There has been so much misinformation spread about us, that your confusion is understandable."

Ben leaned forward. "I wanted Cecil to be the one to tell you these things, but he insisted that I do it. Perhaps in the hopes that you and I could become, if not friends, at least not enemies. I don't know. But I'll give this my best effort.

"President Blanton, much of what you and all the other liberals in government tried to do before the Great War was admirable. Only a very callous or shortsighted fool would deny that. It was very impractical, but admirable. But you were trying, and will probably continue to try, to buck human nature. There will always be poor people, Mr. Blanton. That's the way life is. In any land, on any continent. It has been that way since the beginning of time and will remain that way until God takes a hand and fulfills His promise to destroy the earth and all on it.

"There will be those who will work hard all their lives and never have anything to show for it. There will be hopelessness and despair, tragedy and misfortune, needless suffering of good decent people, and the most terrible and heinous of crimes committed against the weak. There will be winners and there will be losers.

"Mr. Blanton, we, as leaders, can only point people in the right direction, perhaps provide them with some incentive and material, and then turn them loose and hope for the best. We cannot be all things to all people, all the time. Not at the expense of others who can ill afford to foot the bills.

"When people take away from society more than they give, in the form of criminal acts, and do it time and time again, I see no point in keeping those people alive. Not at taxpayer expense. This time around we didn't kill them. I just ran them out and handed them to you."

"I know," Blanton said, very drily.

Cecil had to duck his head to hide his smile at that.

"Now, Mr. Blanton, what you do with those types of people is your problem. You and the rest of the old hanky-stomping, weepy, take-a-punk-to-lunch, soft-line liberal party helped create them, so you can have them. If they come back into the SUSA with anything else on their minds than obeying the law and working hard and respecting the rights of others, we'll bury them.

"Mr. Blanton, I'm telling you all this not to chastise, but to warn you, to urge you, that if you don't adopt some domestic policy very similar to ours, your emerging nation is not going to make it. You see and hear all those protesters outside this office? Why aren't they out working on a home to live in? Gathering up free coal or cutting wood or gathering up scraps of wood to burn? There are millions of head of cattle just running loose all across this nation. They belong to no one. Why don't they go gather up some and start a small ranch and farm? There are literally billions of chickens running loose, laying eggs all over the place. There is no reason for any of those people out there to be hungry. But they're waiting on the government—your government—to do it for them.

"Now there are old people out there who do need help, and they genuinely deserve that help, because you and all the other politicians sure as hell tore the taxes out of them for many, many years. There are very young people and some disabled people in that crowd. They, too, do deserve government help. And you don't need forty-seven house and senate committees to do that. And the rest of those people, Mr. Blanton—they're losers. They've been losers all their lives and they'll die losers. They think nothing is ever their fault. It's always the fault of someone else. The boss didn't like them, he or she picked on them. They didn't get promoted because of this, that, or the other reason. But *never* was it their fault. And if they do find work, they will do just enough to get by. Never more than their share.

"I feel sorry for you, Mr. Blanton, because we've handed you the dregs of society. We've handed you the whiners, complainers, the chronic whip-lash and bad-backers. We've handed you the slackers and the dullards and the underachievers. Those are some of the types of people who are attracted to your form of government. The other type is the high-idealed, idealistic, and out of touch with reality person. They're the smart ones. They have lots of book sense but not nearly enough common sense. They're the ones who will form your staff and make up your house and senate. They will write your speeches and pass the legislation and implement all the glorious and totally unworkable social programs that will lead your government right back to the way it was when you first took office, a decade ago. And you know where that led.

"So, Mister President, here we are. The Eagle and the Dove. The nation that I helped create is going to fly. We're going to soar. We're already so far ahead of your nation that you'll never catch up, not unless you start to copy our ways. And I urge you to do that."

Ben stood up and looked at Homer Blanton. "That's what I came to say, sir. You and Cecil work out all the formalities between our two countries. But you'll have to excuse me; I have a war to fight."

"My war, you mean," Blanton words were softly offered.

Ben nodded his head and walked to the door. There, he turned around. "That's about the size of it, Homer."

# Eight

Far to the north of the new White House in West Virginia, General Revere sat behind the desk in his headquarters building and mulled over the new situation that faced him. It was a brand new ball game now, for sure. The prospect of facing twenty battalions of combat-tested and proven Rebels, plus massive armor and artillery, soured his stomach.

The signing of treaties between the USA and the SUSA had thrown a monkey wrench into Revere's plans. That plan had been to defeat Blanton's poorly-trained and ill-equipped army and then turn the hundreds of thousands of malcontents and whiners and complainers that Ben Raines had tossed out of the SUSA loose against Raines. They would overwhelm the Rebels by sheer numbers, then Revere's troops, coming in force right behind them, would mop it all up.

Now the baby just got tossed out with the bathwater and Revere was back to square one.

Revere's army was larger than the Rebels and Blanton's troops combined, for thousands of foreign mercenaries had arrived to join his forces. But when facing the Rebels, size did not count for all that much. Khamsin, the Hot Wind from the desert, had learned that. So had Kenny Parr and Lan Vilar and Matt Callahan and the Night People and Sam Hartline and all the others who had faced Raines's Rebels over the bloody years. Those people now lay rotting in their graves and Ben Raines was walking tall.

"Shit!" Revere swore softly, as the door to his office opened and the commanding officer of his intelligence section walked in and took a seat. Revere lifted his eyes to the man. "I suppose you've brought me bad news," he stated, not putting it as a question.

The man lifted a folder. "Analysis just finished working this up. If we tangle with Ben Raines head to head in a conventional ground war, our losses would be unacceptable. They would be even worse if we tried to fight him using unconventional tactics. He is considered the world's foremost expert in down and dirty guerrilla warfare."

Revere sighed. The news was not unexpected. "Give it all to me."

"We fall back across the old Canadian border, into the areas that are secure to us, and reopen the factories there while we continue to build in strength. If we run the war factories around the clock, seven days a week, in a year's time we'll have the armor and artillery to successfully face and defeat Ben Raines and Blanton's forces."

Revere grunted. "Your *experts* have taken into consideration that during that year's time, Raines and Blanton will be doing the same thing and growing stronger?"

"Yes. But only Raines will be doing that. Blanton's main thrust will be concentrating on social programs. Blanton is not nearly as security minded as Raines. Our people have been purged from the Rebel ranks, but we have many around Blanton. We have two on the White House staff who feed us information daily. We know everything that Blanton plans. He doesn't polygraph people the way Raines does."

"Can we sanction Ben Raines?"

"Highly unlikely. That's been considered and rejected. Raines has security around him at all times. Most of the time you can't see them, but there is a security circle around the man constantly. Outside of that, there is a uniformed larger circle, then another circle outside of that one. Even a suicide attempt would probably not be successful."

"Damn! How much time do we have?"

"Not much, Paul. We'd better start moving immediately."

Revere slowly nodded his head. "All right. I'll order the pullback. A year is not that long."

"I knew it!" President Blanton yelled when he heard the news. "Revere is all mouth and bluster. I knew he'd back away from us."

"He didn't back away from us, sir," General Holtz corrected. "He just didn't want to tangle with Ben Raines."

"Whatever," Blanton said with a wave of his hand. "Now we can concentrate on really important issues instead of pouring money into the military."

The generals exchanged glances. Same old jukebox, same old song. The generals rose as one and walked out.


After receiving the news of Revere's withdrawal, Ben called for a meeting with all his batt coms. "I don't have to tell you what this means," he said. "You all know. All Revere did was postpone the fight until he can grow stronger. Well, I'm not going to let him do that. We're going into Canada and kick the shit out of him."

"Blanton won't like that, Ben," Cecil warned.

"I don't care what Blanton likes or dislikes," Ben was quick to reply. "I have it on good authority that General Holtz will not commit troops against us. Blanton is going to pitch one of his temper tantrums but that's about all he can do. We've got to cut the head off this snake before it can grow. Start moving supplies out by ship . . . now." He placed a pointer on a map. "Dock in Maine, here, and start moving inland, setting up a depot . . . here. I want four battalions in place on the ground as security before the first ships dock. Dan, have your 3 Battalion parachute in along with Buddy and his special ops group. Georgi, you and your 5 Battalion go in with Jackie and her 12 Battalion. I'll get things rolling here and then join you with my 1 Battalion. Thermopolis, work out the logistics. That's it, people. Let's go."


"He can't invade a friendly sovereign nation!" Blanton squealed. "I'll deny him ground routes and air space."

"With what?" one of his senior advisers asked. "That rabble protesting outside the White House? What are they going to do, hit the Rebels with their placards?"

"You asked for Raines's help," Senator Arnold said. "Personally, I can't stand the man. But he's only meeting the threat the best way he knows how—before Revere can grow stronger. Reluctantly, I've got to support him. Besides," he said with a nasty smile, "the Rebels might be so weakened after a sustained campaign against Revere that we would be able to crush him and put this Union back together."

"Right on!" Blanton said. "Good thinking, Senator." He turned to his secretary of state, the former soap star, Cynthia Barnhart. "Advise Secretary of State Penny that this campaign has our full blessing. God speed and all that crap."

"He's lying through his capped teeth," Ben said, tossing the communique aside. "He hopes we'll be so weakened by fighting Revere that his troops will be able to overwhelm us."

"Regretfully, that is my conclusion too," Dick Penny said. "But I don't believe General Holtz will stand for committing troops against us."

Ben smiled. "Oh, I know he won't. I anticipated this from that goddamn liberal and met with General Holtz and his senior officers two days ago in Tennessee. If Blanton orders Holtz and his troops to face us after the Canadian Campaign, Holtz and his people will turn on him and depose him." Ben smiled at a clearly startled Dick Penny. "You see,

Dick, there are many things I have over President Blanton. He's not nearly as sneaky as I am, and not nearly the one hundred percent hard-assed son of a bitch that I am. Nice guys can't govern a nation this size. It takes a mean bastard to do that. It takes a man able to pick up a phone and order a sanction against an enemy. There hasn't been a Democratic president since Harry Truman with the balls to do that. The Iranian mess could have been avoided if the president had killed Khomeni in Paris, but he didn't have the guts to do it. All he wound up doing was fucking up a hostage rescue. I'd have killed that bastard and not given it a second thought. Khomeni, not the president. We had the deniables ready to go and in place. Blanton is going to make a bad mistake if he fucks with me."

"Ben," Dick Penny said, leaning forward. "Could you kill the President of the United States?"

Ben met the man's steady gaze. "To preserve all we've fought for over the long bloody years . . . I'd have to consider it."